MURDER AT ST. HILAIRE

Lucy O'Donnell series Book 1

Frances McNamara

Rudiyat Press

ONE

Recently retired Boston Police Captain Lucy O'Donnell had a plan. As one of her last acts, she wanted to repay a favor from Bin Yu, her favorite forensic tech. The tall and talkative immigrant from mainland China complained about his mother-in-law. He deserved a break. Lucy took the elevator to his floor in a Chinatown apartment building.

Inside, it was the first time the two women met. The stocky Chinese grandmother wore thick, black rimmed glasses. There were strands of gray in her flat black hair and thick brows, but her cheeks were round and rosy as a girl's. The gaze of her black eyes darted around like a bird. Lucy was curious about the woman who'd spent most of her life in Beijing. "What you going to do now?" Meilan Lin asked. "Can't just sit around." She waved a hand at the Boston skyline outside the window of the apartment.

"People retire in America," Lucy told her. "It's time to sit back and relax, do what you've always wanted to do but haven't had time." Not that Lucy knew how to do that after thirty-five years in the Boston

Police Department. But she wasn't ready to admit it. Meilan hadbeen brought over from China after her own retirement.

Meilan snorted. "You give up such a powerful position, captain of police, to sit around and stare at cherry blossoms? Are you crazy?"

"Lin Taitai, don't be rude to our visitor," Bin Yu told her. He was at the stove cooking pan fried dumplings. He was a tall man in his thirties with wire rimmed glasses. As a forensic technician for the BPD, Lucy considered him something of a magician because of the evidence he had managed to conjure in her most difficult cases. Knowing how much Lucy liked dumplings he'd promised to make some for her. As soon as he heard she would retire, he insisted on coming through on his promise. She was touched by how sincerely sorry he was to see her go.

Meilan snorted then rose with a pile of clothes she had been folding. "I'll take these to Mai and Xi's room," she said naming her grandson and granddaughter. As she left, she threw a parting shot over her shoulder. "Maybe you want to take up Chinese opera, like those lazy old guys in senior center."

"Chinese opera?" Lucy asked. She was sipping a Tsingtao beer at the kitchen table while Bin fried the dumplings. He had set out three kinds of sauces and her mouth was watering in anticipation.

"It's the Chinatown Senior Center," Bin Yu told Lucy. He looked up to be sure his mother-in-law was out of hearing. "She got kicked out. She tried to shut down the opera club to organize a group against the developers who're taking over a lot of the buildings in Chinatown. The Senior Center folks got sick of it. So, they sent a delegation to see us, while she was out. We gave them tea and they politely asked that we find somewhere else for her to spend her time." He shook his head. "Hong's going crazy trying to keep her mother busy, so she won't go over to the Senior Center all the time."

Bin's wife Hong had sent her apologies for missing the meal. She was working on a doctorate in public policy at the Kennedy School of Government at Harvard and had a seminar that afternoon.

Bin waved a spatula. "Of course, Meilan won't listen to me. I told her to cut it out. You don't have a crusade that needs leading, do you? Something we could get her involved in?"

She knew from Bin that Meilan didn't think very highly of her son-in-law. Apparently Meilan told her daughter that Bin was holding her back. Although she had never graduated from university herself, Meilan revered academics and was determined that Hong would become a renowned scholar and return to China in triumph. On the other hand, she treated Bin with contempt. "Laboratory cleaner," she called him. But, despite Meilan's insults, Lucy knew that Bin was very fond of his mother-in-law. He'd told her that Meilan had suffered a hard life in China.

"I have a suggestion." Lucy grinned. Her nephew had gifted his retiring aunt with a week at the Pelican Bay Resort on the Caribbean island of St. Hilaire. It was a two-bedroom timeshare. Lucy had already invited her sister and best friend but there was room for one more. Remembering all the times Bin had saved a case for her, she decided to offer the place to his mother-in-law.

Lucy proposed the trip as soon as Meilan came back into the room. Bin Yu looked at her like she was crazy.

"Island? You have a place to go?" Meilan asked. When Lucy explained about her nephew's timeshare, Meilan frowned and thought for a few moments, then agreed. "Sure thing. We can go see what it's like on the decadent vacation island. That's where big capitalists hide money from the government, right?"

Bin Yu rolled his eyes and Lucy had second thoughts, but Meilan was an enigma she felt like investigating in her soon to be prolific free time. Truth was, she was curious. There were always news stories about China these days. She felt her generation had been brought up in ignorance of that part of the world. They'd paid dearly for that ignorance during the Vietnam War. Besides, having Meilan along would provide a welcome distraction. Although she hadn't let it be widely known, her retirement was not entirely her own idea. It was a fact she didn't plan on sharing with her sister, Norah.

TWO

The Caribbean sunshine was blinding in the late morning. After the gray skies and sleet of Boston, St. Hilaire Island was a paradise. Lucy squinted at the fierce light even though she sat in the shade of their balcony overlooking the infinity pool and the sea beyond it. They could hear the waves break on rocks below them.

Lucy looked at her friend, Mary, who joined her on the balcony. Petite, with red hair and Irish freckles, she was a calming influence on this trip. Mary had urged Lucy to take her time to decide what she wanted to do in retirement. And she was the only one perceptive enough to laugh when she saw the golf clubs Lucy's family gave her. Membership in a pricey golf club just wasn't Lucy's style.

"Well, this is just lovely," Mary said as she handed Lucy a mug of coffee. "I am so ready for this." A medical doctor, Mary was a widow who had raised a son and a daughter by herself.

"I just hope those two get along," Lucy said.

Inside, Lucy's retired schoolteacher sister, Norah, and Meilan were bumping into each other in the kitchen.

"I'm sure they'll manage. We're all here for a good time."

Lucy appreciated Mary's attempt to start them off with the right attitude but, after watching Norah and Meilan argue over how much to tip the van driver the night before, she had some doubts about how this was going to work. So much for her big idea that Norah and Meilan would like each other.

Norah joined them on the balcony. Lucy's older sister was a retired schoolteacher. She was plump with styled hair and blood red nails.

"Tell me again, why did you invite her?" Norah hissed.

"I told you, she's my forensic guy's mother-in-law. She doesn't know anyone her own age in Boston. She came over from China to help them take care of the kids. His wife, Hong, is finishing her doctorate, and Bin has the full-time job. They've got two toddlers." Lucy was thinking that Norah was as much a problem as Meilan. Her attitude wasn't helpful.

"They haven't heard of day care?"

"It's a cultural thing. Besides, she's retired, and Hong is her only child, and they probably want to take care of her, too. She's not getting any younger. So, they brought her over. Anyhow, she likes you."

Meilan had been impressed when she heard Norah was a retired schoolteacher. She revered anyone connected to education. Lucy suspected she had been a teacher's aide, rather than a teacher back in China but she had expected her to get along well with Norah. Now that they were side-by-side, Lucy saw a lot of similarity between them. They were both bossy as hell, and they both just couldn't keep their opinions to themselves. They both tended to be up in your face, convinced they knew all the answers, the right thing to do in any situation, and they were both overly conscientious in pointing out what you were doing that was wrong. It probably came from having to guide a classroom of children firmly in the right direction, but when they tried to extend the attitude to adults, it didn't work.

She saw Norah staring at someone looking up from the pool deck below them. "Look," she said. "There she is. I recognize her from pictures. It's the girlfriend."

Uh oh, Lucy could tell Norah's antennae were up. One of the things her sister was anticipating was getting some juicy details on their nephew's latest fling. Norah considered it a major goal of the trip to find out everything she could about the new girlfriend so she could share it with relatives at home. Lucy rolled her eyes. She couldn't wait to hear Norah grill the poor girl.

Anna Maria Vandergott was a sales rep for the resort timeshares and the famous girlfriend of Lucy's nephew. She was a stunning blonde in a blue and white silk dress that clung to her figure like cellophane. Lucy wondered how much walking she did in the three-inch heels she wore. The women waved and put on their Nike running shoes and 50 SPF long-sleeved sun protection clothing to meet her downstairs.

THREE

"I hope you are enjoying your visit?" The young woman was solicitous in a very European way. Lucy knew she was Dutch, and she wondered what her nephew had told her about his aging, newly retired aunt.

"Oh, it's perfect," Lucy assured her. "We love it here. The balcony overlooking the pool is fantastic." The only thing that had pulled Lucy away from that perch was a feeling of obligation. The previous night, Anna Maria had called to invite them to a free breakfast followed by a sales pitch about the timeshares. It seemed a small favor in return for the free week from her nephew. After an embarrassing breakfast grilling of Anna Maria, Norah ducked out of the tour, pleading an appointment to get her nails done at the spa. Typical. That left Mary, Meilan, and Lucy to follow their guide to the super luxurious part of the resort, which Lucy could never afford, but what the heck.

When the elevator took its time responding, Lucy and the younger woman chose the stairs. Anna Maria climbed the four flights of cement stairs in three-inch heels without a stop. Lucy managed to hike up with some difficulty. As she struggled not to pant, she knew she should have taken the elevator. Mary and Meilan took the elevator to "save their knees." Truth to tell, Lucy's knees were of a similar vintage, but she just hated the idea that they needed saving. Time to get more realistic.

"This is one of the newest penthouses," Anna Maria told her. "I think you will like it. This section was added only last year."

Lucy tried to look duly impressed, although what she was really interested in was Anna Maria herself. According to Lucy's sister-in-law, Steve had already bought his two weeks a year when he met the girl. That particular nephew was known for being a canny investor. Having abandoned the multi-generational occupation of his cop father and uncles, he was having financial success as a CPA. Anna Maria had been polite in her replies to Norah's searching questions, but Lucy thought she'd given nothing away about her relationship with Steve.

There was a flurry of activity as the petite Mary and stocky Meilan trooped along the open balcony to join them. Meanwhile, Anna Maria unlocked the door to lead them into the hushed shade of a spacious apartment. The wood paneling, carpets, and high-end appliances of the new unit made the one where they were staying look a little shabby, but all that luxury also made it formal and stuffy, like the type of place where you were afraid to put down a drink without a coaster.

While they oohed and aahed politely, Lucy could see that Mary was getting the same vibes. They'd both spent their early family vacations in cheap rental cottages near the beach where shabbiness and sand swept grittiness were part of a charm that signaled relaxation. This looked more like the site of an upscale cocktail party in a trendy part of South Boston.

Meilan, on the other hand, was prowling around, opening doors and appliances, sniffing at details, examining every closet and bureau drawer as if she were going to buy the place. Considering that she was an unemployed mother-in-law, and that she had spent her working life as a teacher in Communist China, that seemed highly unlikely. However, Meilan didn't let the reality of a situation stop her. At least Anna Maria seemed to appreciate the interest, so when Mary gave Lucy a quizzical look, she just shrugged. Why disillusion the young Dutch woman?

When they completed their tour of the interior, Anna Maria led them out on to the shaded balcony that overlooked the sea. The heavily populated pool area was off to the right, but the view here was more secluded, with surf splashing on the rocks immediately below. To the left was the channel used by yachts to reach the harbor behind the buildings and a tall, circular, glassed-in tower that had a revolving light at the top. The first night when they noticed its regular signal, Mary dubbed it the "Eye of Sauron."

Anna Maria invited them to climb up a small winding staircase. Her heels tapped on the white iron steps. They followed her up and out onto a roof that was also painted white and was blazing in the sun. They were assaulted by a smell that was both sweet and pungent. A bar with stainless steel sink and refrigerator, as well as a massive gas grill, gleamed in the blinding light. The stools at the counter looked directly into the roof area of the next unit where a grinning young Asian man with black framed eyeglasses was slapping some meat on the grill. A much older, wizened Asian man hunched over the counter beside him. There was a wheelchair in the background.

"Ingrid, good to see you. I'm just showing the old man how the grill works," the younger guy told Anna Maria. Lucy could see the girl suppress a flinch. He obviously confused her with some other young woman. But Lucy figured in the timeshare business, the customer was always right, so the girl didn't bother to correct him, smiling brightly instead.

"Mr. Chin, my, that smells delicious. I'm so glad you're enjoying your grill. This is Ms. Lucy O'Donnell, Dr. Mary Murphy and Mrs. Meilan Lin.

Before she could continue, the air was suddenly sputtering with syllables of Chinese that most of them didn't understand. Needless to say, the westerners were all shocked. Meilan was spewing syllables while the older Mr. Chin growled back, his brow furrowed, and his wiry eyebrows lowered over narrowed little black eyes. The spectators gulped with embarrassment.

"Meilan, stop." Lucy tried to intervene. Meilan ignored her. Finally, Lucy took her arm and forced her back to the staircase, blocking her way when she tried to come back up, and advancing on her so she had no choice but to start stepping down. When Meilan tried to yell over Lucy's shoulder, the former police captain pressed a hand on her arm forcing her down the stairs. "Enough," Lucy said.

Lucy heard the younger Chin bid Anna Maria goodbye, accepting her apologies with a good natured comment. But Lucy wasn't really hearing that. She was too busy herding Meilan back into the unit and towards the door. It reminded her of working the aftermath of a Red Sox game when they lost. Spread your arms, look them in the eye and keep stepping forward one step at a time. When they got into the living room Mary slipped by her and took Meilan by the arm, patting her in a doctorly manner until they were out the door. They didn't wait for Anna Maria. Lucy figured she'd had more than enough of them.

Back at their own unit of slightly chipped stucco on their own shaded balcony overlooking the infinity pool and the ocean beyond it, Lucy and Mary joined Norah settling into the comfortable chairs. But not Meilan. She trudged into the bedroom and was routing around in her suitcase like an animal in its lair.

"What was that all about?" Mary asked in a low voice

"What happened?" Norah had gotten back before them and installed herself in her favorite corner, with a bottle of water by her side.

Lucy bent forward craning her neck to be sure Meilan wasn't close to the door. "Meilan got a little agitated when we met a couple of Chinese guys up on the roof of the timeshare over there." Lucy pointed towards the flank of buildings that overlooked the scenic black rock cliffs, visible in profile. "No idea what it was all about, the whole thing was transacted in Chinese, so the rest of us just stood there gawking."

Norah clucked.

Lucy rolled her eyes. "I tried to ask her what it was about on the way back, but she ignored me." Meilan had a way of just pretending she hadn't heard or didn't understand if she didn't want to hear something. Bin Yu had told Lucy it was a way of not being rude. Smile and deflect was a common tactic according to him. "Don't believe the smiles," he had warned her. According to his wife, Bin himself had not fared well in a society that required such pretense. He was as blunt as his American colleagues, a tactic that was not acceptable in a Chinese work environment. Lucy shook her head.

Mary was more understanding. "I suppose if she wanted us to know what it was about, she would have told us. Give her time. She doesn't know any of us that well. I think the younger Chin was just as embarrassed by his father's reaction as we were by Meilan's. And he could understand what they were saying."

The sliding door to the balcony opened.

"Umm, I think Meilan wants to go for a swim," Mary said.

Looking up, Lucy saw Meilan Lin standing before them. She wore a two-part bathing suit in bright orange, with a long sleeved Australian rash guard in a tiger print. Her face was covered by a large facemask over her black rimmed glasses, and she had a green breathing tube sticking up like a submarine scope. On her feet were dark green plastic flippers. "Great," Lucy said. "I think it's time for a wine cooler."

FOUR

Luella Roberts wiped the smooth teak with her soft cloth. She sprayed more of the lemon smelling oil and massaged it into the top and sides of the cabinet. The scent mingled with the sea air that blew in. She had opened the sliding door to the balcony after unlocking the front door and wheeling her cart into the timeshare apartment. It wasn't a bad job, cleaning for the Pelican Bay Resort, but it certainly didn't pay as well as the dental technician job she had trained for. Still, she wasn't sorry she was here. She would stay as long as it took. She owed Billy at least that much.

She took a folded piece of newspaper out of her pocket, smoothing it out.

POLICE IDENTIFY SUSPECT IN DEADLY SHOOTOUT *St Hilaire Tribune October 17*

Police are investigating the circumstances surrounding the death of 25-year-old William Roberts of Tomey Village near Marlborough Street in Sweet Bay. On Monday, October 16 at 12:05 AM police responded to reports of a shooting in Sweet Bay. According to witnesses, arrival of two police vehicles was followed by an exchange of fire in which William (Billy) Roberts was hit multiple times. St. Hilaire Constabulary Lt. Leonard Strong said Mr. Roberts was wanted for questioning in the beating death of Ingrid Sobel, an Australian widow found in her rented villa in March. Jewelry stolen from the dead woman was reportedly discovered in the taxi driven by Roberts and police had been searching for him for the past two weeks. Roberts was pronounced dead at the scene. This is the fifth time in the past year that police have had shooting confrontations with suspects in violent crimes against tourists. In each case the accused was armed with a pistol and had to be subdued by police fire. None survived. Mayor Justin Smith of Harbor Town said the incident is another example of the commitment of island authorities to making sure the streets and beaches are safe for visitors. "We won't tolerate violence against visitors," he told reporters outside the town hall. "Criminals will think twice about attacking tourists after the brave actions of our officers."

It hurt to think of her brother torn apart by the bullets that had hammered into his body. She could still feel the arms holding her back and smell the cordite as she screamed. She saw it all. Billy had no gun.

They said he had a gun. There was no gun. He had no gun, not ever. But there was one there, in the pictures of his dead body they released to the newspaper. There was a gun in his hand, and they said that made it all right. Sure, she could believe he might have stolen some jewelry, but only if the woman was mean to him, and if she left it around, careless like. But he would never hammer her head and push her down on the rocks like that. No way.

Luella opened her eyes, trying to free herself from the memories. It did no good to cry. She was done crying. She bent to dust the bottles on the lower shelf of the bar. Odd that. Exactly the same bottles as the ones on the top. Rum, Gin, Scotch whiskey. Exactly the same make. She stood up, hands on her hips, comparing those on top to those on the bottom. This wasn't the riddle she had come to solve, but what the heck. She pulled out a small shot glass. She took the bottle of rum from the bottom and set it on the counter next to the identical bottle already there. They had exactly the same amount of liquid, perhaps three quarters full. Shaking her head, she opened the bottle from below and poured a thimble full into the glass, then sipped it. Oh, my, yes, smooth golden rum from a local distillery on another island. OK. She rinsed the glass and poured the same amount from the bottle that was on the counter. Looked the same. She sipped. Not really. She looked at the glass. It had the same amber hue, but it was completely tasteless. Water then? Colored water? What was going on here?

Shaking her head at the unbelievable stupidity of the tourists who visited St. Hilaire, she put the bottle of good rum back on the bottom shelf. If this guy wanted to fool everybody, good luck to him. Was he thinking it made him look wealthier by having two bottles when he was too cheap to buy more of the real stuff? This time she shook her head in wonder. People could be so strange.

But that kind of strangeness didn't get somebody killed. At least not as far as she had ever heard. Footsteps tapped on the concrete outside, but they went by the door and on to the empty condo next door. Good. She had already finished in there. And if they were busy in that unit, maybe she could do the search she had been planning. She packed up her supplies and, cocking an ear, she waited until she heard the door close next door before she went out to the elevator. She just had time to do what she needed to do. She owed it to Billy. Her big brother had always looked out for her. Now it was her turn. Maybe it was too late, but she owed him that much.

FIVE

Before she left for the pool, Meilan announced that she would not be joining them for the dinner cruise that evening. Between her accent and the nasal quality of her voice due to the snorkelling mask, it was hard to understand her. But Dr. Mary managed to interpret. They just nodded and sat in silence until they saw her splash into the pool below them. Lucy wondered what she expected to see on the bottom of the pool with the snorkeling gear. She shrugged. Perhaps she was practicing, that would be like her. Meilan was a very determined person who could be disciplined when she had a goal. No wonder the Chinese opera fans had expelled her. When she got an idea in her head, she could be relentless.

Lucy was relieved there was no aftermath to the scene she had witnessed between the Meilan and old Mr. Chin. There must have been some bad situation between them in the past, but Meilan declined to explain it. It probably was none of their business. Lucy just hoped they could avoid the old Chinese man and his son. She wasn't sure they could get Meilan to drop it, when it came to the Chins. Meilan was an enigma to her travelling companions. She was very prickly since the argument with the old man on the rooftop. Lucy still wanted to learn more about Meilan once she settled in. But Meilan wasn't mixing as well with Norah as Lucy hoped. Meilan displayed respect for Norah as a teacher, but Norah didn't seem to appreciate that. Lucy was annoyed with her sister's lack of patience with the Chinese grandmother. Lucy decided to put aside worries about how the women would get along. This was supposed to be her big vacation.

On the balcony, Lucy savored her wine, rolling a sip around her mouth as she sat with Mary and Norah looking out on the vista before them. A large sailboat with furled sails was motoring into the channel on the left. The brilliant Caribbean blue-green water was dotted with a few other boats as it spread out in front of them, and at their feet was the pool surrounded by royal blue and white striped canvas chairs and lounges. A few people were lying around reading Kindles or sliding fingers over smartphones. A waiter hurried by with a couple of tall drinks that were bright pink, delivering them to a lanky blonde woman lying on her stomach and a distinguished looking, slightly craggy man with a couple of waves of gray hair at his temples lying beside her. Meilan's industrious splashing in the middle of the pool was the only disturbance in the picture of total relaxation below them. It made her sleepy...

***

The next time Lucy saw the blonde woman and the touch of gray man was on the dinner cruise, and that was when she realized they weren't a couple. At least not with each other. Lucy, Norah, and Mary boarded the catamaran for the floating dinner that would sail from a bar with drinks and appetizers, to a full restaurant with a main meal, and on to a coffee and dessert place, all under the stars. They dutifully removed their shoes as instructed by Captain Neil, and found a place on the bow to stretch out for the journey.

They settled on the deck, backs propped against the front windows of the cabin, sipping white wine in small plastic glasses. Lucy saw the blonde woman glide across in front of them, followed by a chunky square man in shorts, tee shirt and matching ball cap. Behind them, the touch of gray man politely squired a woman with a brown page boy haircut and glasses to a spot right beside Lucy.

The man with the ball cap was grousing at the blonde. "You ask me where I want to sit, I say up there, and you sit here." Lucy noticed the blonde ignored him, shrugging him off and positioning herself directly in the middle of the bow, where she stretched out her long legs. She wore a tight-fitting black tee shirt with a sparkly design of the Eiffel tower, and black jeans with a chain belt. On her bare feet, her toenails were painted a vivid red. Lucy thought the outfit looked like a teenager's but the woman was clearly in her forties. She was the type who would remain "well preserved" into her sixties. While she leaned back on her elbows ignoring her husband, he perched on a bulwark.

Meanwhile the other couple took places beside Lucy. Norah and Mary were discussing some jewelry Norah had bought from a local artist that morning. Bored, Lucy surreptitiously examined her neighbors. The brown-haired woman wore a man's dress shirt over a yoke top and shorts all in neutral colors. The cuffs were carelessly rolled up. She sank into the shoulder of her companion. He, meanwhile, arranged himself with an arm draped over one knee, displaying his long-fingered hand while the other arm hung on the shoulders of his companion. He wore trim khaki shorts and a matching shirt with buttoned pockets. When the woman pulled her eyes away from his, she noticed Lucy's glass of wine. "Where did you get that?" she asked.

"They were pouring some when we came in," Lucy told her. The woman patted the man's arm and pushed herself up to go and find some.

"A pleasant evening," the man said.

"Yes, couldn't be better." She detected a faint accent. "Are you staying at Pelican Bay?"

"Our friends are," he nodded to the blonde and the man with the ball cap. "We're all part of a consulting group, but we're taking a break at the moment. Juliet and I are staying on the boat, it belongs to Mike and Rita Blaine over there." He pointed to the blonde woman. "We offer sailing trips, take groups out for team-building, that sort of thing."

"Oh, so you're working down here. That must be something," Lucy said. She introduced herself, her sister, and their friend. She noticed Norah's ears perked up and she turned to hear what this good-looking man was saying. He introduced himself as Guy Laurent. Lucy thought he might be French Canadian. She told him she envied his working conditions. "Certainly, beats three feet of snow."

"Ah, yes. So long as we avoid the hurricanes. We spent the summer up in Delaware near Annapolis, then sailed the boat down last fall. And this is Juliet Raymond." The brunette had returned and handed him a plastic glass of wine. She acknowledged the introductions, but Lucy was amused to see how she settled herself firmly between Guy and the newcomers, laying a hand on his thigh in a proprietary gesture. Lucy noticed that he had not introduced her as his wife. They might not be married but Juliet had definitely staked a claim.

They all sat back to listen to safety instructions as the boat began to slip away from the dock, and Lucy saw that Eliot Chin, the young

Chinese man whose father had argued with Meilan, stood on the deck. She hoped he wouldn't recognize her but she didn't need to worry. He seemed preoccupied and uncomfortable in his bare feet. The captain and his mate had explained that the deck was newly painted and they wanted to keep it pristine so people were asked to remove their shoes. Mr. Chin had done so reluctantly.

Lucy noticed a subtle reaction as the Chinese man gingerly found a place on the bulwark next to Mike in the ball cap. The older man seemed to gather energy to himself. Turning to Chin, he engaged the younger man in conversation. The blonde, Rita, and the couple, Guy and Juliet, all gravitated towards Mike and Chin, like the arrow on a compass. Chin was their center of attention.

The catamaran's first stop was a bar with balconies open to the harbor where they had drinks and appetizers. Then they motored across the bay to a softly lit Japanese restaurant where they slid into cushioned booths to sample a dozen dishes for their main meal. By then the two couples had circled the young Chinese man and herded him to a prominent table where they were joined by the Australian captain of the catamaran.

Lucy, Norah and Mary found themselves seated with a middle-aged couple who were trim tennis players, and a pair of obvious newlyweds from the Midwest. The woman of the older couple, who looked like an aging Barbie, graciously favored the newlyweds with advice. "Good for you, getting married. You can't be too fussy, that's what I told my friend, Carol. You have to go out there and get attached. Why there are so many dating sites and groups now, there's no excuse for not finding someone. Look at us. We were both married to other people, but we weren't happy. You can't not be happy, that's what we say. So we found each other on a dating website and that's that. Now how did you two meet?"

The young bride blushed as she admitted they had been friends and neighbors since grade school. When she talked about their families and the wedding, the aging Barbie bristled. "That's all very well, but you need to keep at it, you know. Keep the relationship fresh. We do that, don't we Kenny?" Kenny was absorbed in his sushi, but he nodded, and Lucy thought she saw a resemblance to a plastic Ken doll her daughter had played with when she was very young. "Now, what about you ladies?" the woman turned to the older group, "you should really try Big Match, I can't tell you how helpful it was to me, and to most of my friends."

Lucy restrained herself from rolling her eyes, stuffing her mouth with fish instead. Norah explained that her husband was on a fishing trip and had approved of his wife's expedition with her newly retired sister and their widowed friend. Barbie pounced on the fact that Lucy was newly retired, going on and on about how she needed to use the Big Match website to find someone to share the bliss of her golden years. Later on, Lucy and Mary agreed the young couple with all their familial ties were a much better match than Barbie and Ken. In a calculated move the three older women extracted themselves from those companions when they returned to the boat, finding a roosting spot that was too narrow for them to follow.

The final stop was at a pretty bakery that stayed open for the catamaran. They were served French coffee and pastries. Lucy and her sister found themselves joined by Captain Neil when he followed Mary back from the buffet table. He had medical questions about a reaction he had developed from the fiber glassing he'd been doing on the boat. He was a sinewy man, of medium height with a thatch of straw-colored hair and sharp cheek and jaw bones. He spoke with an Aussie accent and after Dr. Mary suggested some treatments for the rash on his arms, she asked him how he had come to live on St. Hilaire.

"It's not as uncommon as you might think, yeah," he said. "Turns out a lot of people come to visit, and they stay here. That's what happened to me. We were sailing through, but we put in to make a repair, and what do you say, we never left." It turned out that the "we" was an exaggeration as he was single, and his mate was a local from the island. Delroy Jackson was bartender at the Pelican Bay Resort.

Delroy joined them for dessert and gently ribbed Captain Neil about his sensitive skin. It turned out that some recent regulations required changes to the catamaran in order for them to stay in the tour business. Captain Neil complained the local police chief was a stickler for safety regulations and if he didn't complete his fiber glass changes by the deadline he'd be out of business.

By the time they returned to where they had started and were waiting for the van, Lucy and Norah were teasing Mary about how she had made a conquest of Captain Neil. "Without even visiting Big Match," Lucy told her. Meanwhile the young Chin was surrounded by the group from the team-building firm. It looked as if they had landed a contract with him, and they were all in very good spirits. Lucy wondered if Chin was a little tipsy. Obviously, he was buoyed by being the center of their attention and had turned a bit loud as a result. When the van was late picking them up, he lectured the van driver on tardiness all the way back to the resort.

Back at their unit, Lucy was glad to retreat to the balcony with a glass of Limoncello. Meilan was nowhere to be seen. Mary and Norah joined her, and they left the lights turned off as they watched the moonlight on the gently swaying water that spread out to the horizon. The peace was broken only by the periodic striking of the bright light from the light house in the tower at the far end of the resort.

The pool below was lighted. It glowed softly. Lucy noticed a couple in the pool. The man swam with a strong stroke to the far end. The woman followed more slowly, taking her time, luxuriating in long soft strokes until she was treading water, moving her arms in long arcs just in front of him. Lucy had the impression they were naked, although she couldn't tell for sure. Skinny dipping like teenagers. She squinted in the dim light thinking it must have been Guy and Juliet down there. Norah also noticed and she nudged both of her companions. The lovers were embracing when they heard a door opening near the bar.

Eliot Chin marched across to the hot tub in a little fake grotto on the far side of the pool. No one spoke. They watched as he slipped off his leather slippers, dropped his fluffy towel and plush bathrobe on a chair, and set the water gurgling by hitting the red button. He stepped gingerly into the hot water. Lucy wondered what would happen when he noticed the naked swimmers but when she looked back at the pool, Guy and Juliet had disappeared. She relaxed.

Norah began to wonder out loud about Meilan, asking where she could have gone. Lucy had no idea. She just hoped Meilan would not appear and erupt again when she saw the young man in the hot tub. Instead, they saw Anna Maria Vandergott, still in her spiked heels, tap her way across the deck to where Chin wallowed, steam rising from the hot water. She held a tray with a glass and a pitcher.

"Such service," Norah commented.

"Not as good as this Limoncello, though," Mary said. "But I think it's my bedtime. I'll set up the coffee for the morning."

***

The next morning, they sat in the sunshine on the balcony at seven AM when Dr. Mary noticed that Eliot Chin was still in the hot tub.

"What the hell? That can't be right," Lucy said. And it wasn't. He was dead.

SIX

He was dead. Lucy and Mary hurried down and, with the help of the man who had just started cleaning the pool, they pulled the body out and tried to revive him. Norah went to the front desk and got them to call for help. She returned to the pool side with Anna Maria and the girl's boss, Carlo Menotti. He was a squat Italian in a silk suit and shiny leather loafers. His thinning hair was slicked back, and he wore chunky gold and ebony cufflinks and an expensive looking watch.

"I'm afraid there's nothing we can do," Mary told them. "Was he out here all night?" She was looking at Anna Maria. The poor girl looked distressed.

"I don't know. He came in after the dinner cruise and he ordered a pitcher of rum punch. I brought it to him."

"We have called the hospital," Carlo told them. "They will be here any minute. Can't you keep him alive till then?"

Mary grimaced and bit her lip. "We'll see what they say when they get here." She looked across at Lucy. It was clear that the man was already dead. Lucy supposed that from the point of view of the resort it might be better if the man died in the ambulance or the hospital. She wondered if it would impact sales figures to have the death occur on site. Too much time as a detective had led to a deep cynicism. Maybe it was time to let that go.

"Shouldn't someone tell his father?" she asked.

"Oh, dear. Perhaps I should do it," Anna Maria said. Lucy thought the young woman looked distressed and confused. She wondered if she had seen a dead body before, then mentally kicked herself. Having seen a lot of dead bodies in the course of your career was nothing to feel superior about.

"Yes, you go to him," Carlo said. "We'll send for Livingston. He can take the old man to the hospital. He'll have to carry him down and put the wheelchair in the van." He turned to address some of the staff who started to wander out to the pool deck to see what was going on. "Make sure the ambulance people come right in," he told them as Anna Maria trotted away to tell the older Chin what had happened. Carlo waved his hands giving directions to other staff people to close off the pool area.

Mary remained by the side of the dead man until two emergency medical technicians in bright orange vests rushed in, pulling a stretcher behind them. As she consulted with them, Lucy and Norah backed out of the way. Grabbing Lucy's forearm Norah pointed. Meilan Lin stood huddled with a towel around her shoulders in an archway across from the pool. She appeared to be dripping wet. The sisters hurried across to her.

"Meilan, where have you been?" Norah asked.

Meilan brushed a corner of the towel across her face. "I was swimming. Early swim, good for heart." She stared at the EMTs. "What happened?"

Lucy and Norah exchanged a look. "It's Eliot Chin. He was in the hot tub. It looks like he had an attack or drowned or something," Norah explained. "We're not sure. We saw him from the balcony but when we got down here, it was too late. At least Mary was here to know what to do. Didn't you see him? Were you in the pool?"

"The son?" Meilan asked. "Yes, I saw him in the hot water. Serves him right. Big capitalist."

"Meilan, please, the man is dead." Norah was scandalized and Lucy could see storm clouds on the horizon. This was no time for them to have one of their spats in public.

"Where were you all night?" Lucy asked. There was something going on with Meilan and her detective instincts were on fire. She didn't like it that Meilan had argued so publicly with the dead man's father. "You weren't in the room when we got back last night. Did you get in later?"

There were two bedrooms. Lucy and Mary shared one, and Norah had the other. She had invited Meilan to use the second bed, but Meilan had insisted on using the pullout sofa in the living room instead. The previous morning, she had still been buried in the covers when the others had their coffee on the balcony, but this morning the sofa was made up and in place with no sign of her. They all assumed she woke early and went out before they were up.

Meilan looked at Lucy with a frown. "Late, I got in late. Got up early, for a swim. I saw him in the hot water. Dead? Too bad. Serves him and his nasty father right though."

"Meilan, don't talk like that," Norah said. "It's disrespectful."

Meilan just rolled her eyes, but she followed Lucy and Norah when they led the way back up to their balcony where they could watch the comings and goings. Mary assisted the EMTs, then joined Lucy and the others. They made another pot of coffee and had just poured it out and doctored their cups with cream and sugar when there was a knock on the door. Lucy opened it. Standing there was a dark-skinned black man of medium height with a bald head and square metal rimmed glasses. He wore khaki pants with a crisp pleat and a white short sleeved shirt with a badge on the shoulder.

"I'm Chief Wendall Jackson of the St. Hilaire constabulary. I'd like to talk to you about the man who you found dead this morning in the pool area."

The whole tenor of the thing felt so familiar to Lucy. "Yes, please come in," she said. She knew there was something very wrong about this death. She could smell it.

SEVEN

"I understand you were the ones who found Mr. Chin?" Chief Jackson asked.

"I did," Mary told him. She was peeking over Lucy's shoulder. Lucy led him to the balcony, and she explained that they had noticed Chin in the hot tub the evening before and so they were surprised and then alarmed when they noticed that he was still there in the morning. They went down to the pool area to investigate. He asked about Mary's medical credentials and wrote down their names and addresses. No one mentioned that Meilan had not been with them. He did do a double take when he noticed her, but said nothing. He asked if they knew the dead man. The others let Lucy answer. She knew they were stunned by the seriousness of the situation when both Norah and Meilan kept silent.

"We didn't," she waved vaguely at the others. "We met him briefly when we were on a tour of the timeshares, then he was on the dinner sail that Mary, Norah and I went on last night, but we didn't talk to him. He spent most of his time with some of the other folks on the cruise. I think he had some business with them." With a trained investigator's memory, she even recalled their names, Mike and Rita Blaine, Guy Laurent and Juliet Raymond. She pointed them out where they were settled by the infinity pool despite the police activity on the other side. From the balcony, they could see the resort staff, providing breakfast to the Blaine group and other guests in an effort to restore normalcy.

The distraction was not enough for Chief Jackson to lose his train of thought. "And Mrs. Lin, you didn't go on the dinner cruise? Where were you?"

Meilan looked glum. Her back was stiff, and she was frowning. Lucy thought that did not bode well. "No. No boat. I swam here. Do exercise," Meilan told him, then sank into a stubborn silence. She planted herself on a chair and picked at grains of sand on the toes of her right foot, as if trying to remove every last bit before putting on her sandals. Lucy recognized obstructive behavior in a potential witness. She hoped the chief would ignore it.

"So you all saw Mr. Chin in the hot tub and he looked fine when you retired last night?"

They agreed. Meilan said nothing. It occurred to Lucy that Meilan had known the dead man's father, but the son had not seemed to recognize her, so she let her Chinese friend's silence on the subject stand. She had no desire to be drawn into the matter. The chief thanked them and rose to leave. But before turning to the door, he asked Lucy what she had done in the police department.

"When I left, I was a captain, in an administrative department." It was not a happy memory. "Before that, I spent fifteen years as a detective in homicide and special crimes."

He tapped his pen on his notebook and looked thoughtful. "I see. Well, thank you. You are all here for vacation, is that correct? Please do not leave the island without checking with me at the department."

They looked at each other and Lucy suppressed a groan. She could see where this was going. "We've only got the timeshare for the week, Chief. I hope this won't make us stay longer. We wouldn't be able to. Dr. Murphy has to get back to her practice, and the rest of us have people and appointments waiting for us."

"Yes, yes. It should all be all right, but don't leave without checking with me at the police station. It's in the main town, Hilaire Proper."

There was a stunned silence as he shut the door behind him.

"They can't make us stay, can they?" Norah asked.

"Maybe we need to see if Anna Maria has another unit just in case," Lucy said.

"But that's ridiculous, I have a wedding shower to go to next week," Norah was indignant. "They can't keep us here."

"Capitalist pig," Meilan said. "Dead but still a big pain in the butt."

Lucy was startled, then realized Meilan was referring to the dead man, not the policeman. She wondered if Meilan was really talking about the dead man's father. She was sure here was some history there. All of her instincts were urging her to find out more, but she had to restrain herself. It wasn't her case.

EIGHT

Juliet Raymond watched as Rita and Guy swam an impromptu race in the infinity pool. She had moved her lounge to capture the shade from the umbrella that stood over the round table where Mike Blaine was seated. Ball cap pulled down, his eyes were hidden behind a racy set of sunglasses. He was sipping a very large Bloody Mary with a hunk of celery stick poking out of it. He took the olive on a toothpick out of the drink and licked it before biting it off and gulping it down. She could hear him swearing under his breath.

Juliet's cell phone rang, and she walked off to take the call from her lawyer while stepping back and forth in the shade of one of the balconies.

She watched Guy Laurent's long arms stroking the water and felt her heart leap with every stroke. Her husband, Ted, was being difficult about the house. She knew he didn't want it, and their two daughters were both away at college. She needed the money from the sale to be able to rent something back in Cleveland where she and Guy could live. It had been romantic to run away and live on the company boat, just the two of them, but after the summer in Delaware and the sail down to St. Hilaire, it had begun to wear on both of them. The surroundings that had been so new and sparkling had become dirty and soggy with time.

The escape from the heated exchanges that went with the marital discord had been a blessing. She'd had enough conversations with angry daughters, concerned siblings, outraged in-laws. She and Ted had been growing apart for a long time. When their neighbors Mike and Rita started a team-building business after Mike got laid off, Ted had barely noticed all the time she began to spend with them. As long as he got his eighteen holes in and the meat was tenderized and ready for the grill along with his scotch and soda every night, he noticed nothing. He never asked how she spent her days.

It was rewarding to finally use her background in accounting when she helped Rita get Mike started on a new career. It was Rita's plan that would allow him to maintain his all-consuming passion for his sailboat while still making a living. Juliet didn't know how much she missed the work she had given up to raise the kids until she became involved.

When she realized that the Blaines would be taking the whole enterprise to Annapolis to put the plan in motion, it gave her pause. It was the only way to establish the business by recruiting and taking clients out on sails where they would learn teamwork. After a lot of thought, she proposed Ted take that golf trip he had been salivating about for years while she took a paid position on Mike and Rita's first cruise.

It as such an adventure. She met Guy, a friend of Mike's who was skilled at laying the bait for the clients they needed to attract. What exhilaration they all felt at the end of their first cruise was glorious. They landed a contract for three more sails. After that, the thought of going back to her role as suburban housewife was just impossible to imagine. She couldn't, she wouldn't.

She fell for Guy in a big way, and he was available, long divorced with no children to support. He was a little cagey, too long a bachelor to be able to commit. She thought of him as a magnificent bird, an eagle, that had landed on her porch railing and she was being extremely careful to not startle him into flying away. She knew he wanted his own place, but a stylish place in a city. She had a plan to be able to fulfill that wish and she could picture the two of them entertaining against a backdrop of a city skyline. It wouldn't be Washington D.C. or New York, but a backdrop of Cleveland or Cincinnati had to be better than a rented room in the suburban home of friends. That was how he was living in D.C. before he joined Mike and Rita on the boat. Juliet had a plan.

After listening to her lawyer's description of her soon-to-be ex-husband's latest offer and clarifying her own breaking points, she hung up fairly confident that her lawyer could get what she needed. Then she returned to the pool. She rushed to drape a clean towel on Guy's shoulders as he stepped up from the water, placing herself between him and Rita. Both of them were energized by their swim. Rita strode dripping to the chair beside her husband to get her own towel. She shook herself like a puppy and bent over to towel her long hair, then after a quick brush off she sat down.

"You didn't order me one?" She was looking at the half empty glass in Mike's hands. He shrugged, and she waved at a waiter, pointing at Mike's glass indicating a need for the same for all of them. "I suppose you're drowning your grief?"

"You bet. I don't know what you think we're going to do. We had him in the bag. He was up for having three sails to cover all his employees. Now what'll happen? You think whoever takes over from him is going to listen?"

Rita was still wiping strands of hair with the blue and white striped towel. "Who knows? They might. Anyway, we promised Mike Junior we'd be back for his big game, so I'm not too unhappy. What are you grumbling about? We had a good run up in Annapolis. We should be able to get through the winter. Besides, we'll need to go back there to drum up some more business."

The waiter arrived with three tall glasses of spicy tomato Bloody Marys. Mike pointed at his own glass and the waiter took it away for a refill. Rita frowned at that. "I don't know why you insisted we come down here anyways, if you're that worried about money. It's costing a lot. We could have just put the boat away for the winter and gone back next spring."

"Will you stop it? All you do is complain. I'm sick of it." Mike got up and stomped away in the direction of the bar. Rita snorted.

"Is there going to be a problem?" Guy asked in a restrained sort of way.

Rita looked at him with an appraising gaze. "There shouldn't be. Unless he's been up to something I don't know about." She took a sip of her drink then held up a plastic tube. "Guy, honey, would you mind?" She pointed at her back.

He moved over to spread the sunscreen while she held up her hair in a twist. Juliet took a long pull of her own drink to keep from commenting as she watched them. Soon, the alcohol and the strong sun were making her a little dizzy. Guy finished and rubbed some of the sunscreen on himself, then he laid back with a towel over his eyes. Juliet pulled herself more into the shade and watched jealously as Rita lay on her stomach soaking up the hot Caribbean sun. It just wasn't fair the way some people were impervious to the damaging rays of the sun, while some, like Juliet, had to avoid a tendency to fry up into a crispy, itchy piece of burned toast.

But she had a plan, now, and she was going to stick to it.

NINE

Lucy tracked down Meilan in the exercise room of the resort. She was head down, arms swinging, walking determinedly on a treadmill. It was a sizable room and was filled with shiny equipment. No matter how sweltering it was out in the brilliant Caribbean sunshine, fierce air-conditioning kept the temperature was downright cold.

Behind Meilan, seated on a standing bicycle, Carlo Menotti, Anna Maria's boss in the timeshare business, was steadily pumping his bony legs. He wore a trim suit of knee length shorts and matching sleeveless gray shirt in a shiny modern fabric. He looked quite at home with a towel draped over the handlebars of his machine. Lucy thought he must exercise regularly.

She stepped on a treadmill next to Meilan and started the machine at a slow walk. Looking over her shoulder she could see that Carlo was listening to an iPod and was far enough away not to overhear them. "Meilan," she said, waving a hand to get her friend's attention. Meilan took the earplugs out of her ears. She frowned at Lucy. "Meilan, you need to tell me what you were fighting about when we saw Chin and his father yesterday."

Meilan turned up the rate of her machine and trotted industriously to avoid the conversation. Lucy shook her head. She turned up the rate on her own machine and followed her own prescribed regimen for half an hour. She could see that she had more experience with the machines than the Chinese grandmother and when the other woman appeared to be flagging, Lucy slowed down her own machine and reached over to turn down Meilan's as well. When Meilan's breath was back to something more normal, Lucy stopped her machine and then Meilan's. She beckoned her over to the water fountain where they each sipped from a small paper cup.

"Sit down," Lucy insisted. She pointed to a deep leather couch arranged in the corner overlooking the beach. Meilan wiped sweat from her brow with her towel and reluctantly sank into the couch. Lucy joined her, feeling her heart rate slow down as she relaxed. "Listen, Meilan, that cop was serious. If he thinks we're in any way involved in this murder, he's not going to let us leave the island. We need to make sure that doesn't happen. We all need to get back to Boston on time." She thought about what Bin Yu and his wife would think if they heard their baby-sitting grandma was stuck on the island. They would also worry about her visa status although she did have a green card. Lucy had made sure her immigration status would not be an issue before suggesting she come on this trip. "What was that all about, up on the balcony yesterday? Don't look like you don't know what I mean. You do. Who were they? How do you know them? Did you know them back in China, or what?"

Meilan wiped her square face. "Nasty man, Chin. I know him from the Cultural Revolution, long time ago, you know? Very hard time in China. He was bad. Afterwards he got to be a big shot official in different provinces then back to Beijing. But like all of them he sends his little prince to foreign countries to get a university degree, then go to a business school. Big party big shot has capitalist son making big money in the west. He's a big hypocrite."

"I see. You didn't like him because he was a hypocrite? He's a communist party member but his son is a businessman in the west? That's why?" Lucy could see that the wealthy surroundings of the Pelican Bay Resort wouldn't exactly fit the expectations of a truly socialist society. However, she didn't believe top politicians in a communist country would be dedicated to a Spartan existence any more than politicians in western democracies were. Surely Meilan was too old to suddenly be disillusioned by seeing the old man in these surroundings. There had to be more to it than that. "But you must have known Chin's father personally. You did, didn't you?"

Meilan appeared to grit her teeth. She looked out at the sunny sand where some young people were playing beach volleyball, then over her shoulder to where Carlo was spinning his standing bicycle, wagging his head to the tune on his iPod. "He was a big shot in Red Guards," she told Lucy, looking into her eyes with a fierce glare. Meilan shifted uncomfortably on the leather, unsticking her sweaty thighs. Then she exhaled and told Lucy the story. "My father was a professor at BeiDa, Beijing University. My brothers were all good students They followed father into the university. I was in high school. Mao called all young people to be Red Guard. Supposed to be a big honor. Get rid of old bads was the number one thing to do. The four olds old customs, culture, habits, and ideas. Destroy the old bads."

TEN

Beijing, August 1966

Meilan looked up at the big character posters in disbelief. No. Not again. It was all over when she was eight, now she was fourteen. From six to eight, she suffered through two years of being spurned as the child of a Rightist. Two years of taunts and sitting in the back of the auditorium with other black family kids. Two years of taking turns accompanying her mother on long train rides to the pig farm where her father was sent for rehabilitation. Until she refused to go, shouting at her mother that she hated him, she never wanted to see him again.

But he had come back, and he had been reinstated as a professor. She knew he would never again dare to criticize what the government did, what Chairman Mao did. She knew because she heard her mother warn him over and over never to do that again. If he pointed out that Mao's Great Leap Forward had been ended, that even the party had finally seen he was right to oppose it, he was subjected to the bitter accusations that it was that kind of arrogant talk that had left his wife with two hungry boys and a crying little girl to feed. And she reminded him there had been no help from his family who had all been labelled bad, black, former landowners. It was only her own red peasant background that had kept them from starvation. If Meilan's brothers Shang or Wei ever dared to try to support their father, her mother would rage hysterically. That was over. The bad times were over. With his wife's nagging and her political connections he had risen again. He had become assistant provost of the people's university

Until now. Chairman Mao announced the movement to uncover the counterrevolutionary revisionists. As part of the Socialist Education Campaign, work teams were sent to help the students identify the former Rightists on the faculty. All classes were stopped and there were daily meetings at all the schools, and the university, too. Meilan joined the Red Power Red Guards at her school. They had their own red kerchief they all wore. They stood up in meetings and recited from Mao's little red book from memory. Meilan had a fine memory and she loved Chairman Mao. She shouted slogans louder than anyone else in her group. They called her little foghorn.

She saw three teachers outed as Rightists and removed from their classrooms. They were criticized in meetings in the auditorium. Students got up and accused them of promoting Rightist thoughts. They were assigned to clean the toilets and were followed around by bands of students who yelled "Cow ghosts and snake demons." They all knew these were black monsters hidden among them that had to be exposed and eliminated.

Stoked by the atmosphere and determined to prove her dedication to Mao and the party, Meilan rushed out of her home in the morning to be first to participate in the latest movement. But today her group marched to the administration building of the university. There they saw the big character posters that announced the results of the university work team investigation. And there she saw her father's name emblazoned with five others. Running dogs, traitors, Japanese spies, spies for Chiang Kai-shek. These were enemies, the counterrevolutionaries. They had to be purged along with the other bad old black things.

Meilan stood quivering, as she felt fellow red guards around her pull away when they realized her father's name was listed. But she wasn't quivering with fear, she was quivering with anger, a glare of red flashed before her eyes, and she nearly lost consciousness. Old, old, old. She knew in her heart it was true. Her father had done it again, he had ruined everything with his old values. Meilan knew it was time to destroy the four olds! Mao had told them to. Old customs, old culture, old habits, old ideas. It was all so old. But she was not. She was new.

She felt someone grab her arm and pull her through the crowd away from the Red Guard group. She opened her eyes to strike out, but saw it was her oldest brother, Shang. He pulled her under an overhanging balcony at the corner. "Meimei, you need to go home. It's not safe." He spoke softly into her ear and looked around warily.

She pulled her arm away. "No. Leave me alone. I'm a Red." She struggled as he pulled her back again.

"Meimei, go home. It's going to get bad. Come on, mother sent me to get you, now, come on." But she wriggled, trying to get away from him. He was bigger than her. He was due to complete his degree in the spring and he planned to follow their father into the academic life. Meilan knew her mother had tried to get him to join the party and become a political cadre, but he refused. She felt only scorn for him. She thought she saw a gleam of fear in his eye and that only caused her to hate him.

People were starting to notice them. "Destroy the four olds!" Meilan shouted at him, then she spit, so he let go and cursed her.

"Comrades, what is the matter?" A man in a crisp Red Guard uniform and a hat with a medallion embroidered on it, elbowed his way through the crowd of students. "Ah, Lin Shang!" He pointed a wooden bat at Meilan's brother. "I hope you have come to help your black monster father confess his counterrevolutionary revisionist actions." His eyes narrowed and he swept his other arm around to get the attention of the people. "Here is the son of the traitor Administrator Lin. Quick, grab him. He needs to see what happens to traitors."

"Cut it out, Chin," Meilan's brother said, as he struggled against several more Red Guards who grabbed his arms. "Let go of me. I haven't done anything. I need to take my sister home. Let go of me, you dirty pigs. Let go."

Meilan was furious. Now, Shang had exposed her as related to her disgraced father. If he wanted to be known as the son of a black monster that was his business, but he had no right to paint her with that dirty brush. They were doing it to her again, her father and her brothers. Why couldn't they support the country and the party and Chairman Mao? How could they be such traitors? Only her mother and she were loyal. They were going to ruin everything again.

As they dragged her brother away, the leader, Chin, touched her arm with his bat. "Little sister. What about you? Do you want to support your traitor father? Daughter of black monster Lin, where do you stand?" He raised his voice and the crowd pressed in, eager to find out what was going to happen. She heard some of them cursing her. She began to see red again, closing in on her sight. She felt lightheaded. They were going to grab her and paint her black, all black, just like her father.

"Cow ghosts and snake demons!" she yelled in her best little foghorn voice. "Destroy the four olds! Destroy the four olds!" Some of the crowd took up her chant and she saw Chin smile at her as if he had some sort of evil plan, but she wasn't afraid. "Down with traitors and revisionists!"

"Comrade Sister," Chin yelled loudly to be heard over the chanting. "Come with us. You can condemn the traitors and destroy the poisonous snakes seeking to eat the people's society! Bring her." He nodded to another couple of his Red Guard cronies and Meilan felt herself being lifted by her upper arms and moved swiftly through the crowd. She was happy. She surrendered. She was part of the group again. She saw her own Red Power Red Guards and tried to wave but couldn't get her hands up, so firmly were they holding her upper arms.

"To the stadium," she heard people yelling. She could see some banners swaying above the crowd ahead of her. She was pulled along, hearing some yells, some chanting and then a loudspeaker began to sound as they neared the stadium and people joined in singing the anthem as they moved along. "The east is red, the sun is rising. From China comes Mao Zedong..."

When they neared the gates, Meilan could see between the bodies of the Red Guards that there were people being paraded in front of her. Nearest was her brother Shang who was being pulled along, getting punched periodically. In front of him others were marching with banners. When they entered the stadium and waited for those ahead to mount the stairs to the hastily erected wooden stage, she saw there were five men and a woman. They were all professors, including her father.

When she came to a stop, she could see them pushed to the center of the stage. White glop dripped down their heads, glue used to attach the large cones of dunce caps on their heads. Each wore a plank that hung from rope around their necks. On the plank, large characters labelled them traitors, black monsters, poisonous snakes. Her father was the second figure, beside the university president.

She was furious when she saw him, feeling a huge empty hole in her heart where all her plans and desires were swirling out into the darkness. Why had he done this? Why had her father brought them to this? Didn't he care what happened to his family at all? It was bad enough when he was a pig farmer. If they made him clean the toilets like the teachers in her school perhaps, she could bear it, but this. She had tears in her eyes as she looked up at the people filling the stands, waving their hands, and shouting insults. She forced herself to stop the tears. She would not let anyone think she sympathized with the traitors. She saw her brother being dragged up the stairs and flung down on the floor behind her father. Chin moved forward to hit him with the bat.

Then the five disgraced professors were made to bend over with their hands held behind them. One comrade pushed a man's head forward, and held back one hand, while another comrade held back the other hand. For the woman, Professor Shu, there were two women comrades to push her head forward while they pulled back her hands.

Chin took a megaphone and began to lead some chants. "Destroy the four olds! Destroy the counterrevolutionary revisionists!" He told them to look at the sayings of Chairman Mao, to see what should be done to traitors. People waved little red books. Then Chen began alternately interrogating and insulting each of the traitors. He called up students and professors who read from written sheets their accusations of what the professors had done that was counterrevolutionary. When he charged them with faults, the crowd roared. At the end of each he whacked the person with the bat, and they were pulled back into the position of being bent forward, the charges hanging from their necks on the printed board, the person's name crossed out with red slashes of paint.

When he got to Meilan's father, Chin accused him of corrupting his students and even his own son. He read a list of charges including cooperation with the Japanese and spying for Chiang Kai-shek. Meilan's father was shaking his head.

A secretary from her father's office was brought forward. She read from a sheet of paper how he had looked down on the working people and scorned party orders. One of his graduate students read an accusation that he had been identified as a Rightist in the Rightist campaign for disagreeing with Chairman Mao and daring to rebuke the Chairman for the Great Leap Forward practices. The man went on and on about how elitist Meilan's father had been and how he had dared to put up his opinion as an economist to challenge Mao's wisdom. The crowd booed. Chin finally got that man off and brought on another to condemn her father for what he taught in the classroom. Someone threw a rotten onion at her father, and he cringed. Meilan was furious.

Then Chin beckoned and Meilan felt herself being dragged up the steps to the stage. Out beyond the edge she could see hundreds, thousands of yelling faces in the stands. She was brought to where her brother lay on the ground groaning. He looked up at her and covered his face with his hands, pulling his knees up. Chin growled at him, threatening him with the bat, but he turned to Meilan, took her hand, and introduced her to the crowd as Comrade Meilan of the Red Guards. Her stomach burned with pride. Her father might be a traitor and her brother might be a running dog, but she was a believer. She was a true follower of Mao so when Chin asked her whether she agreed with the Chairman, she shouted "Destroy the four olds! Destroy the four olds!" And when he asked her to condemn her father as a counterrevolutionary and a traitor she yelled "Yes, and I hate him, I love Chairman Mao, and I hate him. I hate any revisionist who doesn't follow Chairman Mao!"

Everyone clapped and hooted, even Chin clapped for her. Then he signaled for them to take her away so he could move on to the next man, the university president. As she was pulled off the stage, Meilan saw her brother weeping but her father just stayed with his head pushed down and his hands pulled back, the board with his crimes written out hanging from his neck. She felt a pang, but she pushed it away, and started yelling again "Down with the olds! Down with the olds!" The Red Guards who were moving her away cheered her on and took her to a place where she was pushed in among a crowd of people near the bottom of the stage. She could barely see anything, but she stayed for hours, cheering when the crowd cheered and booing when the crowd booed.

When Meilan got home she was hoarse and thirsty. Her mother was silent. The next day, after her mother had left for work, her brother Wei told her their father and the university president were dead. Word had come in the morning that they had died during an interrogation in the basement of the university the previous night. Her brother Shang was being criticized and would be sent to a labor camp for reeducation. She just stared at her brother, daring him to rebuke her for her part in the previous day's activities. He watched her warily, like she was a little snake, and he wasn't sure if she was going to bite him or not.

She didn't care. When she reported to her unit, they didn't want to include her. They weren't sure what to do with a girl whose father had been labelled a traitor. She was furious. She told them she loved Chairman Mao and she was a Red Guard. She ran out the door and down to the university. When she found Chin, she told him she wanted to be in the revolution, she wanted to serve.

"Revolution is not a dinner party," he told her, quoting Chairman Mao. "What happened to your father was necessary in order to dig out the counterrevolutionary poison. The revisionist traitors have to be destroyed." He glared at her, as if daring her to blame him for her father's death.

"He's not my father! Chairman Mao is my father!" she yelled.

In the end, they made a place for her with their unit and when they moved out to Shanghai, she went with them. She saw her mother before she left. She told her mother she still recognized her because her mother was a good red comrade, but she never wanted to hear her father's name again. Chin and three of his men accompanied her when she visited her family before they left town. Her mother was silent.

August 1977

Deng Xiao-Ping and the party blamed Chairman Mao for the Cultural Revolution, although they praised him for his work in the original revolution and establishment of the republic. Meilan was outraged when the work of the Red Guards was repudiated. Her brother Shang was rehabilitated and reinstated at the university, which was reopened. Memorial plaques for her father and the university president were dedicated and Wei and Shang spoke at the dedication. Meilan spent five years in Xinjiang on a sheep ranch. When she returned, her brothers got her a job in the local primary school. Their mother had died working on the same pig farm where their father had been sent in the fifties. Her red background had not been enough to save her. Meanwhile Chin had become a party official. He had refused to let Shang go to their mother until after she died, so she was buried on the pig farm. The sons brought her body back to Beijing after they were reinstated.

Chin kept his job and advanced when he crossed over to the side of Deng and the others. He had been canny enough to abandon Mao's faction when Zhou En Lai died and Mao's wife and the others in the Gang of Four tried to keep people from remembering him. Chin knew that public opinion was against her, and Mao was dying. Chin even married a distant relative of Deng's, an ugly woman who had been married to a man beaten to death during the Cultural Revolution.

Meilan hated to accept the help of her brothers. She knew they despised her. But she kept her faith in Mao and the party. Her hatred of the new ways led her to divorce her husband, another teacher, after her child was born. She named her daughter Hong, Red, in keeping with the custom of Mao's time when children were given revolutionary names.

She was disgusted when her brothers sent their children away out of China for university. But she was furious when she kept seeing Chin rise in the party. He was nothing but a running dog who followed any change the people in power proposed. She heard him make speeches repudiating the Red Guards and rehabilitating Mao's enemies. She never wanted to remember that day in the stadium, but when she couldn't keep it out of her mind, she didn't see her father or her brother, she saw Chin. He was nothing but a liar. She kept clippings of newspaper articles where he repudiated every single thing he had said in those days of revolution. He was nothing but a revisionist, a capitalist pig in disguise.

And when one day she met him, at her daughter's graduation from high school, he didn't even remember her. But she sidled up to him and whispered in his ear what she thought of him. When he moved away, she stopped whispering and she yelled it out loud for all of them to hear. "Counterrevolutionary revisionist, capitalist pig," she called him. "Traitor, liar, running dog." Her daughter finally calmed her down explaining that Chin's son was her classmate. Neither of the young people had any idea what she was talking about. But Meilan thought she had exposed Chin and he deserved it.

ELEVEN

"Apparently she knew him during the Cultural Revolution and later he went along with the new government administration that repudiated it. It had something to do with her father, who died when she was fourteen, but she didn't it explain very well. Her English gets bad when she doesn't want to tell you something."

Lucy and Mary were laying on well-padded lounges under the shade of an umbrella. At their feet they could see the waves gently lapping the sand. Meilan was snorkeling, with her backside in the air and her air hose sticking up. She was out beyond a fringe of seaweed that some workers were halfheartedly raking away into piles. Behind them, in the shadow of some low hanging trees, Norah was ordering pina coladas from a convenient bar/restaurant with a thatched roof. The buildings of the resort were off to the left, while the beach in front of them was walkable with some mounds of coral encrusted boulders along the right.

"It sounds like she had a hard life growing up in China, and this Chin guy stands for everything she hates about it," Lucy said.

"Did she tell you where she went last night?"

"Humph, for a walk according to her. She's hiding something, and if it keeps us from going home on time, Norah is going to kill me." Lucy hoped the local police wouldn't find Meilan's explanations as suspicious as she did.

At that moment Norah approached, balancing three plastic cups of frothy white liquid in her hands. They took the cups and sipped freezing sweetness through straws.

Settling on her cushions after a big mouthful, Norah nodded towards the resort. "There they are. I wonder if the husband is going to say anything. And that poor Juliet Raymond, she looks like she's bundled up for the North Pole for heaven's sake."

Lucy and Mary peered beyond her to where some of the people from the catamaran cruise were settling into a group of lounge chairs. They were the ones who ran the team-building firm. The group of Bostonians lay back and closed their eyes. Listening in on the conversation across the way was inescapable, and curiosity about people you met at this kind of resort was inevitable. Just human nature, Lucy thought.

The two couples deposited their towels, sandals and cover ups on the padded lounges, then Rita and Guy ran to the water's edge and jumped in, quickly gliding beyond the line of seaweed. Juliet struggled to open an umbrella while Mike Blaine trundled down to the edge of the water, with a glass in his hand. He sipped as he moved his foot through ankle deep water, entangling some of the seaweed on his toes. Glancing down, he grimaced with disgust under his racy wraparound sunglasses.

"Uh oh, I wonder if he's mad about them yet." Norah had been watching the group at the resort. She invented a sort of soap opera drama, assuming Rita and Guy were having a fling right under the nose of the woman's husband. Lucy thought Mike Blaine was just being finicky about the seaweed, but, unlike Norah, she was trained to stick to the facts. She'd learned the hard way that there were too many possible reactions from people to try to assume anything. Norah had a single script and expected everyone in the world to follow it. Mary was more skeptical. In fact, Lucy often suspected the doctor had witnessed more obtuse and inexplicable behavior than even she had seen in her thirty-five years as a police officer.

"Perhaps I should have gotten Meilan a drink," Norah said with a moue of distaste.

"No, she doesn't like alcohol," Mary soothed her. "In fact, that's often true of Asians, especially Chinese, in my experience. Some of them are very sensitive to alcohol. They don't like it."

Lucy thought of some of the gambling joints in Boston's Chinatown where whiskey flowed as freely as in any Irish bar. There was also some kind of a colorless liquid that was one hundred proof called Baijiu that was popular down there. But, even there, some of the men were unable to imbibe. "She brought her water bottle," Lucy pointed out to her sister. Then she turned to her friend, the doctor. "What about Chin? Was his death natural?"

"Oh, Lucy, do you have to go into that? We're on vacation," Norah said.

Lucy didn't attempt to explain that their vacation could come to a screeching halt if Meilan was suspected of harming the dead man, but she knew that Mary understood her.

"I couldn't say without an autopsy," Mary said. "But we saw him drinking while in that hot tub. That could have an effect on anyone, and if he were particularly sensitive to alcohol, that might cause a reaction."

"He didn't drown, did he? Drink too much, slip down and be too out of it to get his head back above water?" Lucy asked.

Mary frowned. "I didn't think so when we pulled him out. His face was very red. I'd wonder about a heart attack more than drowning, but, as I say, an autopsy should determine cause of death."

"Oh, you two are morbid," Norah said. "I'm going down to see what Meilan is up to. At least she's not up here going on and on about a dead man." Balancing her plastic cup, she got to her feet and, stepping gingerly to avoid stones, she headed for the water.

"He did seem awfully young to just pass away like that," Mary said. "Unless he had a heart condition or something."

"I don't think he was allergic to alcohol," Lucy commented. "I saw him with drinks a number of times, including when we ran into him and the father up on that roof deck. How long will it take for them to know if it was a natural death? We need to know. You heard that police chief. We can't leave if they don't let us. Norah is going to have a bird if she finds out we have to stay because of this."

"I would expect them to have preliminary findings pretty quickly. As long as they did the autopsy right away."

"Oh, I'm sure that will be taken care of. Can you imagine being the one who has to tell the local mayor or governor or whatever that a tourist has just died? I don't know which would be worse, an accident with the resort at fault, or a crime. Probably the accident would be worse for the tourist industry."

"You think they'll make us stay while they investigate then? I suppose you would know more about that than the rest of us. I'm on call the weekend after we get back."

Lucy shook her head. "I think I'd better find out just what they're thinking. If I were them and I knew there was a big argument the day before, and then this guy is found dead the next morning, and he's too young to be just having a heart attack, yeah, I'd be suspicious.

Honestly, this is just my luck. So much for the retirement vacation."
She started gathering her things and took a final slurp of her drink.

"Where are you going?"

"To find out."

"But where?"

"I'll get Livingston to take me to the police station. Don't tell
Norah. Tell her I went to take nap, will you?" Livingston was the van
driver who had picked them up at the airport.

Mary sipped her drink as she watched Lucy trudge away, right
past Rita and Guy as they strode up to their lounges dripping water.
Poor Lucy. Mary knew she had misgivings about retirement already.
It certainly seemed unfair to have a well-deserved vacation spoiled like
this. On the other hand, perhaps it was just what she needed to see that
the world wasn't coming to an end just because she no longer had to
get up and slap on her badge every day. Mary settled a little deeper into
the cushions and decided to wash away her worries by listening to the
slap of the waves on the sand.

TWELVE

"There seem to be a lot of Asian grocery stores on the island." Lucy was in the passenger seat of the resort van with Livingston Jackson driving. He was a tall and bony black man with dreadlocks and a colorful tee shirt. He had greeted them with an entertaining patter when he picked them up at the airport two days before, sustaining interrogation by Meilan Lin for the whole drive. Lucy noticed that he spoke several languages, English, French, a local patois and some German. He told them all the young people were sent off island for university and many did not return as there weren't sufficient jobs.

"Yes, mum, there's a lot of interest in natural gas deposits off shore, don't you know. That draws some of the Chinese all right and they need their special foods. And they like all kinds of foods, you see. So, they up and bought up all the groceries and warehouses now. Yes, there's plenty of chop suey. Uh, excuse me, you won't mind if we just see what's up with this little lady now, will you?"

There was a young woman in a bikini, covered by a swath of pink and blue printed cotton wound round her waist. She had long brown hair, big square sunglasses and she was flapping a broad brimmed straw hat against her thigh after waving it to get their attention. As Livingston pulled onto the sand shoulder of the road, another three young people in beach clothes came out from behind some dusty trees.

"Qu'es que sait?" Livingston guessed they were French. They answered him in chattering tones and eventually he translated. "They say they were left here by their taxi and they have to get back to their cruise ship at the harbor, or it will leave without them. Do you mind if we give them a ride? It's almost on the way. Well, a bit out of the way, but they're going to have a problem." He grinned at Lucy. "You'll see what I mean when we get there."

She shrugged. "Sure." She wasn't looking forward to her interview with the chief of police anyhow. She knew he would resent her interference and she hadn't figured out an approach to find out what she needed to know without offending him. Sometimes you had no choice but to be rude and pushy. She thought this would be one of those times, but she wasn't happy about it.

The young people climbed into the back of the van, chattering away. The girl who had flagged them down, heard Livingston talking to Lucy in English, so she attempted to speak to them in that language. "Thank you so much. We must return to our ship, or we might not make it home," she told them. "The taxi man, he said no ride back, no ride back. We don't understand. Why no ride back?" The others bent forward eagerly, repeating "no ride back" and exclaiming in French.

Livingston pointed to a line of cars ahead. "It's a stopping point. You see all those people?" There was a double line of local people spanning the road, carrying placards saying "No LPCP." Everyone in the van bent forward to see. "They don't want the LPCP, the Land Planning Commission Plan. They have a plan that's based on people back in France having really old titles to some of the land and wanting to sell them. The new owners would take the land away from families who have lived here for years. They want to take away some of the land where people have older houses, yes probably shacks, but family houses that have been there for years and they want to take the land. They'll only sell it to developers to make new resorts."

"Terrible," said the young woman. "But what happens to the people who lose the houses?"

"They want to build higher buildings in the towns, seven, eight story buildings where now there are only two stories. They want all the people to live in those high rises, don't you see, and keep the open land for the resorts."

"Money," Lucy said. "It all comes down to money."

"True, but the local people are protesting. They think if they disrupt the tourists the government will have to do something. It's a problem that all the young people get sent away to Europe for education. It's good to get the education but then there are no jobs for them to come back to, so they have to stay in Europe for jobs and there are fewer and fewer local people. That's a bad thing." It was the same problem he had mentioned earlier.

"I see," Lucy said. "But what about them?" She pointed at the back seat. "How do we get them back to their ship?" She was a little worried that they would have to return to the Pelican Bay resort with more guests and she could just picture Norah's reaction.

"Ah, sometimes it helps to know the people," Livingston told her, then he pulled out of the line of cars to the wrong lane and quickly drove down to the line of protesters. Waving, he didn't even stop, and Lucy braced herself, thinking he was going to plow through the people. She started to protest but, just as she did so, the line miraculously opened up and the van slid through. The young French people in the back clapped their hands.

"I can see you're a man of influence," Lucy told Livingston as she relaxed and turned back towards the front. He maneuvered through the narrow streets of the harbor town and stopped at an opening where the tall sides of two huge cruise liners formed a canyon. The young people jumped out, thanking him, and forcing him to take a handful of euros.

"And now, my influence should get you to the police station, yes? It is outside town, on the other side," he told her, putting the van in reverse to get turned around.

"Very good. Livingston, what can you tell me about the Chief of Police? Anything?"

"Hmm. He is a real SOB," he told her. "You don't want to mess with him. He'll throw you in the clink before you can blink. And he'll throw away the key. He's irrational, stubborn and a pain in the rear. But he's my brother," he said.

Lucy thought he was kidding, or making up a rap song or something but when he didn't follow that up with anything more, she began to wonder. "Really? You mean he's really your brother?"

Livingston have her a tired look. "Since I was born," he told her. "He's the oldest of the Jackson brothers, then me, then Delroy." Lucy recognized the name Delroy--the bartender at the resort and Captain Neil's first mate.

"Oh, so you all grew up here?"

"More or less. Same mother, two fathers. Wendell's was a sea captain on a tanker. Del and me, our dad was a jazz man. My mom, she kept her own name, though, so we're all Jacksons." He slowed down and pulled into a gravel drive in front of a low building of yellow brick with a St. Hilaire seal over the door. Two squad cars with brown and tan markings were parked before the rhododendron bushes in front of the building and two chunky young men in brown uniforms lounged near the door, smoking. "So here we are. St. Hilaire police. I'll wait for you outside," he said.

"Yes. Thanks." She opened the door, but before she got out, she turned back to him. "Any hints for dealing with your brother? I need to find out what's going on about the death of that man Chin at the resort."

"Nope. Good luck with that. He's a real hardass."

Lucy groaned and pushed herself up from the car. The sun was blazing. She thought she should try to play the card of being one professional to another, but the fact that she no longer carried her badge made her feel naked. She wasn't sure she could do this.

THIRTEEN

As Lucy marched up to the glass doors of the police station, she thought she noticed one of the young officers glaring at Livingston. They moved aside for her in a way that made her feel old, but she merely asked if the chief was there. One of the young men held the door for her, directing her to a receptionist inside.

After a preliminary phone call, she was led down a corridor to a small businesslike office where Chief Wendell Jackson sat behind a desk with several piles of papers in front of him. At one side were a keyboard and large monitor. He stood and invited her to take a lightly padded metal chair opposite him. "What can I do for you Ms. O'Donnell?" He peered through his steel rimmed square eyeglasses.

"I've come because I'm concerned about what you said to me yesterday," she told him. "About not leaving without letting you know. We only have the timeshare for this week, and we need to leave on Saturday, so, if for some reason you need all or some of us to stay, we'll have to make other arrangements. In fact, I don't think we can. Dr. Murphy needs to get back to her practice, my sister's husband is expecting her to return, they have other plans the following week, and

Mrs. Lin is needed by her daughter to care for her grandchildren. I want to find out what we can do to ensure we'll leave as scheduled. Can you help me with that?"

He didn't reply immediately. He was looking at a sheet of paper in front of him and his face was gathered in a frown. Lucy wondered if she had said something wrong. But when he spoke, he surprised her. "So, you were in homicide for a long time, is that true?" He said it as if the paper in front of him gave him the information and she wondered if he had, in fact, been checking up on her background. It certainly sounded like it.

"That's right. I just retired. I mean, I'd moved on to some more administrative duties, but most of my time I was a homicide detective." She hoped he wouldn't ask about the administrative duties. Boston politics were thorny to say the least, and she'd had a rocky time after leaving investigative duties. In fact, she'd come to regret ever moving up the food chain. It was the biggest mistake in her life.

"I know your brother, Mike," he said. "He was my mentor in an IACP program."

The International Association of Chiefs of Police was an organization that upper echelon police officials, like her brother, belonged to. Lucy knew Mike had volunteered for a program that helped train chiefs in rural and small jurisdictions to take advantage of expertise that big city departments had on staff. He'd travelled to Wyoming and a reservation in New Mexico. He must have come to St. Hilaire on one of his trips. He was Stephen's father and that perhaps explained her nephew's interest in the island.

"Yes. Mike's still on the job," she said.

The Chief seemed to come to a decision, putting down the sheet of paper and sitting back to look her in the eyes.

"I think you can understand that the crimes we deal with here are usually predictable. We have thefts and scams where visitors are targeted. We've formed a special squad to deal with those, and we make a big effort to protect our visitors to be sure they have a safe and comfortable visit. You can imagine how important that is on an island that depends on tourism as our main economic engine."

Lucy thought he was quite well spoken. She wondered if the chief position was elected. "Then we have the crimes against locals, the usual drunken brawls, domestic disturbances, petty theft. And we have a small number of problems with drug trafficking where they try to move drugs through the island from South America. There's been a big joint task force working on that and I'm glad to say St. Hilaire has pretty much been removed from that drug corridor in the past few years. That's no longer a big problem. But something like this," he picked up a red folder and shook his head as he opened it, "this is not so common. Take a look."

Lucy was surprised when he turned the folder around and pushed it towards her. She sat forward eagerly when she saw it was the coroner's report on Chin's death. The form was different from what she was used to, but it was easy enough for her to hone in on the important details. She read with interest, then flipped through the photographs behind the forms. "Poison?" she asked.

"So, it would seem. Although you can see that there's some uncertainty."

"Typical. The medicos never want to sign off on anything for certain, they always give you probabilities," she told him, and she was surprised to see that he really wanted her input. "This wouldn't be common in Boston either, you know. Most homicides are pretty straightforward." She found herself reassuring him.

It was a tricky kind of situation. There was reason to believe the death was unnatural but at the same time the medical folks wouldn't absolutely confirm it. She'd seen it go both ways, finding out what appeared to be a natural death turned out to be a cold-blooded grab at an inheritance by a supposedly heartbroken relative, and, in a different case, a son was accused of getting rid of an elderly mother when it turned out the woman had mixed up her medications by mistake resulting in a lethal dose.

"Straightforward, yes. You see, Captain O'Donnell, it was captain, wasn't it?" Lucy was startled, he really had been checking up on her. He knew she was retired so it seemed odd that he was insisting on using her title.

"Yes, that was my final rank, before I left." She didn't say that retirement had spared her from demotion. No need to go into that.

"Well, Captain, I can understand your problem with not wanting to extend your stay, but I also have a problem. You see this is the end of our season here, and some of our staff are seasonal, so we are down to a small number of officers. And most of my guys aren't experienced in this kind of investigation. Truth is, every time I get one trained up, they get lured away to the mainland or one of the bigger islands. I just had my best young investigator resign to take a post with that joint task force. And right now there are some other, let's say some complicating factors. As a result, I just don't have the staff to do all the work I need to move this along in an efficient fashion. So, I can't promise you that you'll be able to leave on time. I mean, what would you do in my place? Perhaps some of you might leave, but we'll have to ask Mrs. Lin to stay until we know where we are with this. Look at the file."

Lucy picked up the file and looked through it. She had no idea why the chief was sharing this information, but she read it eagerly. Chin and his father had been staying at the resort for the past month. He had recently sold a startup company and retained only a small staff. He had been touring a number of Caribbean islands, perhaps looking for investment opportunities according to a summary statement by whoever had been doing the research for Chief Jackson. When Lucy got to notes about the interview with Chin's father she saw that he claimed Meilan had exchanged insults with the son, not the father. She cleared her throat. "You know, I was there when Mrs. Lin had words with the Chins. I don't speak Chinese, but I thought it was the father and Meilan who were arguing, not the son."

Chief Jackson looked satisfied. "Miss Vandergott also had that impression. But you can see how it would look if we let Mrs. Lin leave before we have a full explanation. Mr. Chin's father has already complained to his consul. There's no Chinese presence on the island but over on Guadalupe, there's a consulate."

Lucy shook her head. Politics, it was everywhere. "Well, you can't just keep us here forever."

"Unfortunately, I can, but believe me when I say I don't want to. That's why I was thinking you might be able to assist."

"Assist?"

"Yes, as a consultant, perhaps? Your brother suggested it. He knows how limited we are with staff, and he understands the policy of supplementing local talent when something comes up that's more than we can handle. As a retired officer you must have considered going into business consulting? I believe it's often done?"

"Mmm. I haven't been retired long enough to think about it." Her brother Mike had suggested consulting to her. He must be behind this offer.

"We contract for expert services. I have a discretionary fund. This death is just the kind of situation we use it for."

Lucy stared at him. "Are you saying you want to hire me? You can't be serious."

But he was. It turned out he had even already contacted her former superiors at the BPD and had received a glowing recommendation from the Chief of the Bureau of Investigations. He seemed quite confident of her agreement. "So, if you can help us to do a proper investigation, it would ensure that you're allowed to return home as soon as possible."

Lucy considered the fact that she was connected to Meilan who would have to be considered a suspect. Should that disqualify her? She didn't think so. The local department needed outside expertise for this case, and she could always recuse herself it if became necessary. The best result for everyone would be a speedy resolution of the cause of death, so she agreed to the unusual proposition.

She knew it was real when she filled out the paperwork which included her social security number and her previous employment. Jackson was really hiring her. It occurred to her that the chief had probably called her brother for a recommendation of who to ask for outside help. It was only a coincidence that she happened to have the skills and be present on the island. She had no personal connection with the deceased.

When she asked about other officers she might need to work with, he told her she would report directly to him. He even gave her a badge and had her raise her hand to swear her in. But she wondered whether lack of trained staff was the only problem that was causing him to turn to outside help. There was a certain coldness when he introduced her to the two young officers who had been standing outside, as he led her out of the offices.

The chief was unfazed by their reaction, continuing to lead her briskly to his four-by-four with a large police medallion on it. Before she could explain to Livingston, the chief shooed his brother away. The van driver threw up his hands in exasperation before shooting off, leaving behind a spray of gravel.

"Captain, please, let's go and talk to the elder Mr. Chin once again, come."

FOURTEEN

They found the elder Mr. Chin in his wheelchair, on the porch of the luxury timeshare condominium that Lucy had toured the previous day. He sat with a plaid wool blanket over his knees, despite the Caribbean heat, and his head had the sort of immobility that suggested the stiffened joints of arthritis. His hands were curled like claws along the arms of the wheelchair. Anna Maria had conducted them to the condo, and there was a maid cleaning the inside. Lucy and Chief Jackson joined the old man on the balcony. The chief explained that they had additional questions. When Anna Maria quickly excused herself, Lucy thought the young Dutch woman was retreating from a storm cloud that she could see gathering over the old man's rigid head. Lucy took a seat on one of the canvas chairs, and the chief took another.

At first the old man pretended to not understand them. But when Lucy cheerfully suggested that she get Mrs. Lin to translate, suddenly he spoke quite fluent English with a slight British accent. Lucy speculated that he might have learned it in Hong Kong.

"That woman is an illiterate peasant," he told them. "She was jealous of my son's success. No doubt her family is not so successful. She was raised in an ignorant time in my country. She is too stupid to understand the concept of Capitalism with Socialist Characteristics. She is of the old guard. They are not able to adjust to the new century. It is regrettable," he told them.

Lucy felt like she had listened to an election speech by a particularly sleazy politician. She remembered Meilan ranting about how the younger Chin was a capitalist pig, though, so she decided to move the questions to the older man's personal history. "Mrs. Lin mentioned that she knew you from the Cultural Revolution and that you had been involved in some criminal activity at that time."

The old man's watery eyes slithered towards Lucy's face while his neck remained stiffly in place. She saw his tongue move across his lips and thought of a snake. "Old woman, bad memory," he said. "She refers to bad time in my country. Chairman Mao Zedong was great leader, unfortunately led astray by his evil wife and Gang of Four. The Party repudiated that movement. Old woman is mistaken. Ignorant peasant family, she is jealous of party cadre. You can talk to Chinese consul in neighboring islands. Chin family is most respected, high in party structure. Lin woman is ignorant refugee. Those who flee China tell lies. Official American policy is to discredit such lies." He licked his lips again after this statement.

Chief Jackson took over. "We will certainly be talking to your consul. As an independent republic, St. Hilaire welcomes investment by you and your countrymen." Lucy thought he was tactfully pointing out that there was no American jurisdiction involved, and no American policy to be consulted. Of course, they all knew American influence was paramount, but islands that existed by tourism would go out of their way to welcome any visitors with money. And the Chinese had certainly shown they had money in recent days. "We have many local businessmen of Chinese heritage," the chief said. "I understand you are a quite important official of the Chinese Communist party. I confess, I am not familiar with the doctrine you mentioned. Do you mean it is not unusual for a prominent communist in your country to have a son who sells his company in an American IPO for many millions of dollars? I was a little surprised to learn about that."

"Not unusual," the snake eyes blinked. "Capitalism with Socialist Characteristics is doctrine."

"I see. We have a lot in common nowadays, don't we?" Chief Jackson said. "Why, I just read an article about how in your big cities, people were being displaced when their homes were taken by the government and given to big developers in the name of economic development. Did you know exactly the same thing is happening here? Right on this island? It is. We have quite a few demonstrations going on right now about that. People who don't want to go along with that plan. When I read that article about China in this morning's newspaper, I thought to myself, why that's the same thing that's happening here. Is that Capitalism with Socialist Characteristics then? I guess we have Capitalism with St. Hilaire Characteristics that's an awful lot like what happens in your country."

He said it in the most cordial manner and with a slightly hometown hick style that Lucy didn't buy for a moment. They all knew the kind of demonstrations being staged on the island wouldn't have been tolerated for a day back in Chin's homeland. Lucy bit her cheek lightly and looked out at the expanse of water below them to keep from rolling her eyes.

Chin's face was as stiff as if it were chiseled in stone. "Lin woman is mistaken. I do not know her in China. If she says I do, she lies. She threatened my son and now he is dead. I have asked Chinese consul to fly here to assist. Death of Chinese national is not to be taken lightly. Someone must pay."

"We will find out what happened to your son, but I have to ask you again, are you sure he didn't suffer from any health problems that might have caused him to collapse?"

The lizard like tongue shot out and wet the thin lips before the old man replied. "My son was young man. Too young for any problems. What is cause of death? I demand to know. If hotel is to blame, we will seek compensation. If person is to blame, we will demand retribution."

He certainly was fluent, and Lucy felt sympathy for Chief Jackson who would have to face the threat of an international incident if Chin decided to make waves. And Chin seemed determined to be as nasty as he could in the circumstances. Despite the fact that he was confined to the wheelchair, he seemed to be the kind of man who could cause a lot of trouble if he put his mind to it. She didn't envy the chief his position in the coming week.

"According to the coroner's office, you son died by ingesting aconite. It's a vegetable poison that is available in a number of forms. We are currently investigating the source. It could have been in something he ate or drank, although whether it was an accident or done on purpose we have yet to determine. According to the medical people, the aconite paralyzed his breathing and led to cardiac arrest. We are very sorry for your loss, and we will do everything in our power to investigate the causes."

Old Chin grunted.

Before they left, Lucy asked if they could search his son's things in case there was anything that would help them to find out what had happened. The old man refused. She hid her outrage, but Chief Jackson just shrugged as they descended in the elevator. "Stubborn old cuss, but since he's refusing, it may be better to leave him to stew for a while. We can get a warrant, of course, but I'd like to postpone riling the man until we have to."

Lucy just rolled her eyes and suggested they start with the resort staff.

FIFTEEN

There was a loft above the bar at Pelican Bay Resort where the real work took place. Floor to ceiling windows overlooked the infinity pool and the vista of the sea that spread off to the horizon where a few fluffy clouds decorated the sky. A model of the resort sat under glass, displaying a newly proposed expansion around the harbor behind the main buildings. The new structures were like magnificent little doll houses with perfect tiny little pieces of furniture, wine glasses and even artwork on the walls. Lucy wondered how much it cost to build the miniature compared to the cost of the full-sized resort.

Anna Maria Vandergott stood nervously beside a bar of polished blonde wood. There was an espresso machine on another table as well. "Could I get you something? It will be a few minutes before Mr. Menotti will be able to break."

She sidled in front of the glass door to an adjoining conference room where Lucy could see the short Italian gesturing energetically towards a Powerpoint slide of a chart on a wall mounted flat screen. She recognized the newlyweds and the other couple from the dinner cruise. They were strategically placed where they had no choice but to take in the view of the expanse of blue-green Caribbean water.

By the dollar signs on the slide and the gestures of Carlo Menotti, Lucy guessed he was moving in for the kill. Then he stopped for a moment, listening intently, and she shifted her stance to see a figure seated at the very end corner. It was Meilan Lin and she appeared to be an active participant in the session. Lucy rolled her eyes. She figured Meilan had decided she needed that free breakfast again and was extracting a toll for having to sit through the sales talk. Lucy wondered what dialectic would emerge between a dedicated Communist who complained about "capitalist pig" entrepreneurs and a high-powered timeshare salesman.

Glancing at Chief Jackson, who was taking Anna Maria up on her offer of a cappuccino, Lucy thought the local chief was being too patient. After all, they were investigating a murder. On the other hand, she was uneasy when she thought about what Meilan might say to him. The Chinese grandmother was explosive and irrepressible when she got going.

"Captain O'Donnell, you know Miss Vandergott, don't you?" Lucy nodded. She didn't think the young woman's connection to her nephew was relevant in the circumstances, so she let the chief continue without interruption. "Miss Vandergott had the misfortune to experience one of the few violent crimes on the island when she arrived last spring," he said.

"It was very terrible," the young woman said. "I left the villa before it happened, and the woman was only an acquaintance, but it was a very terrible thing. The man who did it is dead now. Didn't you tell me that?"

The chief nodded. "That's true. I'm very sorry you had to experience such a thing." He turned to the frowning Lucy. "You see, Miss Vandergott travelled to St. Hilaire with a young widow, a Mrs. Sobel."

"Actually, we only met on the plane, but I had a few free days before I started working and she had a whole villa to herself, so she invited me to stay with her--until I had to start my job. I was quite lucky, and it was a lovely villa. Nothing bad happened until after I left."

Chief Jackson continued the story. "Mrs. Sobel rented a villa on the other side of the island where it's rather deserted. It seems she had come to recover from her husband's recent death. He died of cancer, in Australia. The poor woman had no close relations, as we found out when she died. Only some grown stepchildren from her husband's first marriage and they weren't close. It was after Miss Vandergott left that Mrs. Sobel was robbed and killed. Her body was found on the rocks below the villa. It was luck that a man found her before the body was washed away by the tide."

"I felt so awful," Anna Maria said. "It happened after I left her and moved here to start my job. They give us lodgings, you see. And it was the taxi man who brought us from the airport who did it. He was the same one we called to bring me here from the villa." She shivered. "To think I was in the automobile with him. I thank God for my safety, but poor Mrs. Sobel, I can't help thinking he might have dropped me off and gone right back to and rob and kill her. I was so relieved when I heard he was dead, shot by the police."

Lucy looked at the chief with surprise. There seemed to be more violent crime and serious police action in St. Hilaire than she expected. A police shooting in Boston was an uncommon event. How much more so on such a small island? At least it ought to be uncommon. The young woman's reaction seemed a little off to her as well. Despite all her years of experience, it seemed rather cold blooded to Lucy to gloat about the death of the man. Perhaps it was the young woman's way of dealing with the shock of such violence. Nonetheless, for a moment Lucy wondered at her nephew's taste in women.

Chief Jackson was gently stirring his coffee. "His fingerprints were found in the villa. When two of my officers went to arrest him, he resisted. There was a shootout, and he was killed. Some of Mrs. Sobel's stolen jewelry was found hidden in his taxi."

Lucy was somewhat alarmed to hear a robbery suspect was armed with a gun on the small island. Of course, big American cities had a problem with guns, but St. Hilaire? "Very dramatic. They couldn't take him down without a shooting?" She realized right away that she shouldn't have said it. Chief Jackson bristled at the perceived criticism.

"We don't have the resources of a large city department. We can't call out a SWAT team to arrest a robbery suspect. They said he pulled the gun right away and they had no choice but to shoot him before he could fire."

Lucy noticed that the description depended on the testimony of the officers. She wondered if there were other eyewitnesses as well, and whether there was something questionable about the shooting. She couldn't help speculating that the shooting must have sent a message to other local thieves and scam artists about what could happen to you if you harmed a visiting tourist. The killing of a tourist had to be bad for the island's main industry, after all. Was someone trying to do something about it?

"Everybody was very happy they caught him," Anna Maria said, and Lucy was sure they would be. No wonder the chief wanted an outside investigator when another tourist was found dead. She wondered if she was being set up to take the blame whether they did or didn't identify Chin's killer. If he even was killed. She shrugged, thinking that if she found out, in the end, that she was only a patsy it wouldn't be the first time.

Carlo Menotti had finished, and they saw him move to the door of the conference room to release his captives. Lucy knew this was the point in the proceedings where he turned the prospective clients over to Anna Maria or one of the other attractive young salespeople to give them a tour. As Anna Maria moved in to take over, they heard Carlo bantering with Meilan.

"Too much," she said. "Too expensive. Have to be a big bucks to afford."

"On the contrary, Madame, this is probably the most affordable vacation plan you will ever have a chance to invest in. As I mentioned, it's because of the new expansion that these prime weeks are available at such a bargain price. But if you don't believe it, it's nothing to me. Believe me, these weeks are so good they will be gone—like that." He snapped his fingers. "No problem."

"Oh, yes, big problem, big problem. You're not going to get rid of them so easy. Not with that price. Big price needs a Big Bucks Daddy." Meilan waved at the couples moving away with their guide. "No Big Bucks here, you'll see." Suddenly she became aware of Lucy and especially the uniformed Chief Jackson. Her eyes narrowed. It was obvious that she didn't like the policeman. "I'll go swim now," she said and bounced out the door.

Carlo watched her go with a glint in his eye that Lucy recognized as a determination to overcome Meilan's objections. She must present a challenge to him. Lucy thought he would have a rude awakening when he found out how Meilan managed on a small Chinese government pension by living with her daughter. But he was an experienced operator, used to parting fools from their money, so she felt no obligation to warn him.

They conducted the interview in the conference room. Carlo Menotti took out a white linen handkerchief and wiped sweat from his brow as they sat down. He told them the younger Chin had purchased two months of time in the penthouse timeshare unit. He had told Carlo that he was looking to invest money from the sale of his company but then he fended off all of the real estate schemes proposed by Carlo.

"He was interested in natural gas," Menotti told them. "I told him they excavated around here and found nothing, but he had his own sources of information. I think the old man knows something. Probably about where other Chinese are planning on investing. I think they planned to get there first, then turn around and sell it, whatever it was, back to other Chinese. But they weren't planning on staying here. That's why the timeshare was enough for him. I tried to interest him in some really good property deals but no dice, as you say. The old man had some interest in the local grocery stores, I think. He used to go meet with some of the owners."

Carlo brushed crumbs from the table in front of him and deposited them on a tray with leftover pastries. "I have another session starting in a few minutes. Why are you asking these questions? We're all terribly sorry for this unfortunate situation. Mr. Chin obviously had some sort of underlying health condition. The hot tub has signs clearly posted, about the dangers and the responsibility of anyone who uses it. I've checked with our lawyers. No matter what the old man may be saying, the resort is in no way responsible. Let me get you our lawyer's contact information." He pulled out a card conveniently located in the breast pocket of his elegant gray silk suit. "We are terribly sorry for this unfortunate event, but we take no responsibility for it." Lucy could see him looking over her shoulder to where two more couples were entering the reception area.

Chief Jackson fingered the business card. "It's not the hot tub that concerns us," he said. Menotti's full attention returned to the chief and he looked alarmed. "According to the coroner," the chief told him, "Mr. Chin was poisoned."

SIXTEEN

They left a startled Carlo Menotti to chew on that one and descended the broad staircase to the resort lobby.

"So, where would you go next? Should we question Mrs. Lin, or would it be better if you did that without me?" Chief Jackson asked her.

"I may be able to get more from her alone and, in any case, we need to talk to the staff. We saw Miss Vandergott take Chin a drink while he was in the hot tub. He was on the boat trip with us before that and we all ate the same food. I didn't notice that he had any problem. Let's ask the bartender about that drink. He might have seen something since the bar's open late." As she plunged around the stairs to the doorway of the resort bar, she noticed a bit of reluctance on the part of Chief Jackson. He followed her more slowly.

The bar was located a few steps above the infinity pool, which was convenient for guests. Behind the bar stood the stocky, smiling young man who had helped Captain Neil with the boat, Delroy Jackson. He smiled at Lucy and held up a shaker. "Guavaberry Crush?" he asked. He'd made the local specialty for Lucy and her friends their first night at the resort and it had become their favorite drink. She was about to turn him down when she saw his face fall. He put the shaker down stiffly. Lucy looked over her shoulder to where Chief Jackson was entering through the open door. The two men were studiously avoiding looking at each other. The stiffness made Lucy change her mind.

"Sure," she said. "Make me one."

The bartender looked at her with surprise but then he grinned and started pulling ingredients together. He seemed to approve of her decision. When she waved over the chief, asking him if he wanted one, the bartender switched on the blender to crush ice. Chief Jackson shook his head no. Of course, he wouldn't drink since he was on the job, but Lucy was still on vacation. She wasn't sure she believed she was really going to be paid as a consultant and even if she was, there was no way she would cut short her well-earned vacation activities. If he didn't like it, he could fire her. She might have been hoping that he would.

When the blender finally stopped, the bartender bent his head over his ingredients. Lucy said, "Delroy, I'm helping Chief Jackson look into what happened to Mr. Chin the other night."

Delroy looked up with a raised eyebrow and Lucy wondered if she'd said something wrong. She remembered what Livingston had told her. The chief was a brother with a different father while Delroy was the youngest brother with the same father as Livingston.

Chief Jackson cleared his throat. "Ms. O'Donnell is a retired captain of homicide from Boston. I've hired her to help with the investigation into the death of Mr. Chin here at the resort," he said.

Meanwhile Delroy was busy adding cream of coconut from a can, evaporated milk, sugar, pineapple juice, rum and finally mango and guavaberry liquers. After shaking, he poured out the mixture into two wide glasses. Lucy decided to continue. "OK, so Delroy, last night Mr. Chin was in the hot tub and never got out, we saw Miss Vandergott bring him a drink and a pitcher. Do you know what he was drinking?"

Delroy served up the glass to Lucy, placed another in front of his brother the chief, and then wiped up the counter he had been working on. "Let's see. It was last night it happened, yes? I heard all about it when I came in. A terrible thing, finding him in the tub like that. I was on, but I didn't make up that pitcher, no. It was his special rum punch. He had a recipe he was very fussy about. Some folks are like that. Anna Maria, now, Mr. Carlo put her in charge of Chin and his father from the beginning. He told her to make them happy. Must be expectin' to sell him something big. So she always took special care of him.

"I was tending to the Blaines and their group. They came in after that dinner boat cruise with Captain Neil and they wanted some night caps. While I was dealing with them, Anna Maria took care of Chin. She made the punch, right here, while I was talking to the others. They had some champagne when they all come in, then I think they tried to buy him a drink, but he said he wanted to change and soak, and then that other couple, that aren't married, they said they wanted a moonlight swim too, so they left. Mr. Mike Blaine, he had a couple more, but his wife left. I think she wasn't so happy with him drinking, if you know what I mean. By then, Chin had his pitcher and we closed down."

Since Delroy had been first mate on the boat trip Lucy asked him, "You were around when they were eating earlier, on the catamaran, too. Do you recall that Chin ate or drank anything that was different from the others?" Lucy asked.

"He didn't eat the meat, I think. He was eating the seafood and I remember the Blaines and their friends, or, I guess they are their employees, they didn't try the eel. Chin wanted the eel something bad, and they brought it to him at the Japanese place. But the others didn't eat it."

Lucy tried to remember if anyone at her table had eaten the eel. She didn't think so. "You might want to check on that," she told the chief. He shrugged. He hadn't touched the drink his bartender brother had put in front of him.

"Did the man order any other food that night?" Chief Jackson asked.

Delroy bristled a bit, but he answered. "Not that I know, man. The kitchen was pretty much closed down by then." Lucy had been sipping the luscious pink colored drink, so he poured more into her glass from the cocktail shaker. She looked at it ruefully, figuring the number of calories involved was probably monumental, but she took another sip, letting it roll around her tongue for the flavor. It was all part of getting a witness statement, wasn't it? At least, when you were retired... and a consultant...

Chief Jackson stood up straight. He had been leaning forward with his arms on the bar. "If you'll excuse me, I'll just go check with the kitchen to make sure Chin didn't order any food that night."

He lumbered away, his brother watching him go with a grim look on his face. Lucy figured there must be some kind of family dispute in the background to make the brothers so hostile. Maybe it was the guavaberry crush, or the rum in the guavaberry crush, but, against her best judgement, she asked Delroy what the matter was.

He gave her a long look. "He's got a bunch of murderers working for him. That's what it is."

SEVENTEEN

"Murderers?" Lucy looked down at her pink drink to see if it was the source of hallucinations. "Did you say murderers?"

Delroy topped off her drink from the shaker and looked a little sheepish. "It's an island thing," he said. "Lou's brother was only the most recent." Lucy's brow furrowed at the cryptic remark, and he expended some energy mopping up imaginary spills on the counter before him. "Look, it's not that I think Wendell would do it, but he knows damn well what they're doing, and he's done nothing to stop it. I'm only telling you, because you're real police."

"Why don't you tell me what you are talking about."

"Past six months, any local gangsters rob the visitors, they get blown away. No, it's true, I'm telling you. It started at beginning of the season. There were a couple of tourists off one of them cruise boats, got beat up and robbed. So that cruise line, they changed and didn't stop at the island anymore. It was right the beginning of the season, so everybody got all het up about it. The cops, they thought they knew who did it but when they brought them in, the judge let them off sayin' they didn't have a search warrant or some such. So that died down, then some woman visitor at one of the resorts got knocked down and the guy ran off with her bag. Everybody was furious. Everybody knows it was that same stupid kid who did the other robbery.

"Next thing you know, that kid's been cornered in the market. Three of them big cops against one skinny stupid teenager thinks he's a big gangster boy. They shot him down. But then they put a gun in his hand and said he was aiming at them.

"Now, everybody in that market saw. I mean, they all ducked and ran away, but they saw. That boy didn't have a gun. That gun was from another bank robbery last year. The police had that gun for evidence. Course they didn't tell no one that, but we heard." He shook his head, polishing the counter energetically. "Everybody knows robbing the visitors is bad for business, but you can't just go shootin' people! And then it happened again. Three more times, and they all say these guys, who they know robbed or beat a tourist, but when they couldn't prove it, they say they had guns. One time it was the same gun as in that first one. Can you believe it? You think people don't know? But Wendell, he just says he can't prove it on the officers. Then the last one was Billy Roberts, Louella's brother. Louella, she's Livingston's girlfriend. She says he didn't do it. It was a woman tourist got robbed and killed. Louella swears he didn't do it. Got shot anyhow. Wendell, he says he can't do nothing about it. Everybody's scared of those cops now, let me tell you."

Lucy sipped the drink. This explained why the chief wanted to hire an outside investigator. If there were a bunch of vigilante cops killing off offenders for messing up the tourist trade, surely Chin's murder would bring them out. She didn't know whether the chief wanted to prevent the murder of a suspect or trap the officers who were doing it. She did think she might have to keep her head down to avoid the crossfire. This part time job was looking less and less attractive.

"I see, Delroy. So, do you have any idea who might have killed Chin? Because your brother the chief told Mr. Menotti he was poisoned."

"Poisoned? So that's why he's gone to the kitchen. No way. What, you think I poisoned the drink? They planning to come after me now? Those f-ing bastards, I'm telling Livingston and we'll get them before they get us."

"Now, calm down. That's not why your brother and I came in here. In fact, I think he hired me to investigate to keep those officers from knowing what's going on. Yeah, I'm retired from Boston police, I did homicide for a long time and when he found that out, he decided to hire. If what you're saying is right, I think he's trying to avoid having those guys go all vigilante."

Delroy regarded Lucy with suspicion, but he set his jaw, and didn't contradict her.

"Is there anything else you can tell me about Chin and what he was doing here, who he was working with? If he was poisoned, then somebody must have wanted him dead, but it hardly seems like a local robbing a tourist."

"His old man was up to something. I don't know what. He got Livingston to take him out to meet with other Chinese on the island. They own groceries, some property. Captain Neil knows Chin from Australia. Chin wasn't too happy when he mentioned it, but Captain Neil recognized him. Chin was doing some deal with the Blaines on the boat. They got a big sloop over in the marina, they take out corporate types, some kind of team building or something. I told Neil, we could do that too, but he just laughs. Ask Livingston, he'll tell you where the old man goes."

"And Captain Neil, where do I find him, on his catamaran?"

Delroy raised an eyebrow. "Mostly, but you want him today, he came over a little while ago to see your doctor lady friend. He's probably still here."

EIGHTEEN

Lucy went looking for Chief Jackson and found him just exiting through the swinging doors to the kitchen. He told her they had not served any food to Chin that night. When she broached the delicate question about the possibility of vigilante cops on his force, he went dead pan and refused to discuss it. His cell rang and after a short conversation he told her he had to head over to the other side of the island where there were more protesters blocking the way for tourists from one of the cruise liners. He told her to let him know in the morning what progress she had made. Lucy thought he was glad to drop the investigation in her lap. It seemed like local disturbances were more in his comfort zone. Weird poisonings of foreigners were just not in his repertoire, but she wasn't sure they were in her own, either.

She decided to go back to the timeshare to see if she could find Captain Neil, who was supposed to be visiting Mary. She found them in the air-conditioned living room. Norah had convinced Meilan to join her when she took the resort van into town to go shopping, so Mary and Captain Neil were alone. The Australian sailor had followed

Dr. Murphy's instructions in treating his rash and he'd come to show her how it was working. Lucy felt a bit awkward interrupting their tete a tete. She decided they should give Mary a good ribbing about her conquest over wine that evening.

"Delroy told me you recognized Chin from Australia?" she asked Neil.

"Yes, I did. But I'm not sure he remembered me," Captain Neil told her. He wore a fresh blue and white shirt and neatly pressed white shorts. A large waterproof watch on his left wrist seemed to emphasize the stringy muscles and weather-beaten sandals protecting his feet. His sandy hair was neatly combed, and the blue of his eyes reminded Lucy of the Caribbean Sea. Not a bad looking guy, but a bit on the hyperactive side, she thought. He spread his arms as he continued. "He might not have wanted to. Many of us have left behind a life we wanted to get away from when we moved here. I think everybody has a right to make a new start. I know that's what I did. So, I didn't mention it when I recognized him, but he didn't recognize me. I just made a comment to Del about it."

"I see. How did you know him in Australia? And when was that?" It seemed strange to Lucy that they would have pretended they'd never met before. It made her wonder about their relationship in Australia.

"Three, no, four years ago. I was still working for a distillery. I think Chin was taking money he made from his internet firm and buying property in the west of Australia. He was still running that company, but he travelled a lot and I think he might have been investing money for other people--probably party officials who couldn't do it themselves. A lot of those Communist party higher ups get their money out of China and invest it in other countries. It's common in Australia and New Zealand, some of the Pacific islands, too. He was making bids on some ranches. I knew a lot of those ranching guys because they were in my sales area and, believe me, they were some pretty heavy drinkers. They often owned local pubs as well, so I supplied them."

"Is there any reason why he wouldn't want people to know that?"

"I don't think so. I mean, I heard he sold his company and was moving on, looking to start something new, but I don't know that there was anything secret about what he did in the past. I think he probably just didn't recognize me, and, as far as I'm concerned, I left that life behind. He would have seen me in two-thousand-dollar Armani suits and silk ties back in Sydney, anyhow, not like this."

Lucy found it hard to imagine Captain Neil in anything so formal. She also wasn't sure she believed his motive for not recognizing Chin. She asked him about what Chin had eaten and drunk on the catamaran trip but there was nothing that stood out in his mind about that.

Mary was getting impatient with the discussion. Lucy hadn't had time to tell her she'd been hired to help with the investigation. At the pause in questioning, Mary showed Lucy a small painting she had in her lap. "Look at this, Lucy. Captain Neil gave it to me, as thanks for my suggestions about his rash from the fiberglass. I told him he really didn't have to do that."

Lucy was going to tell Captain Neil about how they all imposed on Mary about medical issues, but she was struck by the painting. It was an impressionistic oil painting of a green Caribbean sea gilded by a sunset. There was a beach and a small hut in the foreground and somehow the artist had managed to evoke a huge expanse of sea on the small canvas in the background. There was something about the vibrancy of the colors that had been brought under control and formed into a sort of peace that still pulsed with energy. It reminded Lucy of something, but she had no idea exactly what. It just looked familiar to her.

"A friend of mine did it," Captain Neil said. "He's a local artist."

"It's beautiful."

"Yes, and really you didn't need to do it," Mary told him.

"I wanted to thank you. I can't tell you how much better my rash is, and what a relief that is. Jake is an old friend. He owes me for many a night sailing and drinking. But he's a good mate and a better artist."

"Jake?" Lucy asked.

"Yes, Jake Flaherty. He's been on the island more than twenty years, I think. He makes a living selling his paintings. He has a joint gallery with some of the other local artists over in Trenton."

"Oh my God," Lucy thought. But she didn't say it out loud. Jake Flaherty, could it be the same one? Surely not? Surely not.

NINETEEN

Boston February 1972

A loud knocking woke Lucy. She looked around blearily and recognized the room she had grown up sharing with Norah. For a moment she couldn't think why she was here. She'd moved out, she had her own place now. Her head felt awful when she rose on an elbow, so she dropped back down, feeling sick to her stomach. She had gone out with the girls last night. A bachelorette party while Marty was out with his buddies from the precinct for his bachelor party. She hoped he felt as bad as she did. For her, it had been martinis. Oh, she could taste stale something in the back of her mouth. The knocking got louder. "What?" she yelled. It did remind her of when she lived at home. There was never any privacy.

"That commie coward bastard is here. I don't know what he thinks he's doing here on the day before your wedding, but he says he won't leave till he sees you. If you don't come get rid of him, I'm going to beat the bejesus out of him, so get up."

"Good morning to you, too, Dad," Lucy could feel the adrenalin surge in her body based on the tone of his voice. She did need to get up, so she raised her head and shoulders and yelled "I'll be right there. Leave him alone, I'll get rid of him, just give me a minute." She swore to herself under her breath. She might have done it louder, but she didn't want to provoke her father when he was already mad. She knew it was Jake. She'd expected to hear something from him before this, but there had been nothing. Nothing until the day before her wedding. Of course. The men in her life were such drama queens. She still had to pick up her veil and there was the rehearsal dinner tonight, and first she had to get rid of this hangover. Geeze.

She dug out a pair of sweats from her duffle bag, and quickly rinsed her mouth while running a comb through her hair. Looking at her bedraggled state in the mirror of the only full bathroom in the house, she groaned. It had been the site of many a family battle when she and her four brothers and single sister were fighting to use it while they were growing up.

She was supposed to get home early the night before to set her hair in rollers for the rehearsal dinner. Her sister Norah would rag her about it. She pulled on thick woolen socks and ran downstairs to the front door where she struggled into her boots and grabbed her down jacket from the hook. Her father watched from the bottom of the stairs then stomped off into the kitchen. Her mother stood by the swinging door looking concerned. "It's Jake," she said.

"I know, I know."

"Lucy, you need to get him away and don't let him come back. Your father is furious."

"Right, right." Lucy felt for mittens in her pocket and opened the door. There he was, finally. Too late, as usual. His hair was long, and he had a full beard and moustache. His khaki jacket was hanging open over a flannel shirt and jeans. And sneakers, not even boots despite the foot of snow on the ground. He was so damned needy. She turned and rifled through her brother Dan's neat overcoat for a pair of fur lined leather gloves, then she grabbed Jake's arm and slammed the door behind her. "Come on. Is your car here?"

"I just wanted to, you know, wish you luck. I don't want to make any trouble." His deep voice was gruff in the cold morning air, and he was staring over her shoulder at her mother. A frown creased his forehead.

"Right. Let's go. She pushed him down the steps and out to his beat-up station wagon. She recognized it as the one his family had had when they were in high school, she at St. Clare's and he at Catholic Memorial. Sensing a move of the curtains in the front windows of the house, she grabbed his keys and pushed him into the passenger seat throwing the gloves after him. She jumped in and revved the engine. The car smelled of cigarette smoke and old clothes. She cranked down her window as she pulled away, driving along Baker Street and out on to the VFW parkway till she got to the pancake house where they used to go after dances in high school. What a long time ago that was.

She hustled him into a booth by the window. The place was empty. A tired looking waitress gave them big, laminated menus and poured coffee. Lucy thanked her and ordered a special for both of them. She had been on a diet to fit into her wedding dress, but it was too late for that now. She was too far gone to fit into her dress and had to have it altered anyway. She looked across at the clear blue eyes with long black lashes. Jake always did have the most handsome face. All the girls had envied her when she started dating her older brother Dan's best friend. But that was in the past. The long dead past.

"You're getting married," he said.

She took two little packets of sugar and tore them open, emptying them into her mug. "Well, yeah. We sent you an invitation. Did you get it?" She knew she sounded like a nag, but, really, the day before the wedding? That's when he chooses to show up? "Give me a break," she thought.

"To Marty."

"Right again. You got a problem with that?" Marty. She had a flash of memory. Dan and Jake and Marty in their uniforms. It was a picture she had kept with her and fingered every day for a year, that first year when they were over in Vietnam. But it was Jake, in the middle, whose face she had lingered over the most. Jake was he one she had waited for.

"I'm sorry," he said, and she was annoyed that he seemed to be reading her mind. That was all over. That feeling had been beaten to death and she had stamped it out. But it was his fault. He was the one who killed it. He had only himself to blame.

"Well, I'm not," she said after the waitress set plates full of pancakes and bacon in front of them. She grabbed the glass jar of maple syrup and poured the sticky amber substance over her plate, relishing the act of drowning her pancakes. They would be too soggy after the first few bites, but she didn't care. "I'm not sorry in the least, and you've got a lot of nerve telling me you feel sorry. Marty and I are great together. After everything you did, you don't get to feel sorry for me. Marty has a job. Marty is a good cop, and so am I. Marty isn't wallowing in a pool of self-pity, and he's not strung out on drugs and he's not flipping out and getting into brawls and losing it all the time." And getting arrested. That had been the final straw.

When they first came back, finally discharged, she tried to help him. She had spent so much time rescuing him. Again and again, she went and got him when he was drunk or strung out. Time after time she took him home and shared a cup of tea with his worried mother. His father had finally thrown him out when he turned down a job on the force and joined a group of veterans who were protesting the war.

He shrugged, ducking his head as if she had thrown something. "I know, I'm sorry about me. I'm sorry I haven't been able to adjust. I know your dad tried to help and he's mad at me. But that war is wrong. You don't know, you weren't there. I had to say it was wrong." His eyes flitted around looking everywhere except directly at her. Lucy was not impressed.

"My dad is frustrated. We're all frustrated. We tried helping you and it didn't work. You got worse. You know my dad even got you out of jail and got the charges dropped. He never does that, not even for his own relatives but he felt sorry for you, we all did."

Jake grimaced like he was tasting something sour. He'd heard all this before.

"And it's not like you were into a cause, don't tell me that. Are you still hanging around that place in Cambridge? Still smoking pot, dropping LSD? Still sleeping with that girl?" Lucy had finally opened her eyes when Marty dragged her down to the dirty smoky digs in Cambridge where Jake was in bed with some hippy girl. "Come on, Jake. You just don't want to do anything. You just want to sit around. Everybody tried to help you. They got you jobs but you'd just not show up or you'd fly off the handle and walk out. You got yourself into this mess and you need to get yourself out of it."

He looked sorrowful and that just made her angrier. "I know, Lucy, I know. I try but then somebody says something to me, and I lose it. I try."

"Hey, you weren't the only one who went over there. Dan did, and he got his act together and got accepted to med school. Marty was over there. He got through the academy. He's on the force. But not you. How come you're the only one who can't get it together, huh? What happened to you?" Dan and Marty were the first ones to give up on him. Dan told her once they all had their own devils to battle, while Marty just swore at Jake and said he was a dumb bastard.

Jake looked down at the uneaten food on his plate while Lucy shoveled soggy pancakes into her mouth. He mumbled something. "What?"

"I heard you got on the force."

"That's right. You got a problem with that?" After they broke up, she got serious about getting herself on the force. In the academy she was one of the first dozen women who would carry badge and gun on the BPD. And she decided she wanted Marty as well, coming at him fiercely, and, when she found herself pregnant, making the decision to keep the baby and hold on to the job, the guy, and the kid. She knew it would be hard to do it all, but she was determined. Marty might have his doubts, and she hadn't told the rest of the family about the baby, but she was sure she could do it. Jake might fall apart, but come hell or high water, she would hold it together. And with the child on the way, she had no more time for Jake. He'd have to find another mother.

Now, he was looking at her with those big eyes making her feel a pang of regret, but she stifled it. "I don't know what you want, Jake. But you know it's over between us. Whatever there was, you killed it. Please, don't make a scene. You need to stay away." She really couldn't face a drunk or strung-out Jake showing up at the VFW post where they were having the reception.

He wasn't eating his pancakes; he just turned his fork over and over with his long fingers. "No, I won't," he said. "I promise. I just wanted to say I'm sorry."

What she wouldn't have given for him to have said that six months ago. "It's too late, Jake. You get it? It's too late."

"I know that. I know I'm a screw up."

She suppressed a groan. He was on the self-pity thing again. She just couldn't take it anymore.

"I know. I'm happy for you. Really. I heard you're in the academy. That's great. That's what you always wanted," he said.

She resented that. She hadn't "always wanted" this. She had been forced into it. He was supposed to have done the academy with her brother Dan and Marty, not her. She said nothing, hoping she was projecting a stony image.

He shook his head as if he was feeling sorry for her. She burned with indignation. Where did he get off feeling sorry for her? But then he reached across and took her left hand. "It's better this way, Lucy. I'll never be right again, you know. There wasn't anything you could do about it. I'm sorry."

She pulled her hand away as if burnt. He was turning it around. She had taken him out to breakfast to rub his nose in it and he was still trying to play on her sympathy. She wouldn't regret this marriage, he would. It could have been him as the groom, but he had blown it and she wanted him to know it. "The wedding is tomorrow, in case you didn't read the invitation. It's at St. Theresa's at ten and then the reception is at the VFW post starting at noon. You didn't rsvp but I'm sure we can find a place for you at one of the tables if you want to come."

She'd have to put Dan on keeping Jake away from her father. She didn't need them going at each other. Her father hated it that he'd been in anti-war protests, even though he had gotten Jake out of jail a couple of times. It would be a worry but, after all, Jake had always been one of them. Jake's mother was coming, although his father had suffered a stroke and wasn't able to attend.

"St. Theresa's," he said. "Remember the time we toilet papered Sister Mary Dorothy?"

"Hmm. You and Dan nearly got expelled for that one." The nun had deserved it, though. She was a big fat nun who taught the eighth grade, and she hated the boys who got accepted to Catholic Memorial. She used to humiliate them and try to get them to cry. Lucy remembered how she'd cowed Marty one time and Jake and Dan had gotten revenge by sneaking into the break room where she took a nap every afternoon and festooning her with toilet paper. She didn't know how they had managed to knock her out, but she suspected Jake had used some stolen meds. They led their class to the hallway outside the room when the principal, Mother Alexis, found the sleeping nun. What a miserable human being Sister Dorothy had been. It made Lucy think she would never send her child to be taught by someone like that. She felt her heart skip a beat at the thought of the child inside her.

"Yeah, I remember. Listen, I have to get back. There's a lot of stuff I have to do today. Norah's going to kill me for not setting my hair last night and I still have to pick up the veil."

"Don't worry. I'm not coming," he said, grabbing the check.

"I can get it. You didn't even eat anything."

"It's all right, this I can afford." He threw some bills on the table along with his napkin. "Come on, I'll take you home."

When he pulled up to the front of her parents' house Lucy said "Really, you should come tomorrow. You know everybody. They'd like to see you, I'm sure." Except her father of course but they could handle him.

He looked across at her. His eyes were wide in that near crazy look that he had. "No, it's OK, Lucy. Not my scene, you know. You have a good life."

She felt a surge of emotion that was almost more than she could manage, and she clamped her teeth trying to keep tears from forming, but she bent across and kissed him on the cheek. "You, too, Jake," she said, then she jumped out of the car and barely got the door slammed before he floored the accelerator and disappeared down the street. That was the end of that, she thought.

February 1983

"I don't want that room. I want the other one."

Eleven-year-old Janey was just being perverse. She insisted she wanted the room with the street view when they toured the place before Lucy put down the security deposit, but now she wanted to claim the one with the view of the maple tree in the back yard. Lucy didn't care. Anything for peace at this point. "Great, you take it. Move your boxes in."

She left her daughter upstairs and hopped down to the first floor to see where the furniture had ended up. She was on duty when they were delivered and her mother had supervised. The armchair was on the wrong side of the fireplace, but Lucy didn't care. It was a relief to finally be there. The two-family house in Roslindale was owned by her partner's father-in-law who'd slapped on a new coat of white paint after his last tenants left. The man was a burly retired fireman and Lucy felt confident he would intimidate her ex-husband if Marty ever tried to show up on their mutual doorstep. There were steep stairs down to Washington Street where the traffic whizzed by, but there was a two-car garage out back and Janey could get a bus to school at the corner.

Her daughter was unhappy with the split, but Lucy knew it was necessary. She had to get her out of the little ranch house that had become a cauldron of misery and recrimination. It had been coming on for a long time. Lucy put up with Marty's temper and the bills from strip clubs where he claimed he needed to go to recuperate after a shift on vice. She'd stood up to him and tossed him out when he lifted a hand to her. He repented that and never did it again but when he came up on charges for beating a guy while he was on duty, it was the last straw. Not that he hadn't been called on his behavior in the past, but this time she knew it was in reaction to her own promotion to sergeant. He couldn't handle it that she had moved beyond him, above him. So, he took it out on some poor old drunk. She saw the rage in his eyes, and she decided it was the end. There was no way she would let that rage descend on their daughter. With Janey's inevitable move to the sulky teenage years, Lucy knew he wouldn't be able to control it. This way, he could be a foil. Janey would see her mother as the impossible disciplinarian while her occasional visits with her father would be a time for both of them to bond against her. She didn't mind being the imaginary villain, as long ask Janey was safe.

There was a knock on the door. When Lucy answered it, she found her friend Mary on the top step.

"Pizza, pizza," Mary said, and Lucy echoed her, yelling upstairs for Janey to come down. Mary was followed in by her teenaged daughter, Bridget, and her ten-year-old son Mark. Lucy gave them each a hug and they got the kids settled around the dining room table that Lucy's mother had dredged up from some relative. Her mother didn't approve of the separation, but she grudgingly helped with Lucy's move.

The two women retreated to the kitchen where Lucy searched for a corkscrew for the bottle of good Chianti Mary had brought. She rinsed a couple of glasses and Mary filled them and they had a toast.

"To new beginnings," Mary said.

Lucy clinked glasses and swallowed a big gulp. "How are you doing?' she asked.

Mary peeked at the dining room, but the two girls were carrying on a merry conversation. "Bridgie is coping, and so am I. It's harder for Mark. He just wants to sit at home and watch movies, but I figure, if that's what it takes to get him through it, what the heck. So, I bought him his own TV and VCR player."

Mary's husband had died after a yearlong fight with a virulent lung cancer. Lucy had done what she could to help her childhood friend, but since both Mary and her husband were medical doctors, they knew only too well what the outcome would be. Ron had died at home in a haze of painkillers, but the multiple hospitalizations before that had been grueling for the whole family. Despite her own struggles, Mary had supported Lucy and encouraged her to finally leave her husband.

"I brought you something, for the house," Mary said. "I hope it won't make you feel bad. I found it down in Key West." After the funeral, she had taken her children on a family vacation with her priest brother as a way to help the kids get over it. They had only returned the past weekend. She lifted up a small rectangular package in a plastic shopping bag.

"You didn't have to do that," Lucy said. She found herself touched by the gesture. This would be the first place that would be her own since she had moved in with Marty twelve years before. To have something with no connection to him would be a good thing. She pulled out what was surely a picture and unfolded the brown paper in which it was wrapped.

It was a small oil painting. There was a hand on a windowsill, as if you were looking through a window at a small meadow where a figure was dancing. A big maple tree with a rope swing, and a jungle gym were in the background. Closer to the viewer a girl in a checkered dress was waving her arms and twirling around. The brushstrokes were thick and seemed to be holding a violent motion in check. The hand on the sill was gripping very tightly in a strained way. The window, the trees, the grass all seemed vibrant, as if pulsing with an energy that could break out in aggression at any moment. The figure of the little girl was the only thing that seemed light, airy, and balanced. It made for a strong, palpable tension in the picture. The bottom left hand had "JF" in small black letters.

"It was from a veteran's gallery down there," Mary said. She was watching Lucy closely. "Lucy, Jake Flaherty did it. He's been in a home down there and they do painting and art work as therapy. It gets sold on commission in one of the galleries in Key West. They had some fliers with information about the guys who had done it. Here, look." She handed Lucy a folded sheet of green paper. It described Jake and several other veterans who were painters, briefly noting their wartime service and their residence at a VA facility in Florida.

Lucy took a big breath and looked at the painting. "Sounds like he finally got some help," she said.

"I know. We all wondered if he was dead or something, so it was a relief to see this. His parents are both dead, now, so nobody knew where he was. There were several paintings by him, but I liked this one best and it wasn't too big."

"No, it's perfect. Thank you. And it is good to know things turned out all right for him," Lucy said. She carefully wrapped it back up in the brown paper. "I'll have to think about where to hang it. Meanwhile, if you have come over to help unpack, we've still got a lot of boxes."

"Good. Let's go for it. My kids could use it. There's nothing they like better than ripping things open."

TWENTY

When Mary explained to Captain Neil that Jake Flaherty might be someone they had known many years before, he wanted to arrange a meeting. Lucy told him that she'd been conscripted by Chief Jackson to help with the investigation of Chin's death, so she hesitated to make a commitment. Sensing that she might have other reservations, Mary suggested they wait till the next day and she would contact Neil about a time and place.

"Actually, there's a big regatta at the end of the week, Thursday and Friday. Jake'll be crewing for me on Solace," that was the name of his catamaran. "There's a party at the yacht club afterwards. You should come."

"Oh, Lucy sails," Mary told him, after which he tried to recruit Lucy as crew. She handled a spinnaker in races back in Boston and on Cape Cod but she had no desire to race with people she didn't know. And it had been a few summers since she had last done anything more than Wednesday night beer can races.

"It's not serious, believe me," Captain Neil told her. "In fact, they do this regatta once a month and we take out complete novices. It's just for fun, round the buoys stuff. Do consider it. If you change your mind, there's always room, or just come for the party after. And, by the way, Wendell Jackson will be out there in his old ketch, he wouldn't miss it. It's a regular island thing, once a month. It's supposed to be for the tourists, but the locals are all in it. It's an island wide party. You'll see."

Lucy promised to think about it, and Mary promised she'd go to the party, she was sure that Norah would want to go as well. But she declined the sailboat racing saying it was not her cup of tea. Neither Lucy nor Mary mentioned Meilan, they only hoped she would be able to attend, if she could avoid being arrested, but Lucy didn't want to raise the issue with Captain Neil.

When the captain left, Lucy filled Mary in on what she'd learned from the police. She showed Mary the autopsy report.

"Aconite. That's interesting," Mary said.

"Right. He was poisoned according to the chief."

"Not exactly. Cause of death is drowning but they found traces of aconite. Most likely before the aconite killed him it disabled him enough that he sank into the water and couldn't get out. Hold on a minute." Mary took out her iPhone and began typing with her thumbs. She slid her fingers over the screens a few times, mumbling to herself. Lucy waited.

When she was ready, Mary gave Lucy a layman's explanation. "It's an old poison, also known as monkshood for the plant. It was supposedly used in Roman times. Emperor Claudius was poisoned with it. It was also used as a homeopathic remedy in the nineteenth century till they realized how easy it was to get the dosage wrong."

"How do you get it?"

"Hmm. Well, the plant grows in lots of places and it's been used in poisonings. There was a woman who used it in cooking to kill her ex-boyfriend and his new girl in London a few years ago. She got it from a garden. But actually it's sold in pharmacies still, as a homeopathic remedy. Not regulated because it's plant based. And you could buy it on the internet. Oh, and here's something. It's still popular as a Chinese herbal remedy, and sometimes it's given in too strong a dosage by mistake. Was he taking any herbs do you think? Or maybe an herbal tea?"

"Not that I know of. More like a rum punch, but who can say? Maybe when he went to his room to change for the hot tub he took a pill, or a drink or something. We'll have to check into that. I assume Chief Jackson would think of it, but if he doesn't I'll remind him. Chin's father is threatening an international incident. He's calling in the Chinese consul. It'll be ironic if it turns out to be Chinese herbs that killed him. Anyhow, I thought the chief was treating the old man with kid gloves. He'll have to look into it now." She looked out the window at the horizon. "I hope Meilin didn't bring any Chinese herbs with her. It seems to me Bin said she believes in traditional medicine."

"Oh, but lots of Chinese do. That doesn't mean they would poison someone."

Lucy was glum. Her cop mind was sliding down a well-worn path of suspicion. Chief Jackson couldn't help but follow the same road and she knew it.

TWENTY-ONE

When Louella saw Chief Jackson in the bar, she scurried away. She sure enough didn't trust that man even if he was Livingston's brother. They'd already tried to tell him what those officers did, but he wouldn't listen. After he and that Ms. O'Donnell from 3B in Unit 6 were gone, Louella went in to pass the time of day with Delroy. He told her the O'Donnell woman was some kind of cop from Boston who was helping the chief to find out what happened to the man who had wound up dead in the hot tub.

Louella thought about who she could talk to. Delroy was just a gossip, no good telling him a thing. Before she could decide, the Blaines came in with the couple who were staying on the boat down at the marina. They ordered lunch. While Delroy put in their order, Louella took her ginger ale out to the deck. She could still hear them through the open doors.

"Here, I've got the sailing instructions from them, I'm sending it to all of you," Mike Blaine said. "Check your email." He was tapping on his cell phone.

"You mean you already paid the entrance fee?" Rita Blaine said. "I thought we were going to economize since the Chin contract fell through. That's what you said yesterday."

"This is a business expense, it's advertising. We show off the Last Resort and work the crowd at the awards banquet for another contract. That's different from you laying out my dough on yet another sweatshirt, for crying out loud."

"They're for Mike Junior and Laurie. Do you begrudge a little present for your kids now?"

"Listen, I don't begrudge anything. I'm the one working to send them to those colleges, so don't tell me I begrudge them, like I don't care about my kids. You just say that to make me look bad. If you had your way, you'd be buying out those shops downtown every day. So, don't tell me that. I need you all on board. We need to make a good impression in the racing."

"For Christ sake, it's not like it's a real regatta," Rita said. "They run it every month. It's just for the tourists. You act as if it's the America's Cup or something."

"Just because you don't give a damn, you don't have to ruin it for everyone else. The last time we did a spinnaker hoist you blew it anyhow. I told you about that cleat."

"Hey, if you'd fix the damn thing, maybe it would stay on when the pole was set, instead of letting go. Don't blame me when it fails. Fix it."

"You just hate doing the pole."

"Yeah, that's right. Why don't you do it?"

"And who's going to be on the helm, you?"

"Yeah, maybe. Or Guy. He's got more experience than you do on this water." There was a murmur in the background and Louella thought it must be the Guy person denying he was better. She knew that Mr. Mike Blaine was the boss, so that other guy wouldn't appreciate being used to show up his superior. This Rita Blaine was on a roll for sure.

"You're so mean when you drink, Rita. Guy needs to fly the chute, you know that."

"Me, I'm mean when I drink? You're the one chugging those Bloody Marys like they're water. What's wrong with you?" the woman said.

"There's nothing wrong with me. You need to just pay attention and do what I tell you when you're up there with the pole. We should go out for a practice this afternoon."

"Forget it. I've got a spa appointment. And, anyhow, you can take that pole and put it where the sun don't shine. You and that damned boat. You care more about that than you do for your own children."

"That's a lie."

"I've had it. Have Delroy send my sandwich up to the room."

This announcement was followed by some swearing by Mike Blaine and some conciliatory noises from the other man and woman. Louella shrugged and was about to return to her cleaning duties when her attention was caught by a new entry.

"Hey, Anna Maria," Mike Blaine yelled. "Come over here for a minute, will ya? Here's Delroy with our lunches. Mrs. Blaine left, Del, could you send her sandwich up to the room? She's had a fit of temper. And get Ms. Vandergott here a glass of the sauvignon blanc she likes, yes? Oh, don't say no. You can take a quick drink with us, blame it on the customers, we forced you. And I've got a favor I wanted to ask you."

Louella thought the loud man was being even more loud and blustery than usual. "You told me you've done some sailing, right? So, I really really need somebody to handle the spinnaker pole for the regatta Friday. You've done that? Yeah, I thought you told me that. So, what I'm asking is, could you do it on Last Resort Friday? Please? Tell you what, I've been talking to Carlo about buying another week, what if we do that to clinch the deal? How's that?"

There was a murmur, which had to be assent. Louella wondered what Mrs. Blaine would think of this arrangement. But that's what she got for storming off. Louella shook her head. Some women didn't have a clue.

"All right then, that's my girl! So, we just need to take it out for a quick practice this afternoon. Do you need me to tell Carlo? No? I knew he'd be willing. Wants to close the deal, doesn't he? OK, two o'clock in the lobby, we'll get Livingston to run us over to the marina."

Louella frowned. There was something going on with that group. She had to think about what to do. She didn't trust the chief, but she needed to tell someone. Livingston couldn't do anything. She sat longer than she had meant to and heard the chairs scraping as the lunch party finished and rose to leave. At the same moment she saw Lucy O'Donnell coming across the deck, heading for the bar. Was she really a cop? She was neutral. She can't have had any part in the bad deeds of the police but if she was really working with them maybe she ought to be warned. And Luella needed to confide in someone. She rose and took a step towards the chunky woman in a pastel shirt and white shorts.

"Louella, what are you doing out here? You're supposed to be cleaning the second floor, aren't you?" Anna Maria Vandergott stepped through the doors from the bar.

"Yes, mum. I was just on my break." The Dutch girl stood between Louella and Lucy O'Donnell.

"Well, break is over. Get back to it. You know what Mr. Menotti is like if he sees any of the staff lazing around in public spaces like this. This is for the guests not the staff."

Luella felt the hair on the back of her neck rise. She didn't like the implied threat. She decided now was not the time to talk to the Boston cop, even though that woman was looking at her as if she had seen the move to start a conversation.

"Were you going to say something?" Lucy O'Donnell asked.

"No, mam."

"Wait a minute," she turned to Ms. Vandergott. "Anna Maria, I'm working with Chief Jackson. He's short staffed so he asked me to help with the investigation into Mr. Chin's death. I'd like to talk to any staff members who had anything to do with him. Would this lady be one?"

"Oh, but we thought Mr. Chin had a heart condition or something?"

"Remains to be seen. Would you introduce me?"

"Yes, this is Louella Roberts. She's one of our maids. They don't usually take their breaks in a public area like this." Louella cringed. "But I think she cleans the Chin unit. It's Seaview Q3. You do that one don't you?"

"Yes, mam."

"Ms. Roberts, I'm Lucy O'Donnell. The local police have hired me to help with this investigation. Was there anything unusual about the Chin's place when you cleaned it?"

"No, it's one of the new ones. The older man has a wheelchair. Sometimes Livingston helps get him up and down stairs and so forth. They cook some in the kitchen and up on the deck, but they don't make a big mess like some of the young people who come and party."

"Did you notice anything unusual as far as medicines or food and drink?"

Louella hesitated. She felt Ms. Vandergott's frown directed at her. They weren't supposed to snoop but then they were supposed to make sure nothing was dusty or dirty. You couldn't have it both ways. "The old man has some medicines laid out on the dresser. They had some dried mushrooms and peppers and some other things in the kitchen. Used for their Chinese cooking I guess."

"I see. Did you notice any herbs?"

Louella shrugged.

"Hmm. The older Mr. Chin didn't want to let the chief search the rooms. It might be good, when he gets a warrant, to have you to have a look and see to make sure nothing has been taken away that was there before."

Louella looked at Ms. Vandergott to see if she approved. "I guess I could do that. They might have eaten those things, I suppose. They had some drinks stuff, too." She thought about the odd double set of bottles at the bar. "Most visitors keep a bar in their room like that. Seemed like a lot for just the two of them."

"Yes, well, if that's all, perhaps we can let Louella get back to her cleaning. I know we have some new guests coming in this afternoon and it's always a rush to get the units ready. Can she go?"

"Sure. I'll ask you to come when we get a warrant, Ms. Roberts. Thank you for your help."

As she walked away, Louella heard the Dutch girl telling the Boston cop about how she had been hijacked into sailing on the boat with the Blaines. She mentioned that she was worried about the strains in that group. Louella was worried, too, but she still had no proof. She couldn't see how the death of the Chinese man had anything to do with her problem. The cops who killed her brother had no reason to hurt Chin, but she still felt a prickling at the back of her neck.

"Well, that's very interesting," she heard Ms. O'Donnell say. "I'm thinking they were among the last to talk to Chin, and I'd like to see what they have to say. They're leaving to sail at two? I think I'd better have a little talk with them before that."

TWENTY-TWO

"We do team building exercises and teach a little sailing. It's a combined classroom and on-board experience that we tailor for specific companies who contract with us," Mike Blaine said. Lucy had called him, and he agreed to meet her in the lobby with the stipulation that he would need to leave at two o'clock. They found a group of comfortable chairs near the door.

"Your wife, Mrs. Randolph and Mr. Laurent are all involved in this?"

"Yes, they're employees. Guy and I do most of the business development. Juliet helps with some of the investment presentations, and she does the books. Rita mainly helps sail the boat, the Last Resort. It's a thirty-five-foot Beneteau we use for the teamwork. We have to be able to sail the boat ourselves, as a lot of them are novices, but it's part of the teamwork training. We have specific exercises for them."

"You knew Eliot Chin as a client?"

Mike Blaine took off his baseball cap with "Last Resort" embroidered on the crown and wiped his forehead with the back of his hand before putting it back on. "That's right. He approached us after we met him in the bar one night. He was planning on sending us three sets of his employees. He said he had just sold off his startup business and was about to get into another line. He thought it was the perfect time to do some reorganization of his remaining staff to gear up for a new project." He shook his head. "We clinched the deal on the catamaran trip, and he would have signed the contract in the morning. It's really too bad he went like that. I'd like to see if I could talk to his old man in case there's any hope of going ahead with the sessions anyhow, but it's probably too soon."

"You were with Mr. Chin on that dinner cruise. Can you tell me about what he ate and drank?"

Mike looked at her with speculation. "Was it something he ate? An allergy or something?" When she didn't respond he answered the question. "Let's see. We had appetizers and rum punch at the first place. You were on that trip too, weren't you? With your friends? We didn't have anything special, and I don't remember anything that was a problem. No nuts or anything like that. There was shellfish, shrimp, but if he'd been allergic, he'd have known to avoid that, wouldn't he?" Again, she failed to respond. "Hmm. Actually, he didn't like the rum punch for some reason. He stopped at the bar and had them bring him something straight up, whiskey, I think. A lot of people don't like these mixed drinks.

"Let's see. Next was the Japanese place. Now there he insisted on eel. It wasn't on the preset menu that went with the cruise, but he asked the waiter and when he found out they had it, he insisted. I remember they had to get the captain there to OK the extra cost. He was fine with it. When it was served, no one else was interested. All a bit squeamish. I had a bite just because he was pressing us all to try it. Guy may have, too. Sort of a bitter taste. The women refused.

"At the dessert place, he refused coffee. Guy, Rita and I all had a brandy, but he passed on that too. I don't think he was big on the pastry sweets either. That was when we got him to agree to a contract for three sails." He shook his head again. It was a big regret for him.

"When you came back here, you all went to the bar, is that right?"

"Yes, we had a toast to celebrate the agreement, actually. But then Chin said he wanted to use the hot tub, instead of having another nightcap with us. I think he got Anna Maria to make him some special drink he liked. She did that all the time. You could tell he liked having a pretty girl waiting on him, like he was something special. We hung around talking to Del, the bartender, but Guy and Juliet decided to go for a swim, and my wife developed a headache and went upstairs." He shrugged. "I stayed in the bar with Del for a few more, then went up."

"Did you see Chin from the bar?"

"Sure, we all saw him trotting over to check out the hot tub, then he went up to his unit change to a bathing suit. That's when we were talking about swimming, and they decided on a swim. Guy and Juliet. At first Rita was keen on it, but I wasn't up to it. That's when she got a headache and went up in a snit."

"Mrs. Randolph and Mr. Laurent are together? There's no Mr. Randolph?"

Mike Blaine moved to resettle himself on the cushions of the big armchair he had chosen. He bent forward, looking at the stairs to see if anyone was coming. "Juliet is in the process of getting a divorce. She was a neighbor of ours back in Cleveland. She got involved when I started the teambuilding business, and she came with us to Annapolis when we started using the boat. She met Guy. He's an old buddy of mine I recruited to help sell. So, they got to be a number. Guy has always had a way with the women, if you know what I mean. I'm not sure she's wise to count on him when she leaves her husband, but their kids are in college. It happens."

"I see."

"Here they come." Mike stood up as Juliet Randolph and Anna Maria Vandergott approached. "Where's Guy?" he asked.

"He's got a headache, he said he can't come," Juliet said quietly.

"What the hell?" Mike said. "I told him I needed him. What's the matter with him? I'm going to call him." He stamped away bent over his cell phone.

Lucy introduced herself and took the opportunity to ask Juliet Randolph about the previous evening. She had nothing more to add to what Mike had already told Lucy.

"He didn't drink any of his champagne when Mike insisted on a toast after we got back. He left right away to go change for the hot tub. I was a little worried he might be having second thoughts, the way he left and had Miss Vandergott prepare his own drink instead. I thought the atmosphere was a little tense. We needed that contract to break even, you see. Then Guy suggested we go for a moonlight swim. That was a good idea, it was really relaxing. Guy is good about defusing the atmosphere like that when things get a little strained."

"Did you see Chin at the pool?"

"He came down after we'd been in the water a while, and we left soon after."

"And you brought him his special drink?" Lucy turned to Anna Maria.

"Yes. I prepared it for him while he was in the bar, but he left to change into his bathing suit, and it was a while before he was ready for it. He wanted it delivered to the hot tub. I asked Delroy to let me know when he came back down to the pool and then I brought it out to him. It was what he always had, a rum punch with guava berries but he didn't like the way it's usually done around here, he had a specific recipe he gave us, and he wanted me to make it for him. Really, there's no reason Del couldn't make it, but he was just fussy that way."

"So, you prepared that drink while the others were at the bar, and you left the pitcher there for a while before you brought it to him?" Lucy wondered whether the drink had been looked at by the forensic people. Did they have forensic staff on an island of this size?

Anna Maria nodded yes but before Lucy could ask any more questions, Mike Blaine stomped over to them, his face red with anger. "That blazing hypocrite. He's not coming. You two, come on. Livingston is at the door." They looked up and saw the tall black man smiling at them and beckoning. "We need to go."

Lucy thought she had gotten as much as she could from them, and she had no desire to get Mike Blaine riled up any more than he was already, so she let them go. She saw Juliet Randolph look back longingly towards the sunshine of the pool area that was visible at the back of the lobby, but she followed the others out. Lucy wondered what Guy Laurent was hypocritical about. Perhaps she could take the opportunity to find out.

TWENTY-THREE

Guy Laurent was not in his room. Lucy decided to interview Rita Blaine, and when she knocked on that door, Guy answered. After she explained she was assisting the local police, he led her out to the balcony where Rita Blaine lay stretched out on a padded chaise lounge. From the arrangement of furniture, she could see that Guy had been sitting in a chair beside her. There were two drink glasses on the little table between them.

"Sorry to disturb you," Lucy said. "But it would be helpful if you could just tell me your impressions of Eliot Chin the last time you saw him."

The balcony provided shade, but Rita Blaine lay with one arm across her eyes as if blocking out the sunlight. She wore a peach top that left her shoulders and midriff bare, and very short white shorts. Her toenails and fingernails were painted a vivid orange red color. Her long blond hair was falling over one shoulder. A large diamond in a platinum setting with a matching wedding band decorated her left ring finger. She took a big breath and uncrossed her legs as she looked at Lucy from underneath her arm. "It's just a headache. Chin was fine.

He was fine about the contract for the boat, he was fine about the trip. He just said he wanted to soak in the hot tub, and he had that Vandergott girl make him his special drink. She's good at keeping the male clients happy like that."

Lucy thought there was the hint of a sneer in that description. Poor Anna Maria. What she had to put up with from both the male and female guests.

"No more than Carlo does for the female customers," Guy said quietly. He had put Lucy in the chair beside the table and pulled over another of the padded armchairs for himself. The Blaine's unit was away from the pool area, but it was on the side opposite to that of the new buildings where the Chins were staying. Like the Chin unit, they faced the sea directly and glints of sunlight reflected up at them. Off on the horizon a couple of wind surfers moved along at a good clip. Lucy appreciated the breeze that cooled the shaded balcony. Surf broke on rocks below them. They were on the second floor.

Rita lowered her arm and sat up a bit. "Yes, of course, that's true. Anyhow, Chin was in the bar with us, then he left. Juliet wanted to go for a swim, but I had a headache, and my husband was settling in for a few more rounds, so I went up to bed. That's the last I saw of Chin until we heard of the accident in the morning."

"He seemed fine to you in the bar, then?"

"Yes, of course. He certainly didn't seem ill at all, did he Guy?"

"No, he seemed quite fine."

"And I understand from your husband you had just settled on a contract with Mr. Chin that evening?"

Rita sat back and raised her arm to her head again. Guy answered. "Yes, that's right. We discussed it with him on the sail and he was enthusiastic. He had employees who would do our teambuilding sessions for three weeks at the end of November and beginning of December. We were happy to make that deal. We were all very satisfied with it."

"And now, with Mr. Chin gone, the contract wasn't signed, so you've lost that business according to Mr. Blaine. Is that a big problem for your business?"

"A disappointment, certainly. But we are also very sorry such a young man as Mr. Chin should lose his life like that. Do they know what caused it? Was it heart failure?" Guy asked.

Rita dropped her arm to her side and said, "It's a real shame, and we're all very sorry about Mr. Chin, but in some ways it's a blessing. Now we're free to go home and have Thanksgiving with our children. They're in college and they'll be off. Otherwise, we would have had to stay here and work the cruise." She massaged her neck with both hands, her eyes closed. "Mike really wanted that contract but I'm glad it fell through," she said.

"Yes," Guy said. "It is a shame to lose the contract, but not a tragedy. It's a tragedy for Mr. Chin's elderly father that his son should drop dead like that. It makes you think about life and how quickly it can come to an end."

Lucy wondered about finding the two people who were supposed to be too sick to sail, drinking on the balcony but she couldn't see how it would impact the investigation into Chin's death. Besides, she could see that a drink in the cool shade would be a lot more restful than splashing round in the hot Caribbean sun on the boat with Mike Blaine yelling orders.

"Do they know what caused Mr. Chin to die? Did he drown in that tub?" Guy pressed for information. When Lucy turned to look at him, he said, "He looked and seemed fine on the catamaran and at the bar. We were shocked when we heard he had died. Do they know what happened?"

"He didn't just drown," Lucy said. She might as well tell them the truth and see how they reacted. "They believe it was caused by some kind of reaction to something he ate or drank. Do you recall anything that might help to identify what he ate or drank that was different from the rest of you?"

"Oh, do you mean, like a shellfish allergy? Or poison?" Rita sat up straighter. "No, no, there was nothing different. Of course, his special punch, but she always made that for him, all the time we've been here."

Guy frowned as if trying to remember. "There was nothing obvious, and none of us were affected. There was the eel at the Japanese restaurant, but Mike and I tried it too. Of course, we had only a taste, he ate the whole dish himself. It was a delicacy he particularly liked. Then in the bar here, we all had champagne. There was the punch, but as Mrs. Blaine has said, we saw him drink that many other times."

"I'm told the punch was made up then left to sit on the counter for a while. Did you notice that?"

They both stared at her. It was finally occurring to them that the questions indicated the man had been poisoned. "No, when Juliet insisted on a night swim and Mike got all snitty about it, I left. I don't remember seeing the punch," Rita said.

"I saw the pitcher. Miss Vandergott had it prepared as soon as he mentioned it, she was very attentive to his needs," Guy said. Lucy got the distinct impression the slick womanizer did not like the Dutch girl for some reason. "It did sit on the counter when he went off to change for the hot tub. He said he wanted it delivered to him there. But no one touched it. Juliet and I left to change to our swimsuits. We're staying on the boat, but we had bags with us. We use the facilities in the athletic club area when we're here. We changed, swam, saw Chin come and by then we were ready to go back to the marina and the boat, so we left."

"How do you get back to the marina?"

"We rent a small van that we use to transport our clients. We drove back to the boat in that. It's just around the harbor. We returned early in the morning, in case we were needed for any last-minute changes or questions about the contract, but that's when we found out Chin was not going to sign it."

"Because he was dead," Lucy said.

"You can imagine what a shock it was to us," Guy said.

Lucy thought that perhaps it had not been a shock to someone. But she still didn't have a clue as to who that might have been.

TWENTY-FOUR

"That's where they plan to put the stadium," Livingston told Lucy and Meilan, as he drove the resort van down a bumpy dirt road. Lucy grabbed a handle above her window and hung on. She hadn't asked for the guided tour when she put together this expedition, but it seemed politic to let the articulate van driver have his way.

After the interview with Rita Blaine and Guy Laurent, Lucy decided to take a different tack. As far as she could see, Chin's death was a bad thing for the people in the teambuilding group. It was true that Rita was happy that she would be able to spend Thanksgiving with her children, but it hardly seemed plausible that she would have poisoned a client to achieve that goal. From her husband's description she played a less than critical role in the training and sailing, so surely, she could have gone home without him. If she and Guy Laurent were having an extra-marital affair, which seemed likely, Lucy could see no reason how that would be helped by killing Chin. Unless he knew of the affair and threatened to expose them, but she had a hard time imagining that. It was much more likely that everybody in the little group of the Blaines,

Guy, and Juliet were well aware of the attraction between Rita and Guy. Surely it wouldn't come as a surprise to any of them.

Meanwhile, there was the question of what other activities Chin might have been involved in during his stay on the island. People said he had come looking for investments, but no one seemed to know what they were. It was known that he had taken his father to visit some of the islanders of Chinese descent.

Since Livingston was the one who transported them, she consulted him. He said he could take her to meet people Chin had spoken to, but he had no idea what they had discussed. She sensed that Livingston had some sort of a chip on his shoulder about the local Chinese, although some of the families had been on the island for a long time. When he mentioned that they had carried on their conversations in Chinese, Lucy decided to get Meilan to come along. It would help to have someone who could speak the language during the interviews. And in any case, Lucy thought it was only fitting that Meilan should give up some of her vacation time as it was the danger of her arrest that had drawn Lucy into the investigation in the first place. The sooner they could explain what had happened, the sooner they could relax and be assured of getting their scheduled flight home on Saturday.

"The stadium is going to be funded by the Chinese government?" Lucy asked. She wasn't sure of the connection to Chin, but Livingston had insisted they understand the latest island controversy.

"Right. Like a lot of the Caribbean countries, St. Hilaire has recognized Taiwan since 1954. The communist government on the mainland has had a policy for years of trying to get these nations to recognize their government and cut ties with Taiwan. They give grants and loans to build roads, hospitals, or stadiums."

"I see, and that's a reward for changing their policy and recognizing Communist China?"

"Right, the People's Republic of China, but that's not the only string that's attached to the deal. They also give the building contract to Chinese firms, and they bring in Chinese construction workers and engineers."

Meilan looked out the window. "Chinese construction is very good quality. Must be good for the island to get a hospital or stadium. Good of Chinese people to help."

Livingston brought the van to a halt in a spray of light brown dirt. There were piles of construction materials around the flat bottom of this valley, but no work was going on. "Chinese construction may be good, but St. Hilaire construction workers are good, too. If they hired local workers, it would be a boon to the local economy, but, instead, they bring in Chinese and the locals are out of work. A lot of people are pretty unhappy about that." He turned in his seat with an arm over the back, to talk to them. "The island has a big problem providing work for the young people to come back for. All our young folks are drained away because there's no work for them here and this project is bringing in foreign workers so it's not helping with employment at all."

Meilan just shrugged.

"Do you think Eliot Chin had something to do with this construction?" Lucy asked.

Livingston turned forward and hunched over the controls, moving back and forth a couple of times to get turned around and headed back up the hills where palm trees swayed in a breeze.

"Don't know for sure. But he was talking to some of the local Chinese. Or he was taking his father to talk to them." Meilan snarled when the old man was mentioned. "All I know is, this stadium was proposed last year but in the spring, there were big protests about the foreign workers, so they stopped the work. They didn't change from recognizing Taiwan either, and there were some Taiwanese who came and gave the government a grant for some school improvements instead. But the rumor is that the Chinese communists are trying to get the stadium project back on track.

"I'm taking you to the Yun Fat Low grocery store in the middle of the island. That's the best place to find any of the local Chinese islanders. The Chins went there. I waited outside, but they were there for more than an hour one day last week." He pulled into a gravel parking lot and swung to a stop.

It was a big old warehouse building with a painted sign for Yun Fat Low with Chinese characters below the words. There was a smaller building beside it that had plate glass windows and the name Golden Treasure Market. Livingston told them the smaller building was retail while the larger sold to other grocery stores and markets on the island. He said the Chins had met someone in the larger building.

Meilan climbed out of the van with some effort. Her legs were a little short for the steps. Livingston tried to help her, but she ignored him. She looked around with narrowed eyes, then began stomping over to the large building. Lucy started to protest but when Meilan ignored her, she shrugged at Livingston and left him leaning against the van with his arms folded on his chest while she followed Meilan into the warehouse.

Meilan shouted after she entered the door, but Lucy had no idea what she was saying as it was in Chinese. There were two skinny old men sitting on metal folding chairs with a little camp table between them. They were playing cards. They ignored Meilan until she was standing over them. She looked at one man's cards and made a comment. He mumbled something in response and laid down a card. The other man exclaimed and threw in his hand.

The first man, in a faded New York Yankees baseball cap and a sun-bleached pale-yellow tee shirt and khaki shorts, grunted something at Meilan.

"He asked what we want," she translated for Lucy. "I told him we want to know about dirty capitalist Chin." She spewed out a tangle of syllables, very loudly.

Lucy rolled her eyes. "Meilan, don't say that. Say we want to ask them about Mr. Chin and his son. You might tell them there's been an accident and the younger man has died so we are looking into his activity on the island."

"Accident? No accident. He was poisoned. Wasn't he? You told me he was poisoned."

"Well, they think so, but we don't know for sure. Can't you just ask them how they knew the Chins and what business they had on the island?" Lucy looked down the long rows of stacked merchandise. There were cheap metal shelves ranged up and down the length of the building. They rose nearly to the roof in some areas. She wondered how they arranged so much stuff. A workman seated on a machine moved pallets down the far end of the center row. There were a couple of younger men and one woman in a white shirt and blue leggings discussing a list on a clipboard half a football field away from where she stood.

"Something happened to Mr. Chin?" the old man in the Yankees hat asked in unaccented English. Of course, someone who lived on the island would speak English. Lucy began to regret bringing Meilan. "I'm Lucky Yun." He held out a bony hand and Lucy took it. He had a firm handshake. "This is Mr. George Sung." She nodded to the other man who was sitting back lighting a cigarette.

Lucy introduced herself and Meilan explaining that she was helping the local police with the investigation of Eliot Chin's death. Lucky Yun lit up a cigarette as he listened.

"I see." His eyes narrowed as the smoke drifted towards them. Lucy restrained herself from coughing. "It's bad that. For the older ones among us when the time comes, it comes. But for a young one like that, it's terrible to see him cut off. And before his father's very face. Quite awful."

"The elder Mr. Chin wasn't actually there when his son died," Lucy said. "He was sleeping. Eliot Chin was in the hot tub of the resort. He wasn't found until the morning."

Meilan mumbled in Chinese. Lucky Yun looked at her then translated for Lucy. "She says the princeling got his due. Not very friendly with them, was she?"

Lucy felt embarrassed. She was afraid Meilan would insist on her crazy theory that Eliot Chin had been struck down by some deity to avenge the people his father had injured in the past. Lucy thought the Chinese islanders might have a more realistic idea of what the young man had been involved in, so she frowned at Meilan and asked about what businesses the Chins were interested in.

The two old men exchanged a glance but eventually Lucky Yun replied. "The old man has money to invest. Lots of people invest in the island because island banks are very secretive about money. Like Switzerland, you know? But to do that, you need a local business to put a name on the account. Otherwise it's not legal. Americans, Europeans, they do it too. But this one would only invest if the island changes from Taiwan to Communist China. That's what the old man said." He took a puff of his cigarette and blew out a large cloud of smoke. "I told him it won't happen. Too many people are mad about foreign workers. Anyway, I'm not interested. I told him about other guys might be desperate enough, but not me. My family's been on the island a long time. No need to spoil local relations just to make a quick buck out of corrupt Chinese officials. Oh yes, that's it you know. They're getting their money out of China into island bank accounts so if their government goes down, or they go down, they can leave China and live high. Just like American capitalists, don't you think?" He grinned with the cigarette stuck in the side of his mouth.

Lucy thanked him for the information and took down the names of the other men he had referred Chin to. She planned to alert Chief Jackson to this information and have him check on whether Chin had made arrangements with local banks. She figured they would not be open to questions from her about this sort of thing, but the chief should know who to go to get the information they needed.

Meanwhile Meilan was fuming all the way back. "Dirty traitor, big liar. You heard what they said? Old Chin is nothing but a corrupt official. Stealing money from the people and putingt it in banks over here. He's acriminal."

Lucy didn't think Meilan's obvious hate of the old man would help to clear her from suspicion. She kept quiet during the ride, but she planned to enlist her sister and Mary to do a sit down with Meilan where they explained the facts of life to her and got her to shut up about Chin for the rest of the trip.

She would have done that first thing if she hadn't been greeted by a worried looking Anna Maria Vandergott when they climbed out of the van. She saw an ambulance and a police car also pulled in front of the door.

"It's Luella Roberts, one of the maids," the young Dutch woman told her. "She's dead."

It was Livingston Jackson who reeled with shock. "No," he said. "No, no, no, Luella!" He ran up the stairs to the lobby.

TWENTY-FIVE

"'They killed her! She knew they shot her brother for nothing, and she was sure she could prove it and they killed her!" Livingston had been moved to the manager's office on the first floor after he erupted when he saw Luella Roberts' body brought down from the upstairs closet where Anna Maria had found her. He'd lunged at one of the young officers helping with the body and tried to claw his eyes out. He had to be removed by three other men, and his brother Delroy. The chief had the two young officers Lucy had met at the station bring him to the office to be away from the others. Now, Lucy followed.

"What? What proof did she have? If she had proof, why didn't she bring it to me?" Chief Jackson said, pushing his face up into the face of his brother.

"You let them get away with it! You let them shoot down her brother like a dog, you know you did." Livingston hammered his fists on the desk in a rat-ta-tat-tat rhythm. Two officers still had their hands on his shoulders pushing him down into the swivel chair. Tears streamed when he finally sat back and sobbed, his long-fingered hands held up to his face. The chief motioned to the officers to leave but he let Lucy remain.

"Listen to me, brother. I know you're feeling awful about Louella, I am too. But you got to know, I don't want to let them get away with anything." He looked around as if to be sure the door was closed, and he spoke in a low tone. "I know there's some that are doing wrong, but I don't know who all is involved and I don't have any proof. I got to have proof. So, if Louella had some, now's the time to share it, you hear me?" He grabbed a box of Kleenex from a shelf and shoved it in front of his brother. There was a sound of struggle outside the door and the chief got up to see to it, returning with his other brother Delroy who rushed to Livingston's side.

"You all right, man?" he asked.

Livingston snuffled, taking some Kleenex to wipe his face. He stared wide eyed at the chief across from them. Delroy patted his shoulder protectively and turned to his older brother. "What're you doing Wen? You still sayin' there's nothing wrong with those boys even after this?"

The chief was frustrated. "Listen, I need proof. If Louella had proof, then I need it. I can't do a thing without proof."

Livingston swallowed a couple of times then said, "She said she knew something. She knew how that lady was killed and it wasn't her brother. Billy didn't do it and he didn't have a gun. But after what happened to him, how did you expect her to trust you? She don't trust you and she don't trust me because she don't trust you." He gulped back a sob. "She knows something, but she won't tell me. I told her she got to tell somebody. She said she maybe tell the woman policeman, her." He nodded to at Lucy.

"Me? She did start to talk to me this morning but then she stopped when Miss Vandergott told her to get back to work. Are you saying she was going to tell me something about what happened to Chin? Or is this something else?"

Livingston and Delroy took turns in a disjointed explanation of how Louella had left her job as a dental hygienist and taken a job as a maid in an attempt to find out who had done the murder that her brother was accused of. It didn't make a lot of sense to Lucy. "Why work here?"

"She was sure somebody here killed that lady to steal her stuff or for something else."

"Who? Someone on the staff? Or a guest? But the guests weren't here when that happened, that was months ago, wasn't it?"

Delroy looked up. "The Chins were. They were here at that time, and so where the Blaines and all those people."

"Are you sure it was about that earlier death?" Lucy asked. "Are you sure she didn't know something about how Elliot Chin died? How did she die? If she was poisoned, it seems to me it might be the same person who killed Chin. Maybe she saw something."

Livingston looked tortured. "I don't know," he said. "I don't know, but she's gone. All she wanted to do was find the bastards who killed her big brother. She wanted to stop them, and you already know who those guys are. You know them, and you do nothing, man, nothing." He had risen from his chair and was glaring at his brother the chief of police.

"I need proof. I told you so. Wait," the chief put up a hand to ward off Livingston's raised fist, but Delroy had rushed between them. "Listen to me. I have to go upstairs and find out what happened to Louella. I'm taking Captain O'Donnell here with me. She's a homicide detective from Boston. I need her to back me up. They already started with Len Strong." He looked over his shoulder at the door. "I've got to walk carefully till I find out who's involved. Del, you keep

Liv down here. I promise you, if they did it, I'll get to the bottom of it, but you've got to give me time. I can't just fire everybody because some of them are bad apples. I have to find out exactly who's involved and how deep it goes. You just shut up and stay here, and you watch your backs. I'm not kidding now." He glared at them, and Delroy nodded. Then he turned to the door. "Captain O'Donnell, you with me?"

Lucy could see the man was in a bind. Some vacation. To expose corruption in his own force, he was going to use her as a foil, an outside influence, an unknown quantity. She could see what he was doing and why. She'd do the same thing herself. "Right. Let's go."

Upstairs a tall plain clothes officer was in charge. He was introduced as Lieutenant Strong. The two younger officers, Gomer and Duke, were standing around, thumbs tucked into their heavy leather duty belts, keeping staff away. There were two thin young women covered head to toe in disposable white paper suits taking pictures and presumably collecting evidence using equipment from new looking plastic cases lying open on the floor. Lucy got the impression they were eager beavers finally getting to use procedures they had learned in training sessions. She sighed, remembering how competent Bin Yu was at this sort of scene.

Anna Maria had found Louella Roberts collapsed in a utility closet with a bottle of rum in her hand. Her screams had brought others, and the ambulance was called with the police close behind. When Louella was pronounced dead by the EMTs, the patrolman had called the Lieutenant. Lucy noticed they had none of them called the chief until after Strong arrived. There definitely were some tensions in the small department.

They were in the new wing of the resort, where the Chin's had their timeshare. When Lucy heard that complimentary bottles of liquor were stocked in each of these units, she remembered how she had wanted Louella to tell her if anything had changed in the Chin's apartment. At her suggestion they went to the old man's unit where they found the bottle of rum missing. A check of the other units confirmed they all had their full stock of booze.

The chief told the technicians to get the bottle analyzed and the autopsy scheduled and then he insisted on an interview with the older Chin. He sent the other policemen away, but he had to let Strong join Lucy and himself for the interrogation.

Anna Maria Vandergott showed up, sent by Carlo Menotti. Looking uncomfortable, she asked if she could sit in. It was obvious that she was following orders from her superiors. The chief allowed it, although Chin seemed less than gracious about the resort's offer of support. He stared at them glumly from his wheelchair, with the young Dutch woman standing beside him, while Lucy, the chief, and Strong arranged themselves on the couch and armchair across from him. The setup was very adversarial.

"My son did not drink alcohol," he said. The chief had explained that the dead maid had been found with the bottle of rum from the unit and it was being examined for poison. Chin insisted he paid no attention to the maid and that the bottles of alcohol had not been touched by him or his son for themselves. Only when they had visitors who wanted a drink were they ever used. He himself drank only French wines as advised by his doctors. He sat hunched a little in the lightweight wheelchair. Lucy wondered if he really needed it, or if it was for show. His arthritic hands rested on the arms and his eyelids were partially closed. He didn't radiate anger, he seemed very steely cold. Despite assurances that his son was seen to drink, and the unwilling confirmation from Anna Maria that she had prepared a rum drink for him, the old man insisted his son did not drink alcohol. But after a painful turn of his head to look up at the young woman he said,

"My son did not tell me everything. When he was out of my sight, I cannot swear to what he did. There were things he did not tell me."

Lucy thought the younger man must have wanted to get out from under the old man's steely gaze. No telling what he kept from his stern father. But this was an opportunity to get information that she didn't want to miss, so, with a glance at the chief to make sure he didn't object she asked, "Mr. Chin, the maid who has just died was concerned about the death of a young widow from Australia last month. Her brother was accused of that crime, but he died before he could be tried for it." She saw the chief's brow furrow at the mention of this incident, but she plunged on. "You and your son would have been here when that happened. Did your son ever mention meeting or knowing that woman? I've been told that he had spent time in Australia a few years ago. Could he have recognized Mrs. Sobel from his time there?"

The others were puzzled, including Anna Maria who recognized the story of the woman she had known. The old Chinese man ruminated on that before replying. "My son was a businessman. He made some investments in Australia at one time. I don't remember him mentioning any particular woman from that country since we were here."

"Mr. Chin, what sort of investments were you and your son looking for when you came to St. Hilaire?"

A pause. "That is none of your business."

In her peripheral vision, Lucy saw the chief shift in his seat. "But you must see, Mr. Chin, that if someone purposely was trying to hurt or kill your son and that led to his death and the death of Louella Roberts, we need to know what he was doing here. It could help us to find his killer."

Instead of answering her, Chin looked at the chief. "Who is this woman?" he asked.

The chief cleared his throat. "Captain O'Donnell is a consultant. She has experience as a homicide detective in a major city and, as we are shorthanded at this time of year, I have hired her to help with the investigation into the death of your son. We're very anxious to clear that up and to be able to explain what happened as we are very sorry for that terrible tragedy to have happened on our island." Quite the diplomat, Lucy thought.

"The business of my son is confidential. I am a sick old man and I need to mourn my son. The consul is expected this evening. I want to be left alone to grieve my son."

Anna Maria looked particularly distressed, and she shot a pleading look at the chief while she hovered over the old man.

"Yes, we understand, and are very sorry for this intrusion." The chief got up, forcing Lucy and Strong to do the same. "I'll need to have the evidence technicians come in and examine this unit for fingerprints or other evidence. They'll ask for your fingerprints, just to exclude them." He turned towards Anna Maria. "I wonder if Mr. Chin might be better off if he were moved to another apartment?"

"Yes, yes. Let me see to that," she said, moving to where she was directly in front of the old man. "Please, let me get someone to stay with you, Mr. Chin, and then we will move you to a better place. Pelican Bay wants to do everything we can to make this easier on you. We'll do it all, and it will remove you from the sad memories here. Please let us do this."

They left her working out the details with the stubborn old man. Lucy thought that for anyone else she would have felt sympathy. Here was an old man, half a world away from his home, his son had died, it looked like he was murdered, and he was all alone. But, even without the story she had heard of the old man's background from Meilan, he was such a cold fish, she could feel no sympathy for him. She shook herself as she followed the chief and the obviously resentful Lieutenant Strong down the stairs and back to the lobby. Had someone put poison into the rum that Eliot Chin sipped when his father wasn't looking? What did Australia have to do with this? What had Louella Roberts found out, or who had she suspected? Was it Chin himself?

And how was all of this going to be worked out in time for them to be on the plane on Saturday? It was looking more and more like they would have to prolong their not very restful vacation and she dreaded breaking the news to Norah. And what about Meilan. Surely, she wouldn't have poisoned the rum in the Chin unit? Why do that? Was it some kind of revenge thing to kill the son of the man who she blamed for her father's death? She tried to smother such thoughts, but they kept rising up in rebellion.

TWENTY-SIX

T he consul for the People's Republic of China arrived in the late afternoon and the Pelican Bay Resort provided lodgings for him and his retinue, then a banquet in the restaurant, followed by karaoke in the little nightclub at the edge of the beach. Despite his grieving, old Mr. Chin participated.

Lucy lost contact with the chief who was submerged in security and diplomatic duties. Meanwhile she broke it to her roommates that their stay in paradise might be prolonged. Norah was outraged but Mary got on her cell phone to arrange coverage for her on call work at the clinic. When Meilan refused to consider the change of plans, Lucy gave up and called her friend Bin Yu directly to let him know what could happen.

"Bad luck," he said. "Hong and I are so grateful you took the poor old lady with you. We'll find someone to watch the kids." Lucy knew the grandmother's absence would cost the young people more money in childcare than they had planned on, but there was nothing she could do except try to speed up the process. "They don't really think the old lady would have done this guy in, do they? I won't tell Hong.

Her ma's a fierce old girl. I'm afraid of her myself when she gets into one of her snits, but poison the guy? She'd be more likely to clobber him with a two by four." Spoken like someone who knew the woman, Lucy thought. "Do we need to get a lawyer? Or should I come out there?"

"No. Don't do that. If she gets charged, I'll find her a lawyer but we're not there yet and I hope we never will be. The local chief has actually hired me to help investigate. He's got his own problems." She hesitated but finally told him the whole story about the suspected vigilante police and the old Chinese communist recognized by Meilan.

"Wow. I never knew that. I can try to find out more background from Hong about the old Chin guy."

"But don't tell her about it all. Not yet." Lucy didn't want the young couple flying down with their toddlers and making a strained situation even worse. "Listen, what you can do for me is some background research. See what you can find out. And get help from Gary if you need it." Gary was her old partner still doing homicide investigations. He worked with Bin Yu on a daily basis. She asked Bin to look into the background of the widow from Australia and the Chins, and then she added the Blaines and their group as well. She told him what she knew about the poison and forensics involved. Bin Yu gave her a couple of suggestions of things to ask the local forensics people.

"That doesn't help with the local police thing, though, if they're out killing killers. You don't think the old lady is in danger of getting shot by them, do you?"

"No. They seem to concentrate on locals who scare away the tourists, but you're right. If we could get that shut down at least we could concentrate on clearing your mother-in-law. I can't imagine local cops could have had anything to do with Chin's death, but who knows?"

When she hung up, she stayed on the empty pool deck looking out at the water. To make the call, she had excused herself from the karaoke scene and walked back to the quiet area of the resort. Norah had insisted they participate in the resort's evening activity and Lucy had agreed in order to placate her. She contemplated the tranquil scene. The din of the music from the other end of the complex was muffled by the distance. If only they could depend on the local law enforcement, it would be easier for all of them. But if they really had a problem with vigilante cops, it certainly reduced the available resources to clear up the Chin murder, if it was a murder and not just some kind of accidental poisoning.

***

Juliet didn't like the karaoke music. She disliked the noise, the closeness and the flickering lights from the disco ball that hung from the ceiling and slowly revolved. She couldn't drink enough to make it palatable. She wished she could, but it just made her sick to her stomach. When Mike spotted the elder Mr. Chin with the other Chinese in the dining room, he decided there was a chance of reviving the contract. He insisted they follow the Asian party when they all trouped down to the dance club after dinner, hoping to make contact.

Rita was annoyed and she didn't try to hide it. She was huffy when Mike steered her down to the hot and crowded room, all the while ignoring her attempts to discuss booking flights home. The noise of the karaoke muted the argument, reducing it to angry looks. The resident DJ had gotten things started with a hammy performance of "Downtown," then he convinced the young bridal couple to come up on the stage to sing a rousing version of "YMCA," He rewarded them with free drinks, which encouraged another guy who was a would-be Sinatra to try to bellow out "My Way".

The Chinese were encouraged to join in and finally one of them got up to mouth an incomprehensible version of the song the Korean singer/dancer had made famous on YouTube. Everybody clapped for him despite his rather ludicrous attempts at music video style dancing. Juliet found it hard to believe that Mr. Chin, whose son wasn't even buried yet, could participate in all of this, but he sat hunched in his wheelchair with eyes half closed.

Juliet really wanted to get Guy to take her back to the boat and she was about to complain of a headache when Mike got up and gave his own rendition of "Smoke Gets in Your Eyes". She knew he was trying to catch the attention of the Chinese, but she was exasperated by the need to stay and support him.

The whole atmosphere was beginning to grate on her nerves like fingernails on a blackboard and it didn't help that she could anticipate the next step and she didn't like it. He was dropping into a performance that was straight out of the playbook for their team building exercises. And it was a routine that excluded her since she'd never could hold a tune. Never. And they all knew it. So out on the boat when they had worked the group all day and fed them, and then had to entertain them, they would start a campfire routine where Mike crooned this old time ditty and then Rita and Guy would do a really fine duet of the old Cole Porter song "Night and Day." They had perfected the harmony and always got a round of applause. Obviously, Mike had pulled out that routine to get the attention of the Chinese.

Sure enough when he returned to the table, Mike challenged them. He had already primed the DJ who was announcing that he understood another oldie but goody was coming.

Rita was furious. "No. You want that, you do it yourself." She swallowed a mouthful of a pink martini.

But Guy had been quietly watching the Chinese. He reached out and put a calming hand on her left wrist. "Come on. It will be good." He nodded at the DJ. Rita rolled her eyes and Mike just grinned, but not in a happy way. Juliet wondered if he was becoming manic. Why encourage them?

No one paid any attention to her now, especially as the spotlight had moved and stopped on Rita's head. The audience clapped and Rita reluctantly rose after Guy got up and held her chair. The applause increased. Juliet tried to protest. "Really, Mike. You shouldn't have done that, don't you see?"

Mike either didn't hear or chose to ignore her. He was watching the table of Chinese men chaperoned by Carlo Menotti and Anna Maria Vandergott. To Juliet he looked devious.

"Night and Day, you are the one," Rita and Guy sang with a full orchestra on the recording that backgrounded them, and it was soon clear that they actually had voices worth hearing. The DJ adjusted the sound to compliment them and waved at the audience to take advantage of the dance floor. People hesitated, but, in a minute, Mike was up grabbing the hand of the Vandergott girl and spinning her on to the floor. They were followed by others.

Juliet was infuriated. Mike was the one who started this. He put them up there together singing a love song and then he grabbed some young woman and tried to get revenge. But what about her? Juliet was left by herself at the table too sick to drink, and she had to watch as Guy and Rita stared into each other's eyes and trilled away. She couldn't take it anymore. She scraped back her chair and hurried from the room into the darkness.

***

When Lucy returned to the karaoke performance, she saw Guy Laurent and Rita Blaine in the spotlight, singing a duet. Juliet Raymond bumped into her shoulder. The brunette did not apologize as she marched out of the room. Not a happy camper, Lucy thought. But the singers were certainly better than most such amateur attempts. She had seated herself and ordered a beer when the song completed to loud applause and lots of bows. She saw Mike Blaine return Anna Maria to her seat at the table of Chinese men, and then pull up a chair to join them. Mr. Chin sat with his arthritic hands curled on the arms of his wheelchair but the others at his table were clapping enthusiastically. They made room for Guy and Rita when they came down from the stage.

Lucy's attention returned to her own table where a bottle of Guinness was placed before her. She heard her sister gasp. "What is she doing?"

Meilan Lin had left their table to tromp up on to the stage, nearly tripping over wires as she grabbed the microphone from the tall lanky DJ. He wasn't giving it up that easily, though, so he hung on to it as they conversed. Lucy saw the guy chuckle as Meilan gestured and pointed at the table full of Chinese. Finally, he nodded and stepped to his console where he shut off the background music.

"Folks, we have a request for a special song in honor of our Chinese guests. Here is Mrs. Meilan Lin, from Beijing by way of Boston, and she has a special kind of Chinese, I think it's a folk song, right? That she'd like to sing, and she says if you know the words you should sing along—got to admit this is one we don't have on the lineup. So, for a one time only special Chinese ditty here's Meilan, and you'll tell them the name of the song, right?" He handed the microphone to Meilan.

"Oh, my god," Norah mumbled.

Meilan fumbled a little with the large microphone and blinked at the spotlight, but she was not in the least intimidated. Lucy sighed. She ought to video this for Bin Yu and his wife, but she didn't have the heart.

Meilan said, "No, not folk song. This is a revolutionary song, from Chinese Cultural Revolution." Lucy looked over at the table of Chinese wondering what Meilan was up to. It wouldn't be anything good. "A very popular song during the Cultural Revolution."

Lucy saw one of the Chinese officials raise an eyebrow. She hoped Meilan wasn't going to start an international incident now.

"Song has the title 'East is Red'. You know it?" she asked the table of Chinese where there was a stir. "Yes, you know, you know. East is red, sun is rising, Mao Zedong comes from China".

There was an uneasy stir in the whole room, but the Chinese grandmother ignored it and started singing, loudly and from the heart. It was a song with a rousing beat and suddenly the Chinese at the table with Chin, joined in, singing and pounding their feet. Others in the room, who obviously couldn't understand a word of the Chinese language, clapped or pounded along good naturedly. Meilan swung her hand conducting the Chinese singers and several people laughed as the tension in the room dissipated in karaoke good will. Lucy's table reluctantly joined the clapping. She looked across noticing that only old Chin in his wheelchair seemed unmoved by the commotion. He remained hunched down, silent as a stone. Lucy thought she could see Meilan watching the old man with narrowed eyes, but he glared straight ahead.

The song ended to a vigorous round of applause and the DJ wisely wrestled the microphone from Meilan, sending her back to her seat with a lot of thanks and praise for the performance. She returned looking self-satisfied and occasionally craning to look over at old Chin.

Lucy was about to demand an explanation when she felt her cell phone vibrate. It was a call from Chief Jackson, so she excused herself and hurried from the room again.

TWENTY-SEVEN

"Are you sure you want to go through with this?" Lucy had come up with the idea that afternoon, but, at first, Chief Jackson had nixed it. Then, that evening, he suddenly put it into motion. As she sat in his four by four parked in a stand of slender trees watching the moon on the water across a rim of sand, she wondered what had lit the fire under him. They were keeping watch on a small cottage off to the right. Through the open car window, she heard the palm trees brush together and felt the gentle breeze that made the Caribbean such a relief from the cold of New England. She should be sitting on the balcony with a glass of wine instead of cradling a nine-millimeter Glock as she sat hiding somewhere on the other side of the island.

"Yes."

"There's backup?" She released the magazine and checked the rounds in the dim light. She hated using a weapon that wasn't her own. Newer semi-automatics seldom jammed but it did happen. If she had to use an unknown piece, she preferred an old thirty-eight revolver.

The chief hesitated before he said, "Of a kind. I just don't know who I can trust in my department and, until I do, it's a risk trying to depend on them."

"You're not saying it's just you and me?" That would be insane. They only expected two men, but if he was that suspicious of his own department, if he could doubt his officers to that extent, there was no telling what they would really face. She set her teeth as she snapped the magazine back in place and shoved two additional magazines into a pocket of her wind breaker.

"Not just us. But not from the department. We'll be all right. Unless you want out?"

Too late for that. He'd already set the bait, telling his Lieutenant Strong that Livingston was surely the one who was responsible for the death of Chin. Lucy knew he'd done it in a way that was believable. He'd said he wanted to wait to charge his own half-brother until he got search warrants and found the missing money.

Of course, that was a lie, there was no missing money, but it was a sure thing that the news would spread when Strong released the men and told them to take the night off. The chief said he regretted lying to his main detective but he didn't trust his detective's acting skills. Until he was absolutely sure who was implicated, he insisted on secrecy.

Lucy could see why her presence was needed. She was an objective outsider, but she was also a trained law enforcement officer who could swear to what went down this evening. She had been in trickier situations. She and the chief ought to be sufficient to bring the operation off, but, still, it was hardly what she would think of as a vacation activity. On the other hand, she had a sneaking feeling that this would make this vacation more memorable for her. She just wasn't sure that was a good thing.

"It's fine," she said.

"You OK with that gun? I have a permit for you in the back in case anyone asks. You good with a Glock?"

"Oh, yeah." As silence settled down Lucy thought about guns and the job. She'd never liked them. Her father's mantra had been that they were meant to remain holstered and if you even had to take one out, never mind discharge it, you failed. Keeping the peace was the job, and shooting a gun was no way to do it. Just pulling it out was a failure in his eyes.

To overcome her own dislike of the guns in the testosterone filled locker rooms of the police department, she'd gone overboard in the other direction. It was something she always did, a sort of overreaction she supposed. Rather than just putting in her time at the range and passing the periodic tests, she'd become a crack shot and won competitions. It was her own perverse nature that made her do it. If she didn't like something, she'd rub her own face in it. So, she'd mastered the skill, won a shelf full of trophies, and still, when she did have to draw her weapon a few times on the job, she found herself agreeing with her dad. Drawing the gun was a failure to keep the peace, but sometimes you had to do it.

It seemed like this was certainly going to be one of those times. After all, they were looking to shut down some gun carrying cops who were out shooting suspected perpetrators without the bother of a trial. It made her uneasy that she could understand why they did it. She recognized the impulse only too well. Still, she didn't think it was the best way to deal with the situation, and she was grimly aware that if everything went sideways it would be a real mess. She was not sanguine about this, not sanguine at all.

They heard an engine as a car came down from the road.

"It's them," the chief said. His own car was in the trees, hidden behind a hedge that lined the dirt drive up to the house. The lights of the approaching police patrol car went out and the engine died but they could hear the car still rolling down the incline and turning left so it was a few hundred yards in front of them on the drive beside the cottage.

It was almost a shack. Like most of the structures right on the beach it was raised on stilts so an unusually high tide would run freely below the main house. It was made of weathered slats of wood painted a light pink, with a wooden door that was peeling, two multi-paned windows, and a deck that ran all around the outside of the two-room house. The slanted roof was covered with pieces of tarred paper. There were lights on in the house and a single light over the screen door. A steep set of wooden steps led up from the sand.

Car doors opened quietly. Two dark figures climbed out. Leaving the doors open, each man took a little tour of one side of the house then returned to the pool of light at the bottom of the stairs. Chief Jackson touched Lucy's arm and they quietly exited their own car, also leaving their doors open so as not to alert the men of their presence. Lucy followed the chief's hunched over figure through the tree trunks to the edge of the stand of trees.

The two policemen were Gower and Duke, as the chief had suspected. They conferred and drew their guns. Lucy didn't like that. She shook her head in the darkness at the stupidity of the male animal. Why ever did they think they would get away with this? The chief looked around but no one else was in view. One of the men climbed the steps and pounded on the door. "Livingston Jackson, it's the police. Open the door. We need to talk to you."

Livingston appeared in the doorway, backlit by light from inside. Lucy thought she heard the flap of a screen door. Probably Delroy going out the front and circling back. She wondered if he was also armed. She thought she heard another car door behind her faintly, and she hoped it signaled reinforcements. Gower and Duke were telling Livingston to come out, but he was stalling them. Finally, he came down the steps slowly with his hands raised. Meanwhile Chief Jackson had silently risen to his full height.

"Don't you know you can't go knocking off the tourists, man?" Gower was asking Livingston. Both he and his partner were pointing their guns.

"I don't know what you're talking about."

"Oh, yeah? Sure, you do. Your brother knows you did it. He knows you stole the money after you did the Chinese guy. That's what we heard. Right, Duke? So, you think you're gonna get away with it, cause big brother is the top cop but we can't let that go. No sir."

"You mean you're going to shoot me, like you shot Billy Roberts?" Livingston growled.

"That's right. But we don't have a choice, now do we? We just came by to talk, but you went and pulled a gun. Show him, Duke. We figure you stole it from your brother, see, and you pulled it out so there was nothing we could do."

"Put the guns down." Chief Jackson had made sure Lucy had her Glock pointed at Duke before he came right up behind the loquacious Gower. "Move slow and easy or you'll both get it in the back of the head. Put the guns down."

There was a pause at that. Lucy could see Gower keeping his gun on Livingston while he partly turned to see the chief.

"I'm not kidding, you put that down now or I'll shoot," the chief said.

There was a noise behind them, but Lucy couldn't take her eyes off Duke who started to lower his gun and then stopped. This was getting treacherous, she hoped that was the reinforcements.

"Sorry, chief, your turn to put down the gun. You and the lady cop." The voice came from behind. Not reinforcements then.

"Strong? What do you think you're doing? You're in on this too? What's the matter with you?" the chief asked. He kept his eye and his gun on Gower, so Lucy kept hers on Duke. Stalemate?

Suddenly, on the right, she saw a figure jump out from behind a bush, and rush behind her, a shot went off, then a scream. It was Captain Neil who had rushed by her. She ducked and shot the dirt at Duke's feet. He dropped his gun, jumping backwards, and held up his hands.

Meanwhile on her left she saw the chief jump at Gower and roll on the ground, another gun went off. She stepped up to grab Duke's gun from the ground and shove him into Livingston's arms, then turned around to find herself looking down the barrel of a huge gun in the hand of Strong.

She tasted metal in her mouth as she waited for a flare but instead, with a huge whomp, the gun was knocked out of the large man's hand and, when he sprang back clutching his wrist to his chest, another whack of a bamboo pole hit him from behind. A huge screaming zombie with long hair and his eyes rolled back into his head jumped onto the Stong's back pulling him over backwards into the dust. There was a vicious struggle with grunts and swears and then the apparition was sitting astride the lieutenant who was face down with an arm pulled back. Strong wailed with pain.

Meanwhile, with the help of his brother Delroy, the chief disarmed and handcuffed Gower, while Livingston took another pair of handcuffs from Duke's belt and put them on him. As Lucy continued to provide cover with the Glock, the chief took over the subdued Strong from the longhaired fiend who then ran to cradle Captain Neil in his lap.

Neil was bleeding and the chief radioed for an ambulance and more police. Lucy hoped if any of them were part of this conspiracy they would either be too cowed by the take down to admit it or would turn on their co-conspirators in an effort to beat them to the punch by ratting on them.

She was so busy watching the prisoners until sirens and flashing lights filled the dirt road that she still didn't know who the long haired, bearded, pole swinging hero was until the EMT's loaded Captain Neil into their ambulance. When he stood to follow, she got a look at his face. "Jake?"

Cold blue eyes looked back. "Lucy. They said you were on the island. I have to go with Neil." And, with that, he climbed heavily into the ambulance, and it pulled away.

"Jake," Lucy said to herself. He looked so much older, broader, softer, hairier. But she supposed she probably looked like a blurred and smudged version of her younger self as well. She blinked. His presence still hung in the air like an after image. That was really Jake. He was alive and he had just saved her from a gun barrel. Unbelievable.

The chief looked after the departing ambulance. "He's a good man in a tight place," he said.

TWENTY-EIGHT

"What do you mean, we still can't leave?" Norah was appalled to hear the entirely expurgated version of the happenings of the previous evening, but she quickly concluded that the assistance Lucy had rendered to the local police ought to prove the innocence of their whole party. The police ought to know now that none of them could have been involved in the death of Chin. Furthermore, they should be able to understand that she had a bridal shower to attend on Sunday and needed to get back to Boston.

"The vigilante policemen didn't kill Chin. The chief still has to investigate that," Lucy told her.

Actually, it was worse than that. The interrogation of Lieutenant Strong had not gone well. The man had been proud and defensive of his actions, even when confronted with the fact that he had been about to shoot a totally innocent man. When he heard there was no money stolen from Chin, and that implicating Livingston Jackson was a ruse, he'd been angry, saying that, if he hadn't been tricked, he would have found the real culprit in Luella Roberts' death.

He even tried to turn the tables, accusing the chief of conspiring with Lucy. Strong claimed he'd been about to arrest Meilan Lin when the chief identified Livingston as the murderer. Before clamming up and asking for a lawyer, he told them that old man Chin said Meilan had come back to the timeshare the night of his son's death and that she had poisoned the rum bottle that killed both his son and the maid.

Since it was obvious, he was going to have to investigate this accusation aggressively, Chief Johnson rescinded his job contract with Lucy. She was too close to the main suspect. That effectively cut her off from the official investigation which would necessarily have to center on the Meilan now. The chief did it reluctantly, but he had no choice. He offered to loan Lucy the Glock, just in case, but she refused.

"What does she have to do with these Chin people anyhow? Has she told you?" The "she" in Norah's complaint was Meilan. "She was gone again last night. God knows where. What is she up to? I don't know why you had to bring her, anyway, Lucy. How well do you know her, anyway? Are you sure she didn't do it?"

"Norah, calm down."

"Don't tell me to calm down. This is your fault. We're supposed to be here relaxing and you're off getting involved with the police, getting shot at, for god's sake. You're supposed to be retired. You're supposed to be getting your blood pressure down, not running around having shootouts like you were twenty again. This is ludicrous. I'm going to call Jim and Mike. You're out of control here."

Lucy rolled her eyes. Jim and Mike were her older brothers one retired, one still on the force. She hadn't told Lucy that Mike was the one who had suggested her name as a consultant. She didn't need Norah running to them about this. "Norah, stop it. If there was anything either one of them could do to help, I'd be the first to call them. There isn't, so stop threatening to go cry baby to them. There's nothing they can do that I can't. You're not in danger. I'm sorry if you're inconvenienced so you might miss the goddamned bridal shower but be real here. It's Meilan who's in trouble, and I'm the one who'll have to answer to her daughter and son-in-law about it. So, you're going to be a little late getting home, tough. She's in danger of not going home at all."

"And whose fault is that?"

"Norah," Mary was standing beside Norah, and she reached out to touch her arm, but the angry woman stomped to the chintz covered couch and plopped down, her face dangerously red.

Lucy glared at her from across the room. "It's my fault. OK? It's all my fault. And I'm trying to deal with it. Just go get your nails done, will you? Go shopping. Do anything, just let me deal with this."

Norah could have exploded but, instead, she grabbed her cell phone, stomped to the sliding door and went out on the balcony, shutting the door as hard as she could behind her.

"Jesus Christ," Lucy said.

Mary was standing with her arms folded. "Lucy, what about Captain Neil? Is he all right?"

"Mary, I'm sorry, she just makes me so mad. He's at the hospital, they were working on him. The wound was not as bad as it might have been, so he should be all right, but I don't know the specifics." Lucy could see her friend was worried.

"And you said Jake Flaherty was there? How did that happen?"

Lucy had a picture of the screaming, gray haired maniac on the back of the big police detective and then those cold blue eyes looking into her own. She shook herself. "I don't know. I guess he's a friend of Neil and the chief. The chief stopped answering my questions after Strong accused him of conspiring with me." It made her angry to remember it, even though she knew in his place she would have done the same thing. "Look, they won't give us any information about Neil over the phone, but we could go over to the hospital and maybe, as a doctor and friend of his, you could get them to tell you something."

Lucy didn't say that she really wanted to ask Captain Neil some questions about Australia. She needed to know more about the Australian widow who Billy Roberts was accused of beating to death. She had a hunch that it was no coincidence that Chin had spent time in Australia and Neil was the one who had told them about that. At the same time, she was uneasy about meeting Jake Flaherty again, but she could weather that if she needed to.

"I'd like that. I'd really like to know how he's doing," Mary said.

"Good. I'll go down and get someone to drive us. You let *her* know we're going." She nodded at the balcony. "I don't want to talk to her right now."

"I get it."

In the lobby, Lucy learned that Livingston was not available to drive the resort van. The clerk got on the phone to find an alternate driver. As she turned to take a seat, Lucy saw Meilan talking to Carlo Menotti through the glass door to the timeshare office. She was debating confronting the Chinese woman when her cell rang. It was Bin Yu. She really didn't look forward to filling him in on the situation, but she accepted the call and headed for the patio overlooking the beach for some privacy.

"Got some news, boss. Not sure you're going to like it," Bin said. "How's it going there? Are they letting you come home yet?"

Lucy stifled a groan and told Bin what had happened and how the police investigation was even more concentrated on his mother-in-law.

"Tough stuff," he said. "At least you got rid of the vigilante cops." Bin was always an optimist. "Afraid I've got bad news, though. Hong talked to Uncle Shang. He said Old Mother Lin really knew this Chin guy."

He gave Lucy a version of the Cultural Revolution death of Hong's grandfather, and Meilan's history with Chin, how she left with him and worked with his group of Red Guards through most of the Cultural Revolution. "So, afterwards, she accused him of being a traitor to Chairman Mao. Like he supported Deng Ziaoping, you know? She got sent down to reeducation then, after Mao died. So that's why she always hated Chin, and it gets worse. A few years ago, he resurfaced in a central party position and she started trying to accuse him of things, being corrupt and stuff like that. When he moved back to Beijing, she started trying to get to him, following him or the son. She was stalking him! Do you believe it? She even followed them to Australia one time. She never told Hong and me about all this. But that was the last straw. She got forcibly retired from her job and she was being sanctioned by the party when the family got together and sent her over here to be with us. She wanted to fight it. She was always a big party person. She thought she could accuse him and get away with it, like she was doing the party a favor. Wow. The family made her come, she wanted to stay. That was four years ago, and they were happy she stayed in Boston, so, seeing that guy now, no telling what she would do. Not good, huh? You sure we shouldn't come down there?"

Lucy looked out on the beautiful green blue Caribbean waters lapping at the sugar fine sand of the beach and wondered how it had happened. How was it that her good deed could turn out so bad? She had wanted to get Bin Yu's pushy mother-in-law off his back for a week. Instead, she had brought Meilan Lin face to face with her nemesis on the beautiful island of St. Hilaire. So much for good intentions.

"No. Stay there. Did you find out anything else?"

"Australia. The widow was a Mrs. Ingrid Sobel, married to an older man, Andrew Sobel, a rancher with grown children. She was nurse to his first wife when she was dying, married the husband afterwards. When he got sick, he sold the ranch, eventually he died. There was a dispute over the will with his children but that was going through the courts, she would have won, apparently. But the money went back to the husband's heirs when she died.

"More stuff. The younger Chin had an internet firm, partly owned by the government. He did a trip to Australia looking for acquisitions but a couple of years later he sold out and that's why he was looking for new investments in the Caribbean. Those high-level Chinese officials do look for places to put their money overseas in non-communist countries, it's common practice. Elliot Chin wasn't in the party, but his father was still a big shot when he retired."

Lucy glanced over to the new wing. She could see the silhouette of the old man in his wheelchair on the balcony of the first-floor unit. She wondered if he really was as stoic as he seemed in the face of the death of his child. She shivered. It was unnatural. It made her wonder about the country and culture that had produced him and Meilan. The shadow of the Cultural Revolution seemed to extend through the years even down to the sunny present on a beautiful Caribbean Island.

"About the teambuilding group. The Blaine's lived in Cleveland since forever. He lost his job, started consulting. Mike Blaine and Guy Laurent worked for the same big conglomerate at one point, and they did do a business trip together to Australia a few years ago. Laurent is from Montreal originally but naturalized US. He's a management consultant in and out of lots of companies. Known as a ladies' man. It's in the report I emailed. Rita Blaine was housewife till the husband lost his job. Julia Raymond is in the middle of a messy divorce with her husband. Two daughters in college. No record of a trip to Australia for the women. It's all in what I sent."

"Thanks. I'll look at it." They discussed other research he could do and forensics that he had looked at. "Keep digging," Lucy told him. She saw Anna Maria Vandergott heading towards her with a worried look on her face. She wore a pale blue linen suit, a bright white silk tee, and strappy sandals with three-inch heels. "I have to go now. I'll check back later. Tell Hong not to worry." "At least not yet," she murmured under her breath as she hung up.

"I heard you're looking for a ride to the hospital. I'm so sorry, we don't have a van driver. It's to see Captain Neil, isn't it? I heard he got hurt last night. How is he?" Anna Maria asked. Lucy realized the island grapevine would have broadcast news of the dramatic shootout the night before even if the local officials tried to keep it out of the news media where visiting tourists might see it and be put off.

"That's what we want to find out. Dr. Murphy wants to go and see how he is. Can we call a taxi if the van's not available?"

"Certainly, but I wanted to offer to take you in my car. I have a mini coupe. I'll be happy to take you. Mr. Menotti said it was all right. We're all very concerned about Captain Neil. He's a regular around here and our visitors always have a wonderful time on his cruises."

"Great. Here comes Mary."

They followed Anna Maria out to the car. The morning sun was still bearable but as Lucy put on her sunglasses, she noticed a neat white BMW convertible with a blue canvas top pulling out. When she saw who was in it, she did a double take. Carlo Menotti was driving and Meilan Lin was in the passenger seat. What was she up to now?

TWENTY-NINE

Anna Maria dropped them off at the entrance of the contemporary glass and steel building in the middle of the island that was the St. Hilaire Hospital. Lucy noticed a brass engraved plate dedicating the construction to the ongoing friendship between the Republic of China, Taiwan and the island. It reminded her of Livingston's speech about the competition between mainland China's Communist government and the government of Taiwan for recognition by Caribbean islands. The People's Republic in Beijing might be wooing the local officials, but obviously Taipei had got there first.

Inside, Mary quickly got directions to Captain Neil's room on the second floor. The utilitarian linoleum floors, metal trays and busy people in sheet-like green scrubs were part of a world that was so different from the lay back tourist vibe of the resort island, it made Lucy shiver. Maybe it was the cold temperature of the air conditioning, the smell of disinfectant, or bad memories of other hospital visits to wounded fellow police officers. When they stepped into the private room with the door propped open, the medical environment seemed even more at odds with the blue sky and Caribbean sun that spilled into the room through floor to ceiling glass windows.

The high bed was in shade, but a visitor's chair on the window side was in full sun. A broad, bearded man in print shirt, khaki shorts and sandals had his eyes closed against the glare. If Jake Flaherty inhabited this thick waisted body with salt and pepper hair, it was a Jake Lucy would never have recognized. Not until the eyes opened. Then, somewhere behind those crystal blue irises, she sensed the essence of the boy she and her brothers had grown up with.

He stared back at her for a moment, and her spirit shrank at what he must be seeing. Sandy colored hair with darkening roots pulled back in a short ponytail, an aging body sacrificing seductive curves to the pounds of middle age, and a face that was sagging under years of experience that she was old enough to be glad to have survived. Those were all things she saw in the mirror when she bothered to look.

And yet when she looked at this older Jake, she still felt that pull, like a magnet. Just looking at him, she could see the image of the handsome young man he had been superimposed on his older self. Did he see her younger self? She shook herself mentally. If she weren't so concerned about the state of things with Meilan in serious danger of arrest, she would have had a good laugh at her sudden reversion to the self-consciousness of a teenager.

Mary's attention was concentrated on the man in the bed. His eyes were closed in a very pale face. The cheek and chin bones stood out sharply, and his sandy colored hair stood up on one side where he had been sleeping. Tubes were taped to his left arm, and wires protruded from his chest. There was a panel of important looking medical machines against the wall, beeping and clicking. A bulky bandage covered his right shoulder and the top of that arm. Lying under the sheets and blankets wearing the thin hospital gown, white with blue polka dots, he looked cold to Lucy. Mary felt his wrist and scanned him before stepping to the foot of the bed where she pulled a clipboard from a container.

Jake Flaherty watched her. "The round went through and through. They said he lost blood but should recover. Only, they keep coming in and checking, like there's still something wrong. And he didn't wake up."

Mary didn't answer. She was reading and rifling through the chart, biting her lips. Jake looked weary and Lucy assumed he'd been there all night.

Chief Jackson had told her that he called on Neil and Jake Flaherty as backup along with his brothers when he wasn't sure who he could trust in his own department. The chief had no inkling that Lucy knew Jake. The chief told her he completely trusted the local artist, especially in a tight place, but that the Vietnam vet refused to take a gun. Nonetheless, he had a reputation for being able to handle himself, and Lucy had the impression this was not the first time Chief Jackson had called on him.

"Did the chief get those guys straightened out? He didn't come check on Neil."

"He's got his hands full," Lucy told him. In the light of the beautiful Caribbean sun, it was hard to believe the events of the previous night had happened. But it was even harder to get her head around the fact that Jake Flaherty had come out of the dark like a screaming banshee to jump on the back of Lt. Strong.

And yet here he was now, looking soft and gentle as a sea breeze. But she'd seen the manic gleam in those blue eyes the previous night. Some softened version of the boy she grew up with and a still wild version of the man who had come back from war were still inhabiting that aging body. She felt wary about approaching him and tried to keep from staring at him. All the confusion she'd experienced back when she had tried to help him in those faraway days was surfacing again. She was too old for this. She stopped it.

"Captain Neil told us you were living here. He gave Mary one of your pictures. You remember Mary, don't you? Mary Curran, Mary Murphy now." Somehow Lucy couldn't bring herself to mouth the conventional words, so nice to see you again, etc. It wasn't nice to see him again and that was the truth. It only confused the issues. There were things she had to do, and she didn't have time for Jake Flaherty. She remembered only too well how he could enter her world and take it over, becoming the center of attention as if he were a huge sun pulling everything into his orbit. She didn't have time for this. She heard someone enter behind her and turned.

"How is he?" It was Anna Maria. She hesitated on the threshold.

Mary came out of her reverie over the chart. "They've treated the gunshot wound, and it should heal completely, but he's not responding to the drugs as they would expect. He's getting weaker, and they can't tell if he's having a reaction to something they're giving him or what." She turned to Jake. "Do you know if he's allergic to anything? Like anti-biotics, aspirin, anything?"

Jake rose from the chair and stood poised as if on high alert. "I don't know." He was staring at Anna Maria. "Did she come with you?" he asked Lucy abruptly.

"This is Anna Maria Vandergott, she works at the resort where we're staying, Pelican Bay. Livingston Jackson usually drives the van but he's out after all the excitement last night, so Anna Maria gave us a ride."

"I know Jake," Anna Maria said. "I know him from Captain Neil's boat. I've crewed for him sometimes and Jake does, too."

Jake said nothing, moving to look over Mary's shoulder. "What's wrong with him?"

Mary shook her head and closed the chart, dropping it back into the basket at the end of the bed. "They don't know. They're trying to figure that out." She moved back to Neil's side and held his wrist again.

Jake was watching her, occasionally glancing at Anna Maria. Lucy wondered if he had a relationship with the young woman. Something was making him uneasy. He shifted from foot to foot as if undecided where to move. Lucy was apprehensive. She could see a little gleam growing in his eyes. She was afraid he would have one of his outbreaks. Realizing how many years it was since she'd seen him, she was amazed at how tense she was, waiting for him to go off like a bomb. She remembered how much she hated the feeling, and she resented his presence.

As if he could hear her thoughts, suddenly Jake announced, "I need to go home and change. I'll see you later. Lucy, Mary. Sorry not to stay, but I need to leave." He shuffled to the door, pausing to look back, then disappearing.

"Poor Jake," Anna Maria said. "He's a very strange man, but he was a friend of Captain Neil's. I think he felt sorry for him."

THIRTY

Lucy left Mary at the hospital and got Anna Maria to drive her back to the resort. Lucy could no longer count on the police for information. And Chief Jackson was going to be concentrating on Meilan as the main suspect in the deaths of both Chin and Louella Roberts. He had to in order to counter the accusations from Strong. Lucy was disappointed that Captain Neil had not been able to answer questions, and she was disconcerted by the unexpected meeting with Jake Flaherty.

"Anna Maria, you said you actually spent time with the Australian widow that Louella's brother was accused of murdering, isn't that right?"

"Yes, Ingrid Sobel. I only met her on the plane, but she was very kind to invite me to spend my few free days at that beautiful beach house. I was grateful. It was so tragic, what happened to her."

"Did she talk about her background, or Australia while you were with her?"

"Australia? No. I mean, she came from there, but she didn't want to talk about the past. She was sad about the death of her husband,

and she said she didn't want to talk about it. She said she came here to get away from bad memories of a difficult time. I think she meant when her husband was dying. He was sick for a while or something. Is that important?"

Lucy hesitated to confide in the young woman, but she was frustrated about getting information. "Did she know Chin? Or anyone else here? The reason I ask is that Captain Neil told me he'd met Chin before in Australia. And then Mrs. Sobel was from Australia. So, I was wondering if there could have been a connection between Chin and the Sobel woman. Were you aware of her knowing anyone or meeting anyone on the island?"

Anna Maria thought about that as she navigated a roundabout in the bright sunshine. The roads were congested with vans and taxis delivering vacationers to resorts or the cruise ships that docked each day in the main port. "She went out sometimes, the few days I was there," she said when she had maneuvered on to a two-lane road that had fewer cars. "And she talked so someone on the phone. I was mainly at the beach or the small pool she had at that house. I just wanted to relax to get ready to start my new job. But Mr. Chin never mentioned knowing her, and neither did Captain Neil. I'm sure they would have. They knew I stayed with her before it happened." Lucy could see her shiver a little at the memory. Lucy wondered if Captain Neil would have mentioned knowing the Australian widow. It might depend on how well he had known her.

"What about Louella Roberts? Did you see her the day she died?"

"Poor Louella," Anna Maria downshifted as they headed up a steep hill. "That was so terrible too. Carlo is wild. How could two people die like that? It's a disaster for the resort."

"I'm sure it is." It occurred to Lucy that she might find allies in the resort staff since they would be anxious to have the deaths explained.

On one hand that might make them anxious to accept the accusations against Meilan, but it could also mean that they would be open to her questions. "Did you see Louella that day?"

"No, not that day. She didn't report to me, but I usually saw her when she took her break down on the patio. She would have a ginger ale. The staff aren't supposed to use the public areas, they're for the guests, but Louella always sat out there. I spoke to her about it the day before because Carlo told all of them not to do that. I reminded her about it. So yesterday, I looked, and she wasn't there. From what I heard; she was drinking some of the rum from the Chin's unit. They're saying that's what killed her. Is it true?"

"I don't know for sure, but that's what the police were assuming when they were still talking to me."

"And they say some of the police went after Livingston because they thought he had killed Chin, is that true?"

"That was a trap laid by Chief Jackson to find vigilante cops."

"So, Livingston didn't poison Mr. Chin?"

"No, they just put that rumor out to trap the bad police officers. They were the ones who framed Louella's brother for the murder of your friend Mrs. Sobel and shot him down. Apparently, there were some other similar murders of locals who had attacked tourists."

"Oh, there were rumors about that. That's terrible. Did they get them all?"

They had reached the top of the hill and as she shifted and headed the little car down, the Pelican Bay Resort lay below them. Boats filled the harbor behind the buildings, and sun glinted off gentle waves along the beach. Lucy longed for some time on the balcony, but she knew the peaceful scene was misleading. If she didn't do something, they were going to be trapped on this island and embroiled in a legal mess. The police were sure to be pressured by the older Chin and his influential countrymen to arrest someone for the poisoning of his son. And Pelican Bay would be anxious to clear their staff of the suspicion of negligence either for the hot tub or the rum. Meilan Lin was bound to be seen as the solution to a messy problem by the islanders. It was inevitable that they would look for an outsider to blame.

"As far as I know they got them all." Lucy wondered why she had thought that finding the vigilante cops would help the investigation into Chin's death. When the smoke cleared, Meilan Lin emerged as the most obvious suspect, so obvious the police might stop looking at other possibilities. "Anna Maria, it's possible that the authorities will want us to stay beyond Saturday. Can you look into what it would cost and if it's even possible for us to extend our stay if we have to."

"Oh, really? My goodness. I will find out for you. We're pretty booked at this time of year but let me talk to the reservation people and Carlo. I'm sure he'll work something out if he can. And if you are really pressed you can stay with me. I have a unit that is one bedroom, but you're welcome to use it if you have to. I could move in with one of the other girls." She was driving into the resort now, passing the harbor that bristled with sailboat masts on the left and pulling into an assigned parking space. "It's because of Mrs. Lin's argument with Mr. Chin, isn't it? What was that about?"

Lucy shook her head. What was that about? She really needed to find out from Meilan. The story she had told Lucy didn't make a lot of sense. "I'm not sure. I think they knew each other a long time ago, but that was the father, the older man, not Eliot Chin."

She started to open her door when Anna Maria put a hand on her arm. She had thought of something. "About Louella Roberts, another thing they're saying is that they found a piece of the jewelry that was missing from Mrs. Sobel's house, after the robbery and her death."

Lucy hadn't heard this. She would have to try to get information from Chief Jackson. Anna Maria squeezed her arm. "And another thing. When I saw Louella on the patio the other day, I think she was eavesdropping. Mr. and Mrs. Blaine were in the bar with Mr. Laurent and Mrs. Raymond. One of the reasons I reminded Louella about the policy on public places is because I had the impression she was listening to them. I don't know if it's important, but there is something wrong with that group. There's a lot of tension. You know what I mean?"

Lucy remembered her sister Norah's guesses about a love triangle involving the Blaines and Guy Laurent and thought she did understand what Anna Maria was suggesting. She couldn't see how it related to the deaths of Eliot Chin and Louella Roberts, but she had to agree with her nephew's girlfriend, there was something not right there.

THIRTY-ONE

Juliet Raymond headed down a narrow alley behind the strip of tourist traps that ran along the street where the big cruise liners docked. She wore a broad brimmed straw hat with a colorful scarf tied around the crown and very big yellow sunglasses. Her dark hair was all stuffed up into the hat and for once she wore a sleeveless silk blouse and a short, ruffled skirt. She would have been unrecognizable to anyone who knew her, but that was the point. She was already feeling itchy from the sun exposure, but she gritted her teeth and tried not to hurry to her destination.

She turned into the open door of a crowded little shop she had been told about. It seemed more like a walk-in closet than a shop. Floor to ceiling shelves filled the right side and then continued behind the tiny counter made of slats of grey weathered wood. The left wall was covered by a cabinet of small plastic drawers filled with dusty looking herbs. A skinny man with a Rastafari set of beaded braids perched on a rickety stool, reading a magazine in front of a short and stocky Chinese woman who filled up the rest of the space. Juliet almost turned and fled when she recognized the woman as a guest of the resort. It was dark enough to make her want to remove the sunglasses, but she remembered in time that the point of wearing them was disguise. And she fought back the panic she felt, realizing that if she left abruptly, it would be more memorable than if she just stayed where she was.

The Chinese woman zipped a fanny pack closed, then pulled it around into place. She hesitated for a minute, as if she had more to say to the man on the stool, although he was ignoring her as if her purchase had ended whatever feeble interest he had in her existence. Glancing at Juliet, the woman brushed past and exited to the alley.

Relieved, Juliet stepped up to the man to do her business.

***

Meilan Lin trudged along the alley to the corner, then hurried through several more streets to the center square of the port side town. She passed the high-classed jewelry and couture shops to enter the imposing building of the Federated National Bank of St. Hilaire. The fiercely air-conditioned inside had the hushed atmosphere of a self-consciously affluent institution laboring to make its customers feel at home. Lucy might have expected a committed comrade of the Chinese Communist Party to be uncomfortable in such overwhelmingly capitalist surroundings, but she would have been wrong. Meilan marched up to the broad desk of tasteful mahogany that was tucked into a recess on the right as if she were "to the manor born" as they used to say. And the exquisitely dressed and made-up young woman behind it quickly rose and ushered her even further into the sacred precincts.

Lucy would have been astonished to see the former grade school aide interrogate the older man behind another desk where even the flat screen of the computer was shrouded in a sleeve of polished wood.

Meilan grilled him about the security and privacy policies of the bank. After a lengthy discussion and review of a slick booklet, the Chinese grandmother was supplied with multiple printed forms and a silver pen to complete them. But what happened next would have astonished Lucy completely. She would have been shocked to see Meilan turn over the completed papers along with the passport and a paper check, then leave the bank clutching the passport and a folder full of materials on the secret numbered account she had just opened.

***

While the former Chinese Communist teacher's aide was doing her financial transactions, Anna Marie Vandergott was hesitating outside the door of the Chin's luxury unit. She dreaded the task she had been assigned by the resort management. It was often her job to smooth ruffled feathers of unhappy guests, but in Mr. Chin's case, the circumstances were thankfully unique. Never before had she been asked to cater to the needs of a grieving father who might potentially sue her employers for negligence in the death of his son. She knew that was what the higher ups in the timeshare business feared. Carlo Menotti had not expressed it quite that way when he gave her the assignment, but that was what he meant.

She thought about the last time she'd seen the younger Chin in the hot tub beside the pool. He might have been a successful entrepreneur in the software field, but he had been a stupid man when it came to people. In fact, she couldn't imagine how he was able to persuade investors to believe in him. She had to wonder if it was really the commanding presence of the older man that mattered. After all, if Chin was on the island for business, why had he brought the old man at all? She sensed that the father was the power behind the operation, whatever that operation was. She also sensed he was a lot more dangerous than his entrepreneurial son. She had no idea what beef Mrs. Lin had with the old comrade, but she could believe it was rooted in something substantial. And from what Lucy O'Donnell had said, the police were focusing on Mrs. Lin as the main suspect in the younger Chin's death.

Anna Maria was quite positive that Eliot Chin's death was not caused by some nefarious scheme of his. On the contrary, she was certain it was due to his stupidity. He knew something and was too stupid to know how dangerous that knowledge was. She thought that was a mistake the older man would never make. So, she had to wonder if the son had told his father what he knew. It would be like him to do that, even if he hadn't meant to. Perhaps she could find out. As long as she was assigned to the old man anyhow. Maybe she could sympathize enough to get him to confide in her. She wondered if Lucy O'Donnell, her friend Steve's beloved aunt, would want to hear what the old man knew. You would think she would, but what if it implicated someone, she had reason to protect?

Anna Maria stood up straight and threw her shoulders back. At least it would give her the chance to do something, and the sooner the police arrested Chin's murderer, the sooner she could get on with her own plans for her future life. She had to admit, she was already dreaming of what type of a bridal gown would look best on her figure. She knocked briskly and called out. "Mr. Chin, can I come in? I'd like to make sure you have everything you need."

***

Meanwhile, back at the St. Hilaire Hospital, Dr. Mary Murphy was reading the results of the drug screening done on Captain Neil with disbelief. It couldn't be. She looked down at the barely breathing figure on the bed. He'd been moved back to the ICU when he failed to recover from the surgery. Even more electronic equipment was hooked up to his unnaturally pale and still body.

He'd taken a turn for the worse overnight and when Mary found out they moved him back to the ICU, she insisted on a consultation with the attending physician and strongly suggested the drug screen. The Indian born doctor naturally resented the interference and, normally, she would have been more tactful. But she was alarmed by the sudden decline, and she could be quite forceful when it came to her own domain. She worked in an inner city trauma unit early in her career and she knew that recovery from a gunshot wound should not take this trajectory. There was something seriously wrong. Something in his body was interfering with a normal recovery. Whether it was an undetected infection or an unexpected allergic reaction, there was something wrong and the patient was in no position to help with the diagnosis.

She hadn't expected what she was seeing in the lab test results. With a worried glance at Captain Neil, she grabbed the chart at the foot of the bed and riffled through it looking for some explanation for the unexpected amounts of potassium that had been found. There were also repeated instances of the need to return him to assisted breathing devices. There was no explanation, and she had a suspicion, but it had to be impossible. She corrected herself. Improbable but not impossible, especially in light of what was going on at the resort.

Unlikely as it was, she took the test results and the chart out to the central counter of the nurse's station and told them why she thought a follow up analysis was needed. This led to a flurry of activity until the attending physician could be reached by phone and give his weary permission. The charge nurse let Mary talk directly to the lab about what needed to be done. It would take a few hours. She emphasized the critical condition of the patient and they agreed to give the work the highest priority.

She hung up with a queasy feeling in her stomach. If her suspicions were wrong, they would still need to find the source of the problem. If they were correct, Captain Neil might not make it through the night. She apologized to the nurses and then obliterated the goodwill she had achieved by that gesture when she conducted a meticulous interrogation into the exact treatments and dosages that Neil had received. She also insisted that he remain on the breathing device. This made her no friends. The three nurses on duty were affronted by the questions and they also were quick to defend the professionalism of their colleagues on the other shifts. Two of them went off in a huff to tend to patients and the charge nurse, a neat looking middle-aged black woman with a nametag that said Sherry Long, brought the conversation to an end.

"Captain Neil's condition began to deteriorate before he was moved here," she pointed out. "And since he has been here, we've been able to stabilize him. I don't know what you are looking for but the only treatment or drugs he received are contained in his chart and the only people who have been by his side are our nurses, yourself and a few people who looked in very briefly to see how he was doing. Captain Neil is well known and liked on the island, so he has many well-wishers."

"Exactly who did visit?" Mary asked.

With a frown, the charge nurse took the chart from Mary's hand and flipped through to a page near the end and handed it back. "Now, if you could return the chart to where it belongs, I have other patients

I need to see. I'll let you know as soon as the lab calls with results." She turned away.

"OK. Just keep him on the ventilator to be safe. Please." The nurse did not respond. Mary looked at the list which she presumed had been typed up from a set of visitor signatures in a ringed binder at the nurse's station. A dozen islanders had looked in on the patient. Mary knew the ICU would allow them only a few moments with the sick man, but it was the policy here as at some other hospitals to allow such drop-ins because the patient could sense there was support for him, and many responded positively to the contact.

There were a dozen or so names. She wasn't surprised to see Jake Flaherty, Delroy and Chief Jackson listed or Anna Maria since the girl had said she sometimes crewed on his catamaran. She didn't recognize the other names except the last two. What was Meilan Lin doing checking on Captain Neil? She was listed right after Carlo Menotti. Perhaps she had merely accompanied him?

Mary wondered as she returned the chart to the foot of Neil's bed. It hardly seemed likely anyone had tried to do anything in an ICU, but the fact that Chin and Louella Roberts were poisoned weighed on her mind. They had ingested poison. Captain Neil had been shot. His issues had to be complications based on the wound. He had an IV and had not eaten or drunk anything. She was giving way to a tendency to be overly cautious. She felt a little rueful about the test she had demanded from the lab but it was better to eliminate as many possibilities as she could, so she settled down in a chair beside the bed to wait for the results. Unlike Lucy O'Donnell she was so preoccupied with the medical problem it never even crossed her mind that she should have been sitting at the beach, sipping a Margarita.

THIRTY-TWO

Back at Pelican Bay Resort, Lucy was lying in wait in the lobby when Meilan returned. Norah was on a rampage about the need to extend their stay, so Lucy wanted to confront their Chinese roommate before she went back to the unit. She was just about to retreat to the restaurant to order lunch when she saw the white BMW pull up to the door and Meilan got out. The car pulled away.

"Meilan, we need to talk." Lucy was on her feet blocking the way of the stocky woman who trudged with her head down.

Meilan looked up with surprise, then suspicion. "No time. Busy day. Got to go do exercise." She attempted to sidestep, but Lucy took her by the elbow and steered her towards the restaurant overlooking the water.

"No. We need to talk. Come on." Lucy waved to the hostess and led Meilan to an isolated table by the window. When a waitress came over, she told her they would be doing the lunch buffet and didn't need drinks. When she left, Lucy frowned at Meilan. "Listen. You're in a lot of trouble. Why didn't you tell the police you knew the Chins and that you were accused of stalking the old man back in China? Don't you think they'll find that out? And what are you up to? You've been disappearing, staying out all night, going off by yourself, what are you doing? Do you have any idea what kind of trouble you'll be in if they think you poisoned Eliot Chin?"

She wasn't surprised when Meilan wouldn't cooperate. "I told you. Chin is a bad man, a very bad man. He came here to do bad things. Police should look at what he is doing here. Crooked politician. Corrupt official. Lots of enemies. There's no reason for me kill young Chin. I expose crimes of old Chin."

"What crimes? What were you doing in China following him around? You even followed him to Australia and got in trouble there, I hear."

"Crimes against the people. You will see."

"So, tell me about it."

"We need to get lunch, yes? We told them we're doing lunch." Meilan got up and headed for the long tables full of food that were the buffet. Lucy rolled her eyes, threw down her linen napkin and followed.

As Lucy filled her plate with salad, she kept an eye on Meilan who was examining each dish, but choosing only from a few of the fish, shrimp and vegetable hot dishes. She appeared very suspicious of the food, as if it might bite her. When she headed back to the table Lucy looked down at her own plate of healthy lettuce, mushrooms, tomatoes and cucumbers, then grabbed a couple of deep-fried chicken thighs and dropped them on top of it all. She stopped at the waitress's shoulder on her way back to the table to say she had changed her mind and wanted to order a beer.

"Meilan, I'm not kidding. What have you been doing? Where have you been disappearing to? Where were you the night Eliot Chin was killed? And where did you go today with Mr. Menotti?"

The Chinese woman tried to avoid answering by commenting on the food on her own plate and on Lucy's but when the former officer continued to glare at her, she finally replied. "Timeshare boss gave me ride to town. It's necessary to expose old man Chin. He's the one who did it. He and some old cronies steal money then bring it here to hide it. You'll see. They'll will see."

"What cronies?"

"Cronies, buddies, his old fellow comrade friends back in China. They steal money, bring it here, hide it."

"How do you know that?" Lucy asked after the waitress delivered a bottle of local beer.

Meilan was munching on a mouthful of asparagus, looking at Lucy like she was sizing her up. She took a sip of water then shrugged. "Old Chin handles money for big shots. The son's not reliable. Son makes a big mistake with money. Chin, he's a smart old guy. He knows how to find herbs here on the island. Vanderdander woman told him, and he gets the son to take him to buy it." Lucy realized she meant Anna Maria Vandergott, although why she would think the girl told Chin where to buy poison was beyond her. "He gets something to get rid of his son, who's a big embarrassment. That way big shots don't find out about bad money trades by the son. Only he father has codes for secret accounts. He can hide the son's errors."

Lucy stared at her. "What are you talking about? You're saying you think old Mr. Chin poisoned his own son? Why?"

Meilan was shaking her head. "When he loses money for big shots, he can't go back to China. Go back and get arrested, he gets the firing squad. This way nobody knows, old Chin can go back."

Lucy remembered that Bin Yu had found out Chin was suspected of investing money overseas for Chinese Communist officials, but it was only a suspicion. "Why would he kill his own son? And why now?

Sounds like the younger Chin had been doing that kind of investing for party officials off and on for years. Why is it suddenly a problem? Besides, what proof do you have of this anyhow?"

"Proof! Old man went to the herb seller. Vander girl told him. Van driver took him."

"How do you know he wasn't just buying other herbs? Why do you think it's poison?"

"Old Chinese method to get rid of enemies."

Lucy thought it was ludicrous that Meilan wanted to paint the old man as a Fu Man Chu type of character. She was going to say so, but she realized Meilan would have no idea what she was talking about. Fu Man Chu was a character an American might recognize but a mainland Chinese person probably wouldn't. No point confusing an already difficult conversation.

"Meilan, the night that Eliot Chin died, did you talk to him or his father? Did you go back to their unit after that argument you had with the father that day? What did you do while we were on that dinner sail on the catamaran?"

Meilan looked down at her food, while working a bit of green out of her teeth with a toothpick. Lucy thought she didn't want to answer the question and she was about to give the woman a piece of her mind when Meilan finally spoke. "Went to see the old man. He wouldn't open door. Waited till room service brought dinner food, then I followed him in. Old man yelled. I told him he won't get away with stealing from the Chinese people. Waiter made me leave. That's all. Didn't really see son."

"Didn't really see him? What does that mean?"

"Afterwards I was sitting near the pool. In darkness. I saw him in the hot tub. Stupid capitalist turncoat. I spit at him but too dark for him to see. Went up late. You were all sleeping. Slept on the couch but didn't open up bed part. Trying not to wake you. Had stiff neck in the morning, went to exercise to stretch it."

Lucy pushed her plate away. She'd eaten the chicken but left the salad. Meilan had returned to the Chin's unit that night, although she claimed she was not there for long. Lucy wasn't sure if it would be useful to find the waiter who'd witnessed the exchange or if that would just be more damaging for Bin Yu's mother-in-law.

"Anyway, Vanderdander girl gave him the drink, right? She's probably working for the old man. Very attractive to old men that girl. She gives son the drink all the time. Maybe she poisoned him."

Lucy realized Meilan resented Anna Maria, probably because the poor girl had been assigned to take care of the Chins. You couldn't' reason with the Chinese grandmother when she took a strong dislike to someone, so Lucy moved on to another topic. "What about the maid, Louella Roberts. Did you talk to her ever?"

"Maid?"

"Yes, maid. The maid who was killed. The maid who apparently was poisoned by drinking from the bottle of rum that was in the Chin's unit. A bottle of rum they will say that you poisoned."

"No. No maid. Don't know her. No bottle of rum. I don't like alcohol." Meilan had finished her lunch. Her plate was bare.

"Why were you stalking Chin in China? And you followed him all the way to Australia?"

"Stalking?"

"You followed him around." Lucy was exasperated.

Meilan sat up straight and pointed a finger at her chest. "I know. He is counter revolutionary capitalist running dog. I know what he does. Steals from the people. Lies about people. Sends good comrades to labor camps by telling lies. He pretends to follow Mao but really he betrays him first chance he gets. Everybody needs to know what a bad man he is. He needs to admit what he is."

Lucy didn't get it. Even if the old Chinese man was a corrupt official, she couldn't see how Meilan's following him around trying to embarrass him with accusations would do any good. She didn't appear to have contemplated actually harming the guy, she just wanted to malign him to all and sundry. Maybe that would have some important consequences in China, but in the U.S. or Australia people would just think she was crazy.

Meilan glared at her. "Operation Fox Hunt. China finds corrupt officials like Chin. Xi Jinping says it is 'killing tigers and swatting flies.' Old Chin is a big tiger. We need to turn him in to Wang Qishau. He's a big shot in anti-corruption campaign. Need to report old Chin."

Lucy had no idea what she was talking about, and she doubted the local police would either. She would have to ask Bin Yu if he knew what his mother-in-law meant. Meanwhile she asked her about the herb shop and was appalled to learn that Meilan had gone there asking for different poisons and she even bragged about purchasing an herbal remedy that had aconite. She pulled out a dusty plastic bottle. "Here, give me that," Lucy said, grabbing it from her. It was marked with Chinese characters but a small print translation in English mentioned aconite. Oh, great, just what they needed. Meilan had no sense of self-preservation whatsoever. Lucy would need to show this to Mary. She tucked the bag into her purse and asked, "Did you find out that Chin had bought some of that?"

"No. Seller wouldn't say. He could have though. Chinese store, black guy sells herbs but it's owned by local Chinese people. I want to tell the Chinese consul. Chinese government needs to know about big traitor. Wang Qishao needs to know."

Lucy thought about all the Chinese at the table with old man Chin the night before, and she thought Meilan was really living in a pipe dream. For those men, Chin was probably the goose that laid the golden egg. No way they were going to put him in jail. Meilan was the one who was in danger. Lucy frowned. "Meilan, I don't think the consul is going to believe that Chin killed his own son. You have no proof, only suspicions and even those are pretty weak. If you try to accuse Chin of these things, it could backfire on you. It could make trouble for you instead of for Chin."

Meilan frowned. Lucy could see that she didn't want to hear it. "Consul works for Chinese people. Party does Operation Fox Hunt. Consul will act. You'll see."

THIRTY-THREE

Juliet Raymond sat at a round table with a view of the beach and ordered drinks for all of her party. She'd purposely arrived early. Before that, she'd changed to a more comfortable outfit in muted shades of gray but now she clutched her straw purse as she waited for the drinks to arrive and stared out at the water without seeing it.

When she returned from the sweaty frustrating sail with Mike and Anna Maria the previous afternoon, she got the phone call she was waiting for from her lawyer. That sent her racing off in search of Guy to tell him the settlement was drafted and only required her signature for the house to be put on the market.

Excited by the prospect of getting the money they needed, she was deeply disappointed in his reaction, or lack of reaction to the news. Of course, he was still suffering from a migraine, and he pleaded a need for complete dark and silence in the cabin of the boat in order to recover. He rejected her attempts to help him and insisted she go to the resort and use the shower then eat with Mike and Rita, leaving him in peace. When she did return to the boat there was no response to her whispered greeting, and she didn't want to disturb him, so she slept in the outer berth by herself.

He still wasn't himself in the morning. She suggested he might want to skip breakfast with the Blaines as they were sure to bicker in the most irritating manner possible. She joked that if he didn't already have a headache eating with them would be bound to bring one on, based on her experience at dinner. He agreed wanly and returned to the darkened cabin.

When she went to breakfast to take back something for both of them, Rita was leaving on a shopping excursion. Juliet thought she might be doing it to annoy her husband. The night before they'd argued again about going back to Cleveland and she thought Rita was going to answer Mike's refusal to book tickets by spending money. Mike was holding out for a chance to talk to old Mr. Chin about the teambuilding training contract to try to get him to sign it. Juliet was gleeful as she described this to Guy but he was not amused, only glum. So, when he returned to bed, she thought about it and went in search of something to fix the problem.

She was unsure where to turn for information on what she wanted to get but she tried approaching Anna Maria Vandergott and was surprised to be successful. The young Dutch woman suggested the herb seller in the port town and gave her directions. She offered to try to book the van, but Juliet opted for a taxi. She knew the girl would be discreet. She obviously handled all kinds of requests from guests at the resort and did not seem at all curious about Juliet's query. In town, Juliet had accomplished her mission and made it back in time for this lunch.

The waitress set out four large glasses of spicy Bloody Marys on the table. When she left, Juliet looked around. Mike, Rita and even Guy were going to join her, but she was still early. She noticed Lucy

O'Donnell, someone had pointed her out as a retired police officer from Boston, and that awkward Chinese woman named Lin leaving the room. They looked like they were arguing.

She waited until they disappeared and then took out a small plastic bag from her purse. Pulling one of the glasses closer, she carefully scattered some of the contents of the bag into it, stirring with the celery stalk and pushing the glass back in place when she was done. Then she tucked the plastic bag back into her purse and slid her own drink over to take a hardy sip. She liked the bite of spiciness she tasted while she thought about what she was going to say to the others. She was determined to convince them that they needed massages in the spa. She had already booked for all of them. It wasn't the kind of thing she usually did, but she knew it would be good for them and she was hoping that, afterwards, she and Guy could slip away, back to the Last Resort.

When she glanced back towards the door and saw Rita and Mike entering, she also noticed the Vandergott girl. She was staring at Juliet with speculation in her eyes, but as Mike greeted her, she put on her most hospitable smile and wished him a delicious lunch. Juliet saw Guy entering tentatively after them. It was time to put her plan into action.

THIRTY-FOUR

"Operation Fox Hunt?" Bin Yu said. "Ah, I think I know what she means."

After her unrewarding lunch with Meilan, Lucy didn't have the energy to face her sister Norah back on their own balcony, so she found a soft chaise lounge in the shade of the porch overlooking the beach and called Bin Yu.

"Ah, I think that's the big anti-corruption campaign the Chinese government launched last year or the year before. Let me look it up." Lucy closed her eyes, picturing the tall and lanky young man leaning towards the large flat screen of his computer in the crime laboratory where he spent most of his time. He was a northern Chinese, so he was taller than the Cantonese southerners who made up most of the older people in Boston's Chinatown. In recent years, immigrants from all over China had diversified the Chinatown population. Bin had gone to school at Beijing University, but he came from a small village in Shenyang. He was the youngest of eleven children and the only one to leave the village and attend university.

"Yes, Operation Fox Hunt. It's a big anti-corruption campaign. Of course, sometimes that's just a way to get rid of political enemies. But, anyway, this started with the phase called 'killing tigers and swatting flies.'"

"Yes, she said those words, what does that mean?"

"Oh, Chinese language. Lots of times they boil things down to a four-word slogan like that. In this case it means they're out to expose corruption in 'tigers' which would be high level, powerful cadre, as well as 'flies' which would be small time local crooked officials. Of course, they say that, but then you don't know if they're really doing it or just putting on a show. But they did convict a really high level former central committee guy last year, and it says they put in an anti-corruption czar named Wang Qishao, They say all the politicians are afraid of him."

"I think she mentioned his name, too."

"Grandma Lin keeps up on her politics," Bin said. "Sounds like the old man Chin is or was a higher up in the Communist Party. So, a lot of times the children of those people are called 'taizi' which means 'princelings.' They're the little red princes who can do no wrong and get spoiled, like the heirs of emperors in the old days. It's a common criticism of the system."

"Well, your mother-in-law thinks Chin killed his own son to cover up his corruption."

There was a pause on the other end. "Hmm. That doesn't seem very likely. Chinese people really want their children to live on after them to look after their graves. It would be really unusual for a father to kill his own son. Of course, corruption charges in China can lead to a death sentence, you know. So maybe, if he felt really threatened..."

"Really? A death sentence?" Lucy thought of all the crooked pols she had run across in her career. Imagine if a conviction meant the death sentence, wouldn't that be something? She put that thought away to ponder at a later time. There were more pressing issues. "I can't see that she really has any evidence, though. It sounds like she's just saying what she wants to believe. She went and bought some poison to prove he could have, I guess. Don't worry, I took it away from her. But I'm afraid the local police are looking at her as a serious suspect, at least for Chin's death. I can't imagine why she would want to poison the maid."

"Maybe it was a mistake, if she poisoned the rum, and Chin drank some and then the maid just came along and thought she could get a free drink. I'm not saying she did it, of course. She wouldn't, I don't think. Jeese, what am I going to tell Hong?"

"Don't panic yet, she hasn't been charged with anything. Did you find out anything else?"

"Australia. Ingrid Sobel, the widow who died, was Ingrid Van Ness before she married. She was a nurse. She nursed the wife of Andrew Sobel, who had a big ranch. The wife died. She had been sick with breast cancer, and Van Ness lived at the ranch that last year of her life to take care of her. So, after she died, the husband and the nurse got married. There was nothing wrong about it. He just got to know a good-looking woman while the wife was sick, and he was probably lonesome when she was gone. My source said not every woman wants to live in the outback, so the fact that she had already lived on the ranch must have been a good thing in his eyes.

"He had three older children by his first wife, two sons and a daughter, and they weren't too happy with the marriage, but they were all grown up and out in the world, one with his own ranch, one a stock trader and the daughter married with kids. But after a year or so, Andrew Sobel developed some kind of condition. Running the ranch was getting to be too much for him. He was already in his sixties, she was much younger, half his age. But it's useful to have a wife who's a nurse if you get sick, so maybe he chose her for that.

"Anyhow that's when Chin was in Australia and he was buying property as investments for other people back in China who couldn't do that sort of thing openly. Party officials and things like that. Because his company was what they call an S-chip incorporated outside of China and on the Singapore Exchange, it might have been a way for people to invest money the government wouldn't know about. He didn't buy the Sobel ranch, but a few months later it was sold to someone else. The husband was getting sicker. The money went mostly into some accounts he left to his wife, and some went into some investments in jewelry, mostly emeralds. I guess he was a bit of a collector. When he died, the wife got the jewels outright and she got the money for her life to go to the children on her death or remarriage. The sons tried to contest the will and that was still in the courts, but they were certainly going to lose from what I found out. But that all went away now. They'll get the money."

"So, when she died, that meant the children from the first marriage got the money. Do we know where they are exactly?"

"We know who they are, and I'm looking into where they're supposed to be now but that will take a little digging. None of them are in the Caribbean, as far as I know."

"See if you can check on that. That money would be a big motive to kill the widow."

"But what about Chin?"

"Well, maybe he knew the children. He would have known Mrs. Sobel. Maybe he recognized someone from Australia, one of the heirs, or someone who was close to them."

This idea excited Bin Yu and Lucy was a little afraid she was getting his hopes up for nothing. "Wow, so somebody could have killed her for the money and been recognized by Chin, so they killed him. Maybe the maid saw something…"

"It's possible, anyhow. There were some pieces of jewelry found on the man who was accused of killing Mrs. Sobel and also a piece on the maid. See if you can get a list of the jewelry. How much was it worth?"

"A couple of million, I think. I'll see what I can find out. So, do you think the old lady is going to get arrested for killing Chin? Do you think we should come down now? Or maybe just me? Although I know Hong is going to insist on coming to take care of her mother."

"No, Bin, really. I think you can do more from where you are. If it comes to it, I'll tell you and we'll find some place for you to stay but hold off on that as long as you can."

"As long as I can hold off Hong, you mean."

"Do what you can." Lucy saw Anna Maria looking like she had something to say but hesitating to interrupt the phone call. "I've got to go. I'll call you when I have any information and you call me if you find anything else."

Anna Maria approached. "I talked to Mr. Menotti, and he has a suite of rooms in the new wing where you and your party can move if you have to stay next week. The cheaper units are rented but he'll give it to you at a special rate because he knows it's not your fault."

"Thank you very much, Anna Maria. I really appreciate it. Right now it's looking like we'll need to take him up on that offer. But if we move to that wing, can you put us somewhere that's not near Mr. Chin? It would be awkward, if he was next door."

"Oh, no, of course." She looked horrified. "Ms. O'Donnell, there's one more thing. I don't know if it means anything but remember when I said there's something wrong with that group that includes the Blaines and the other two?"

"Yes, has something happened?"

"It's just that one of them, Juliet Raymond, asked me to recommend a local herbalist. She said it was for something private, I assumed some condition she might have. She's very sensitive to the sun I noticed. Anyway, I told her, and I think she went there this morning but she was back for lunch. And before the others joined her, I saw her put something into one of the drinks. I think it was the one for Mrs. Blaine. I didn't see any bad effects. I watched and they all seemed fine after eating and they went to get a massage at the spa. But it worried me a bit."

Lucy stared at her. "Yes. I can see how it would, considering what has been going on around here. You keep an eye on them and for my part I'll see if I can get any information about them." It was strange, but as usual, she couldn't see how that uneasy group fit into the puzzle. It worried her, too.

THIRTY-FIVE

When Mary returned from the hospital, she had bad news. Captain Neil was also suffering from poisoning. That was why he was not healing as he should be. The doctors had been stymied by his lack of improvement but when Mary pointed them in the right direction, they found traces of the poison in his blood. It had already nearly killed him more than once, and, while they were keeping him on a ventilator just in cases.

"The same poison that killed Chin?" Norah asked.

"Actually, it's not the same poison that killed Chin. It's SUX, succinylcholine. It's a special muscle relaxant they use in emergency rooms when they need to intubate, put a tube in someone for them to breathe. It paralyzes the patient for five to ten minutes. He would have died if there wasn't breathing equipment right there."

"How would anyone get that drug?" Lucy asked.

"It's not available to the general public. It's widely available in emergency rooms, though, because you use it if you have to intubate. But you give oxygen to compensate till it wears off. It's only because I saw him stop breathing twice and I saw higher than normal potassium in the blood reports that I had them test for metabolites. They have to use a mass spectrometer to identify them. And they did. The thing is, you don't put this in somebody's food or drink, it has to be injected. The fact that he has an IV means someone could add it to the drip, but you have to know what you're doing."

"They're sure it's not a mistake? Some nurse didn't give it by accident?" Lucy asked.

"No mistake. It's not the kind of drug that you would give by mistake. They'll keep a close watch now. It would have to be someone who knew what they were doing, but they think it was removed from one of the ambulances. They're still checking inventory."

Norah was outraged. "That proves it. This place is dangerous, and we need to go home Saturday. We can't stay here with a poisoner running around."

Lucy took a big breath. She told them the resort would move them to a luxury suite if they had to stay. This only infuriated Norah who stated she was going to pack and stormed off to the bedroom where they could hear her slamming drawers and pushing things around.

"We move now?" Meilan asked.

"No, we're not moving now, Norah is just having a temper tantrum," Lucy said.

"I'll go exercise."

"No, wait a minute, Meilan," Mary said. "I want to ask you about something."

Meilan turned to her with a blank look on her face. "Ask."

Mary glanced at Lucy and then at the doorway to the bedroom as if she wanted to be sure Norah was not listening. "Meilan, did you go to visit Captain Neil in the hospital? I was looking at the log of who had visited last night and I saw your name there."

Meilan looked down at the floor, as if she were deciding how to answer. Lucy thought she had never seen the woman stop to think before she spoke. That was new. "I was with Mr. Menotti, big timeshare boss. He stopped to see Captain Neil, I was with him."

"Mr. Menotti?"

"Yes, he is a friend."

"I see. While you were there, did you or Mr. Menotti do anything or give anything to Captain Neil? Or did you see anyone else do that?"

Meilan frowned. "Give something? Like flowers?"

Mary grimaced. "No, more like a drug." She glanced at Lucy. "Someone tried to poison Captain Neil. They did poison him. The hospital went over all the drugs that were prescribed and given but someone else had to somehow give him the poison. Most likely it was injected into the IV."

"Poison? Like Chin? Old man Chin, was he there?"

"Meilan thinks Chin poisoned his son," Lucy said.

"Why? Does he have access to the poison that killed his son?"

"Yes and he's a bad man," Meilan said.

"You don't know that," Lucy said. She turned to Mary. "Meilan thinks the old man went to a local herb seller on the island and bought this." She pulled out the plastic bottle of herbal concoction.

Mary took it and read the English on the label. "That has aconite, all right. But it's a mild dosage. You'd have to use more than what's recommended but I suppose it could be done. It's not what was given to Neil, though. That was a drug you would only find in a hospital or ambulance. And, besides, I didn't see Mr. Chin in the log of visitors. It was all local island people who visited."

Meilan grunted. "Hire somebody. He can hire somebody to do it for him."

Lucy was getting annoyed. "Meilan, you have no proof whatsoever. Why would Chin want to get rid of Captain Neil? You're the one who the police can prove bought this poison." She held up the bottle and shook it at Meilan. "You're the one who went to visit Neil. Your name's in the log. Don't you get it? They're going to think you did it."

"Why should I poison Captain Neil?" Meilan asked. "I don't know him."

"It's not clear why you do anything." Lucy was trying to restrain herself from shouting. "Why do you follow Chin around and try to hassle him? Why did you buy poison? Why do you insist on doing stupid things that are bound to make the police think you killed Eliot Chin? Do you want to get arrested?"

Meilan stared at her. "Me, arrested? Why? I don't care about the spoiled brat princeling. Old Chin is a bad corrupt counter revolutionary. I want to expose him to the party, make him lose face."

"Well, good luck with that, because all you've managed to do so far is to make yourself the prime suspect in this murder."

Meilan frowned. "No. Not me. Chin." There was a pause as the two of them faced off. Mary rolled her eyes. Finally, Meilan said, "I'll go exercise." Then she turned, picked up a gym bag lying on the floor and marched out the door. As it closed forcefully behind her, they heard the closet door in the bedroom slammed shut by Norah.

"Somehow," Mary said. "I don't think this is helping."

THIRTY-SIX

Chief Jackson avoided Lucy's eyes and looked around the bar. Delroy was making some kind of complicated drink while he talked to the honeymoon couple. The rest of the bar was empty in the late afternoon. Through the tall windows they could see people still sitting on the blue lounges around the infinity pool in shade from the waning sun.

"So, you think one of the Sobel heirs came to the island, killed the widow then poisoned Chin because he recognized him or her from his time in Australia?" the chief said.

That he was skeptical was only to be expected. Lucy had had a hard time convincing him to even meet. His relationship with her was suspect in his department and he was being pressured by the Chinese consulate to make an arrest in the Chin investigation. Lucy took a sip from the brightly labelled bottle of local beer.

"What about Louella Roberts? And now Captain Neil?" he asked.

"The maid could have seen something. Anna Maria said she thought Louella might have been eavesdropping on the Blaine party. But she could have seen something in the unit. I asked her to be ready to help us to see if anything was changed or out of place when you got a search warrant. Of course, by the time we would have done that she was dead. But what if she could have sworn that rum bottle was tampered with or something like that?"

"If she knew that, why would she be dumb enough to drink from it?"

"Maybe she didn't. Anna Maria told me she always had ginger ale on her break. What if someone poisoned her ginger ale, then planted the rum bottle on her after she was dead?" The chief took a long pull on his beer bottle without commenting. "Really, it could happen. What if the killer thought she was snooping around and kept an eye on her? He could have known about her daily break. He could have found a way to poison her drink, then follow her and replace that with a poisoned bottle of rum from the Chin's. Or maybe she found the rum and tried to blackmail the killer and he managed to poison her. Livingston said she was determined to prove her brother was innocent of the widow Sobel's murder."

The chief moved uneasily at the mention of his brother, as if he wanted to shake that off. Lucy had not seen Livingston at the resort since the night they arrested Strong and the other vigilante cops. She assumed he was grieving.

"And Neil?"

"Probably he recognized the killer from Australia, too. He knew Chin there. He might have known the Sobels. The point is, if the reason for all of this is because of the suit against Mrs. Sobel back in Australia, you need to find out from the Australian authorities if the stepsons and stepdaughter are at home or if they are travelling and could be here. Or it could be someone they know or hired who is here. But it means following up on Mrs. Sobel and her connections even though that murder was supposedly resolved. Now that you have the vigilantes you need to reopen that case." He probably wouldn't appreciate her telling him what he should do, but he was a reasonable person. He might listen.

"If Neil recognized this person from Australia, why wouldn't he have come forward and said something? No, I think you're over-looking a different theory that covers all the facts. We've found out from the Chinese that your friend Mrs. Lin had a grudge against Chin's father. The consul came to see me. He says Lin's father died during the Cultural Revolution and she blamed Chin. He says she even followed Chin to Australia, and she was about to be arrested for stalking him when her relatives got together and shipped her off to her daughter in America. When she saw him here, she decided to get revenge by poisoning his son. Louella Roberts must have seen something that threatened Lin, so she killed her. Maybe Louella was trying to blackmail her. And Neil probably knew something about her time in Australia when both the Chins were there, so she's trying to keep him quiet too. We know she was at the hospital. If Neil knew something we should be able to find out what it was when he's better."

"And Mrs. Sobel?"

"That was a robbery. Maybe Billy Roberts did it, maybe somebody else, but it was just a robbery plain and simple."

"What about the jewelry found in Louella's pocket?"

He shook his head. "Who knows? Maybe her brother *was* the thief and she got it from him. Maybe it wasn't Lin who gave her poison, maybe the poison was in the rum and Louella had the bad luck to choose that bottle to steal. Lin was in the Chin's unit the night Eliot Chin died. She could have put the poison in the rum bottle then. The younger Chin came up and had a drink, then went back to the pool and died. Louella decided to take the bottle aside for a little tipple and it was still poisoned. Something like that."

Lucy thought the explanation was pretty sloppy. Were there fin-gerprints on the rum bottle? Why hadn't they taken away all of the bottles in the unit for testing when they knew the man was poisoned? Of course, he died down by the pool, nonetheless they should have known he could have gone up and drunk something then come back down. But she held her tongue. She didn't want to risk having the chief stop talking if he thought she was too critical of the procedures of the local police. She needed to get him to look seriously at the theory that one or all of Mrs. Sobel's heirs might be involved. She took a swig from her bottle.

Before she could try to argue her case, Anna Maria Vandergott came over to the police followed by two tall Chinese men in suits.

"Chief Jackson, Mr. Chin and the Chinese consul are asking for you to come to Mr. Chin's unit right away. Mr. Chin says he found Mrs. Lin trying to plant a bottle of poison in his bathroom."

THIRTY-SEVEN

Chief Jackson didn't object when Lucy followed him over to the new section of the resort and to the door of the ground level unit where Mr. Chin had been moved. Inside, Chin was sitting in his wheelchair. The Chinese consul, a thin older man in an expensive looking gray suit, sat beside him on one of the chairs from the dining room set. Meilan Lin was standing in front of them, surrounded by three bulky looking Chinese bodyguards. Anna Maria and Carlo Menotti followed Lucy and the chief into the room, and the two men who had accompanied Anna Maria joined the three encircling Meilan. Lucy sighed.

"Chief Jackson," the consul greeted him. It was obvious that he was in charge, and he expected to conduct the interview. "We have just discovered Mrs. Lin trying to 'plant' poison in Mr. Chin's personal possessions in an effort to 'frame' him for the death of his son."

Lucy stopped. She felt in her pocket and found the plastic bottle. Was that not the only one Meilan had purchased? Her mouth felt dry

Meilan snapped at the consul in Chinese and there was an exchange before the he said in English, "We will discuss this in English, Mrs. Lin, so that the chief of police will understand." He looked coldly at Chief Jackson and Lucy. Lucy felt an unnerving rivulet of icy water move down her back.

"Please explain exactly what happened," Chief Jackson said. He pulled out a notepad with a pen attached.

"As you know, I have come here from our consulate in Guadeloupe at the request of Mr. Chin to help him deal with the terrible tragedy of his son's death and to ensure that the person who committed this crime is found and punished. Mr. Chin is a member of the Chinese Communist Party who held many important positions before his retirement. I have made you aware of the threats against Mr. Chin by Mrs. Lin which led to her expulsion from our country."

Mei Lan began to protest, but the consul raised a hand for silence, and she stopped, glaring at Chin instead.

"Due to our concern for Mr. Chin's safety, I asked my security chief, Mr. Zhang, to provide protection. You may say that was unnecessary on your island, however I had to follow the advice of my staff on this matter. Mr. Zhang had men quietly watching this suite of rooms. Tonight, they saw Mrs. Lin sneak in and when they stopped her, they found she had poison on her person." He nodded at one of the men who held up a small cloth bag. "Mrs. Lin admits she intended to put this in the rooms in order to implicate Mr. Chin in the death of his own son."

Chief Jackson moved to face Meilan while Lucy suppressed a groan. Unfortunately, she could believe that Meilan would do something like that and she could even believe that when discovered she would admit it. Meilan had wanted to accuse Chin of crimes against the Chinese people. It seemed she had found a forum where she could do that.

"Is this true, Mrs. Lin?" the chief asked.

"Chin is a criminal. He steals money from Chinese people and hides it here on the island. He is the one who got poison, killed his son and the maid. He hid poison after using it. He is corrupt official stealing from Chinese." She was shouting directly at the Chinese consul while she said this. "'Kill the tigers, swat the flies.' Kill this tiger." She was looking at the consul and pointing at old Chin.

"Mrs. Lin, did you try to put poison in Mr. Chin's rooms today?" Chief Jackson tried to keep her on point.

She shifted her gaze to him. "It is necessary to stamp out corruption, get rid of corrupt official Chin."

The chief gingerly picked up the bottle of poison. "Mrs. Lin, did you poison the rum in the Chin apartment? Did you kill Mr. Eliot Chin in order to get revenge on his father?"

"I am not the criminal," she shouted, pointing to herself. "HE is criminal." She pointed at Chin, who sat unmoved by it all. Lucy wondered what kind of cold fish could hear someone accuse him of murdering his own son and be able to sit there waiting for it all to play out.

"Mrs. Lin, I'm going to have to take you to the police station to discuss this further. You may want to consult a lawyer," said Chief Jackson.

Meilan glared at him, then looked at Lucy. Lucy held out her arms helplessly. If Meilan was going to keep doing these things to implicate herself, no one would be able to help her. She would have to find a way to follow them to the station, then find a lawyer. Norah would be enraged. Lucy thought Meilan would not leave the station once she entered it. At the very least she would be charged with trying to plant evidence on Chin, but Lucy was pretty sure the chief would also decide to charge her with Eliot Chin's death. Everything Meilan had done contributed to the case against her. Lucy's stomach lurched at the thought of her next call to Bin Yu.

As Chief Jackson reached out to put a hand on Meilan's arm the consul raised his hand to get their attention. "Excuse me, Chief Jackson, but I would like to convey to you a formal request from my country to extradite Mrs. Lin to face charges in Beijing for political crimes against Comrade Chin. This is an issue of great importance to the Chinese government, and I hope you will be able to help us to take Mrs. Lin back to China to face punishment for her crimes."

THIRTY-EIGHT

"They want to extradite her back to China?" Mary was incredulous. "Can they do that?"

Lucy had called Mary and asked her to come down to the lobby. She really couldn't face Norah with the latest news. "I'm not sure. As far as I know the police have her in custody. She'll need a lawyer."

"You can't very well ask the chief to recommend one."

"I already asked Carlo Menotti. I'm not sure exactly what he has to do with Meilan but when I told him he looked alarmed and swore he would get her the best lawyer on the island. I figure he's lived here for a while, so he probably would know."

"What can we do?"

Lucy threw up her hands in frustration. "I don't know. I'll have to call Bin Yu and his wife to tell them, but I think I'll wait till Carlo tells me the lawyer's name and let them talk to him or her. Meanwhile I'm off the case as far as the police are concerned but I think I need to follow up on leads about the stepchildren who inherited when the Sobel woman died. The police won't do it now that they've arrested Meilin. Finding out one of them did it is her only chance. It's still possible that one of them is on the island and was recognized by Eliot Chin. If they hired someone, it's going to be a lot harder to track down. I need to ask Captain Neil whether he knew the Sobels when he was in Australia."

"He's really out of it. He's not going to be talking to anyone for a while. What about Jake though? It looked like he was pretty friendly with Neil. Maybe he would have told him about something like that."

Lucy had wanted to avoid thinking about Jake. Somehow, she was afraid connecting with him would incite an eruption of feelings, ones that she had been tamping down ever since her retirement. She didn't want to regret anything or think about roads not taken. It wasn't her way of coping. She had always put the past behind her and faced forward. But Jake Flaherty seemed to be a piece of her past that kept resurfacing. Mary was right. It was worth a try to question Jake about whether Captain Neil had ever talked about his past in Australia. She had to put aside her personal doubts and ask him.

They consulted Delroy in the bar who told them Jake had a small house in a local settlement out at the end of the island. Anna Maria heard them talking and offered to take them out there in her car. "I'm so sorry about Mrs. Lin," she said. "Mr. Menotti insisted that I support Mr. Chin but then he was furious when he heard Mrs. Lin had been arrested."

"There's nothing you could do about it," Lucy said. "Mr. Menotti is getting her a lawyer."

"Oh, thank heavens."

"Meanwhile, Captain Neil is still unconscious, and I want to talk to Jake Flaherty, in case Neil ever told him anything useful about Australia. Is there something wrong with that?"

Anna Marie stood looking at the shiny surface of the bar, making a pattern with her finger by stirring some drops left by a wet glass. She looked up at Lucy. "It's just that Jake Flaherty is a little, how do you say it? A bit unstable?"

"Anna Maria, that's no surprise to us," Mary told her. "We knew Jake a long time ago. He had some serious mental issues after he came back from Vietnam. We know about that."

The girl looked troubled. "Captain Neil was friendly with him, it's true, but he warned me that Jake takes a dislike to people sometimes. He's actually well-known on the island for his paintings but he's also known for being something of a recluse. He's not friendly. I mean, I can take you to him, but the captain warned me not to believe everything he says."

Lucy reflected that Anna Maria's reluctance might give her an excuse to put off the confrontation, but she could sense that Mary wanted them to go, so she reassured the girl and they met her outside a few minutes later to be driven out to Langsome Point, where Jake had a cottage. As they drove, Anna Maria pointed out some of the other resorts and beaches and then the part of the island that had remained in the hands of local families. The cost of extending water and electricity to this point of land and the frequent destruction caused by storms and hurricanes meant that only a few small and easily replaced cement houses had been built there. They were mostly inhabited by local people who worked in the tourist industry on the island but also did some fishing and boating off the rocky shoreline of the point.

The houses were painted pale pastel colors with white shutters and steeply slanting white roofs. The ground was sandy and rocky but some wild roses and other thorny bushes with graceful blossoms in bright colors grew around the walls. The paths were paved with crushed seashells.

Jake Flaherty's small house was slightly off the road and stood by a little inlet of water. He had his own somewhat rocky beach with a couple of raggedy canvas beach chairs and a tall fishing rod in a plastic pail beside them. Anna Maria pulled her coupe on to the sand, and they got out. The girl hung back as Mary walked to the open doorway, and Lucy followed, looking around. So, this was where Jake had wound up. It didn't bode well that Anna Maria appeared to be a little afraid of him.

"Jake, it's Mary Murphy and Lucy O'Donnell, are you here? Can we come in?" Mary wore a pastel green beach cover up, a long-sleeved white shirt to keep out of the sun and a tightly braided straw hat. She took off her big square sunglasses to peek into the dark of the interior. Lucy removed her own glasses and tried to see.

"Mary, Lucy, of course, come in." His greying hair fell in curls and was pulled back in a sparse ponytail. The beard and moustache were unfamiliar but the gleam in the crystal blue eyes was just as Lucy remembered it. He still had wide shoulders and wore a soft looking Hawaiian shirt printed with leaves in shades of green against a beige background. His hands were spotted with different colors of paint, mostly shades of blue. He wore khaki shorts with deep pockets and rope sandals. He was wider and softer than he had been when they were young, but he was still a good looking man. Lucy flinched mentally when she realized that he had done the same scrutiny of her appearance while she was looking him over. She grimaced. No surprise they were all getting old.

Jake looked over their shoulders at Anna Maria and Lucy saw a shadow pass over his eyes before he lowered them, stepping aside to wave them over the threshold. "And Miss Vandergott, of course. She brought you. Why don't you come in."

The cottage appeared to be a single large room. Where they entered there was a neat little kitchen, a door to a bathroom, a small table and two chairs for eating. On the right was a substantial ladder to a sleeping loft above the kitchen.

The rest of the room was his painting studio. There was a big skylight and along one wall were tables with paints, brushes, cans of linseed oils and turpentine, a neat set of shelves for unused canvas and wood, with hammer and nails for stretching canvas over frames. On the opposite wall were hung a set of paintings of different sizes, and a lot of paintings leaning against each other on the floor. In the far corner was a desk with cubby holes and a laptop computer. There were three easels set out with canvases propped on them.

The pictures displayed around the room were made up of swashes of blue, green, and white with points of red and orange. They mostly portrayed the light and reflection off bodies of water on the island and they gave Lucy a feeling of airiness and openness that was like the feeling she got when she walked along a beach with waves lapping softly at her feet. They were extremely peaceful looking scenes, and happy. There was another set with people portrayed in everyday occupations, setting a table, serving at an outdoor bar, fishing or digging, selling handcrafts at a flea market. There was an odor of turpentine in the place that made it seem clean somehow, despite the splotches of paint on floor, tables, and utensils.

"They're beautiful," Mary said. "Captain Neil gave me one of your paintings and it is lovely, but these are wonderful. He said you were very successful. I can see why."

"Neil's a friend. I haven't done badly, though. Turns out taking a picture home is something a lot of tourists are willing to pay for. And some of them even get home and decide they need another one and I work on commission. I don't do too badly. I've been here for fifteen years now. Came out from Florida with a friend who had a boat. We put in here and I never left." He looked at Lucy.

"It's a great place," she said. "You're right on the water." She walked over to a large window that looked out on his little beach.

"It means you have to have a generator and truck in some water, but it's doable and pretty cheap all things considered," he said. Lucy noticed the hum of the generator when he said that, but it blended nicely with the gentle slapping of the water against the shore.

"Why don't you come out to the beach, it's a little pungent in here with the paint and all." He led them out to the sandy beach, grabbing a couple of folding chairs as he ushered them through the door. He set them up in the shade where they could look out at the water, then dragged the other chairs back so all four of them could sit. There was a nice breeze. "What brings you out here? Is Neil all right?"

He was looking back and forth between Lucy and Mary and seemed to avoid Anna Maria. Lucy remembered how the girl had said he disliked her. His icy blue eyes raked over the young woman every now and then as if looking for some sign of danger. Lucy thought it was odd.

Mary explained that Captain Neil had not recovered as expected and that they had found out he was poisoned, like Eliot Chin and Louella Roberts, only with a different poison. Jake frowned as he listened, and Lucy could almost count the number of wiry white hairs in his bushy eyebrows. He bent forward with his elbows on his knees and his hands clasped between them. "Poisoned? What kind of poison? Who was Chin? I knew Louella, of course, she was obsessing about her brother's death. She refused to believe he killed that Australian widow. That was why those vigilante cops killed her brother. I hope Wendell has them all under lock and key at least."

Lucy remembered her shock when Jake had flung himself on the back of Lt. Strong just when he was about to shoot her. He appeared so calm and reasonable now. But she had to admit to herself that his mad actions had certainly saved her. "Yeah, he's got them. It was a good thing you were there the other night. Strong was about to shoot me." Lucy turned to Mary and Anna Maria. "Jake came out of the dark and jumped him just as he was pointing a gun at me." She was glad Norah was not with them. She had downplayed the gun battle when she described it to her sister, but she didn't mind Mary knowing what really happened. And perhaps Anna Maria needed to understand why she trusted the man—if she did.

He looked up as though surprised. "Wendell wasn't sure who he could trust so he asked Neil and me to back him up. Turned out he was right. Strong was like his second in command and he was rotten."

"Yeah, well he's arrested now. But that's not what we came to see you about." Lucy felt his concentrated stare as she told him about the death of Eliot Chin and how Meilan Lin had been arrested and the Chinese were asking for extradition.

Periodically, she looked off at the calm water to escape his gaze. When she finished the background explanations, she looked him in the eye again. "The thing is, somebody poisoned Chin and Louella. I don't believe Meilan's theory that his father did it. So, I'm trying to find out if it could have been someone Chin recognized from Australia. The woman who was killed here, the one Louella's brother supposedly killed, was a wealthy widow from Australia. She inherited money and jewels from her husband but his children by an earlier marriage were contesting the will. As I understand it, they were going to lose that court case but when she died, here on St. Hilaire, then they got all the money from their father. There's also some very valuable jewels she was supposed to have taken with her that were never found. I wanted to ask Captain Neil if he knew that woman, Ingrid Sobel, in Australia and whether there was anyone connected to her that had turned up on St. Hilaire."

Jake sat back, crossing his arms on his chest. "You think one of the husband's kids killed her and was recognized by Chin and that's why he was killed?"

Spoken bluntly like that, it sounded unlikely. "Yup. It's a thought worth following up on. Did Neil ever tell you about Australia? Did he mention seeing anyone from there? Did he talk about Chin or Ingrid Sobel at all? I wanted to ask him, but from what Mary has told me, he's not going to be able to answer questions for a while."

"We don't want the Chinese to take Meilan away," Mary said. "Even if she's proved innocent, who's to say they would let her come back? It's not clear what the local authorities will do since they apparently want to promote relations with mainland China these days."

"That's an ongoing dance with islands like St. Hilaire going back and forth between the People's Republic and Taiwan," Jake said. Then he looked off into the horizon for a few minutes. Lucy and Mary exchanged a glance. Lucy wondered how recovered Jake really was from the mental illness he had suffered when she knew him before.

Finally, he spoke. "He talked about Australia when he was drinking sometimes. And he did mention Chin as someone looking to invest in the island, although I don't know in what. He wasn't an art lover that I know of. In any case, Neil had some regrets about things he had done in the past, in Australia. He looked on St. Hilaire as a new chapter in his life. That's probably why he and I get along. Getting past the past, as he used to say. He didn't like to bring it up and I think if he met someone from the past he'd assume they had also started a new life and he wouldn't bring up how he knew them before. That's his philosophy."

"I see. Well, it's too bad but it was worth a try," Lucy said. She felt a profound sense of peace in the surroundings, and she realized it was a relief to her. Somehow the very disturbed Jake Flaherty that she had known had found his way to stability on this island. She was glad for him.

"We should catch up," he said. "I should probably ask you about Dan and the others and how they're all doing back in Boston. I confess, since my folks died, I haven't made an effort to keep up. You're looking good."

"She just retired after more than thirty years on the force," Mary said.

Lucy got up. "Right. We should catch up but not today. I've got to get back and see if there's anything else I can do for Meilan and I need to talk to her son-in-law. It looks like we'll be stuck here for a while, so there should be time before this is all over. We need to get back now, though."

Jake motioned them through the studio to the front where the car was parked. Lucy noticed Anna Maria scampered away as if she was anxious to leave. Mary cast an eye on some of the paintings on the way out and Lucy found herself beside Jake at the end when the other two were getting into the car.

"Lucy, one thing before you go," he murmured.

She looked at him, surprised.

"It's Mary. I get the impression she likes Neil."

"She's a widow. Has been for a long time."

He looked bashful. "It's not that. It's the girl." He nodded toward the car. "The Vandergott girl. Neil's been having a thing with her. You might warn Mary. I wouldn't like her to be disappointed."

Lucy stared at him, then heard Mary call to her from the car. "OK. Thanks for telling me. I'll take care of it." She looked into the clear blue eyes. He was frowning with his concern for her friend. "It'll be OK, we're big girls, Jake. I have to say, I'm glad to see you so well settled. Your place is lovely, and your work is really good."

"Thanks. Big surprise, huh?" He sounded rueful. "You thought I was homeless in a shelter somewhere, didn't you? I don't blame you."

She felt her face flush. That was exactly what she had been thinking and she turned away in embarrassment to return to the car.

As they drove away, she watched Anna Maria Vandergott, realizing she really didn't know the young woman they thought her nephew Steve was serious about. Still, all things considered, her nephew's love life was the least of their problems. She had been avoiding it all day, but she still had to face Norah with the bad news.

THIRTY-NINE

When they reached the resort, Anna Maria put a hand on Lucy's arm to hold her back as Mary went up to their unit. They stopped on the drive leading to the lobby. Lucy was afraid she wanted to confide in her about Captain Neil, and she wasn't sure how to react. The girl was supposed to be the love interest of Lucy's nephew, but she was an adult, free to have any relationships she wanted. And, after all, they were living thousands of miles apart and Lucy wasn't sure how serious her long-time bachelor nephew was about the girl anyway. Visions of weddings might only be the wishful delusions of Norah and their sister-in-law. Lucy was hesitant to become involved, so she was relieved to find that was not what was on the girl's mind at all.

"It's the Blaine group," Anna Maria told her. "Is there any way to find out if one of them is involved? Mrs. Raymond, in particular. There is something very strange about her. Could she be related to Mrs. Sobel do you think?"

"What makes you think Juliet Raymond might be related? Do you see a resemblance? Or has she said something?"

The girl stopped and closed her eyes as if trying to remember something. "I don't know," she said, opening her eyes but not moving. "It's just that Mike, Mr. Blaine, insists that I crew for him in the race tomorrow, but I think his wife usually does the spinnaker pole and it's because of some argument they're having that she's refusing to race. So, when I went out to practice with him, only Juliet Raymond was with us. Both Mrs. Blaine and Mr. Laurent stayed behind. Juliet seemed very anxious about them, and Mike was making rude comments about what they might be doing back at the resort together. I just took it as a joke. He was needling her about Mr. Laurent staying with his wife. I didn't think he was serious, but it was really getting under her skin, I could tell. It was pretty tense. I just think there's something wrong about her, but I don't know what. Maybe I did see some kind of resemblance to Mrs. Sobel. I never thought of that, but now that you mention it, there is something about the shape of her jaw that seems familiar."

"Norah thought she detected a romance between Mrs. Blaine and Mr. Laurent, but even if they were having an affair, I don't see what that would have to do with Chin's death," Lucy said.

"Perhaps he recognized her."

"Oh, I see what you mean. But if there was some connection between her and the dead woman from Australia, I would expect the police to track it down. The problem is, they have Meilan and they're concentrating on her, so they may not be looking into other people. I've asked Meilan's son-in-law back in Boston to see what he can find out."

"Maybe I could find out more. I'll be sailing with them tomorrow." Anna Maria looked at her watch. "In fact, Mike wanted to take the boat out again this afternoon. They're probably looking for me now."

"Anna Maria, don't try to play the detective. There's no evidence that Juliet Raymond or anyone else in that group had anything to do with Chin's death. But if they did, you'd be putting yourself in danger if that person thought you suspected. If the deaths of Mrs. Sobel, Chin and Louella Roberts are connected, and that's a big if, then the person responsible is pretty ruthless. You need to be careful."

"Oh, of course. But no one would suspect me of knowing anything. I'm just one of the staff, so people tend to not think of me, if you see what I mean. I'm always asking people about their past and things like that, it's part of my job. I can ask questions without anyone being suspicious. In fact, really, it would be suspicious if I didn't."

Lucy was not at all comfortable with the idea of the girl going off asking questions about the murders. It was true that she had actually known the Australian widow and that might give her a reason to discuss the woman, but if there was a murderer and they suspected that Anna Maria might guess a connection, she could be in real danger. "Anna Maria, I mean it. You should not become involved with that. If you even suspect someone in that group is involved, you should stay away from them. Tell them you have to work or you're sick or something. Really."

Lucy could just imagine what her nephew would say if his girlfriend was harmed trying to help her with an unsanctioned investigation. No matter how serious or superficial his relationship was with the Dutch girl, he wouldn't appreciate it if she were hurt trying to help investigate a crime. Lucy had quite enough guilt to deal with when she thought of Bin Yu and the plight of his mother-in-law. If only she hadn't invited Meilan along. So much for trying to do him a favor. She suppressed a groan. "You should get out of sailing with them. Just to be safe."

"Oh, I couldn't do that. I already said I'd crew for him and it's too late for him to find someone else, if his wife still won't sail. I really must go, but I'll be careful. I promise."

Somehow Lucy was not reassured but she followed when Anna Maria led the way to the lobby where they found Mike Blaine confronting Guy Laurent.

"Come on, man. I need you. It's a quick run through, so the girl can get the hang of it. Oh, look, there she is. Anna Maria, you ready to join us? Just a quick sail to get the kinks out." Mike Blaine's face was red from the sun, and perhaps a drink with lunch. Lucy noticed that the tall and lanky Guy Laurent looked less than enthusiastic about the jaunt. He wore a neatly ironed long-sleeved shirt, blue Bermuda shorts and deck shoes. Mike Blaine was in one of his sleek looking outfits made of high-tech materials. He carried a safari hat with a chin strap and wore a complicated looking waterproof watch.

"I just have to run up and change," Anna Maria told him, and she hurried away.

Mike Blaine fidgeted, looking at his watch and Guy Laurent murmured something.

"No, you have to come," Mike said petulantly. "We have to make a good showing. Here's Juliet, at least she showed up yesterday. Don't be such a wimp, Guy. We need the practice."

Lucy sat down on one of the deep cushioned sofas and watched surreptitiously as Juliet joined them. Her dark hair was pulled back in a ponytail that was threaded through the back of a baseball cap embroidered with the boat name, the Last Resort. Her nose was white with protective cream, and she wore long sleeves and long pants in a beige color. Her eyes were obscured by heavy looking tortoise shell sunglasses.

Lucy couldn't hear her voice, but she asked something because Mike Blaine cleared his throat and said, "No, Rita's got a head ache. Anyways, I've got the Vandergott girl lined up and we're just waiting for her to hurry up and change. And just because Rita's a sore sport, that's no reason for Guy here to poop out. I told him he's coming whether he likes it or not. I'm not spending another hour working the boat while he and Rita lounge around by the pool. We're down here to work, you know. See if you can talk some sense into him, will you? I'll get the van." He stamped out of the front door while the other two rolled their eyes.

Lucy pretended to peruse a brightly colored magazine while looking at Juliet Raymond but she had only seen a fuzzy photograph of the dead Australian widow, so she had no opinion as to whether the brunette resembled her at all. She was about to head back to the unit when Mary appeared in the lobby looking like she was in a hurry. "Lucy, there you are. I got a call from the hospital. Neil is not doing so well. He had another episode. I want to go back, in fact his surgeon asked for me. No, you don't have to come. I called and Livingston can take me. I can see he's out there now. I just wanted to let you know. I told Norah, she's up on the balcony. I'm not sure when I'll be back but call me if you need me."

She hurried out the door and Lucy sighed. She couldn't put it off any longer, she needed to go up and talk to Norah.

FORTY

Lucy found Norah on the phone making arrangements to reschedule various activities when they did not return on Saturday. While Norah was talking, Lucy got a message about the contact information for the lawyer that Carlo Menotti had hired for Meilan and she called Bin Yu with the information.

He called back after talking to the man to say that he and Hong would not arrive until Monday. They were sure the Chinese would not be able to get action on their extradition request before then and there was nothing the lawyer could do on the weekend. Bin Yu feared the Chinese might spirit his mother-in-law away in the blink of an eye, but Lucy assured him no legal system ever worked that quickly, no matter how influential the petitioners. She didn't say that it was more likely to be a long, drawn out and costly affair, but she thought it. She was determined to send Norah and Mary home as soon as possible but to remain herself to try to help the young couple. What a mess.

Bin Yu was still digging for information on the Australian stepchildren who would inherit the Sobel money, and until they had more to go on, Lucy was stumped. She told her sister that Meilan had been arrested, listened to her rant, then took a morose Norah down to the pool and wandered over to the bar to get Delroy to make one of his complicated rum drinks to try to cheer her up.

Taking a stool beside Rita Blaine she watched while he made the concoction. Rita looked haggard. Long nails painted bright red tapped against the stem of a martini glass. She wore a terry cloth cover up in a soft pink color over a red bikini and chunky gold earrings and necklace. Bright lipstick matched her nails and a red straw hat sat on a stool on her other side. "I heard your Chinese friend was arrested. Did she really poison Chin?"

Lucy frowned. "She says she didn't but that's what she's being held for."

"That old man is getting his way then." She nodded towards the buildings off to the left, and when Lucy turned around and looked up she could see the silhouette of old Chin in his wheelchair on the balcony of his unit on the first level. He was an evil looking old man. "I think he's a dangerous old codger." Rita Blaine seemed to be reading her mind.

"If he gets his way, Meilan will be extradited to China." Lucy turned back to the bar to watch Delroy. He was chopping, measuring and dumping ingredients into a blender. She turned towards Rita. "How well did you know Eliot Chin?"

"Not well. He was a client. Or a potential client. My husband was wooing him to sign up some of his employees for teambuilding training on our boat. We have a business doing that sort of thing."

"I see. Did he know your husband or Mr. Laurent or Mrs. Raymond before you met here?"

Rita raised an eyebrow, but she answered before taking a sip of her martini. "I think Mike and Guy might have met him in Australia, a few years ago. They were both working for a big conglomerate back then.”

“What about Mrs. Raymond?”

“Juliet? I don't think so. She never mentioned it. I think she does have some distant relatives there, but I don't think she knew Chin. She barely noticed him. She's got other things on her mind these days, if you know what I mean.” She took another sip.

“Oh, yes. I heard she's in the middle of a divorce. Have you known her a long time?”

“Juliet was our neighbor for years. We had adjoining back yards. She has two daughters who are about the same age as our kids, Mike Junior and Laura. They grew up together.” She pulled the toothpick with an olive out of the glass and slid the olive into her mouth. She seemed to be thinking, remembering. “Do you have kids?”

“A daughter, but she's grown with kids of her own so I'm a grand-mother,” Lucy told her. She asked Delroy for a bottle of the local beer. He stopped his complicated preparations to uncap one and hand it to her. She sipped.

“Grandmother. I suppose it will come to that someday,” Rita said. “They grow up and life changes. Happens to all of us, you know?”

Lucy nodded.

“Well, for me it was when Mike got laid off. He was down. I knew all he really wanted to do was to sail his boat, the prize of his life. But we still had to get our kids through college. So, Guy and I came up with the idea of the teambuilding sails. Don't get me wrong, Mike does most of the work, but Guy used to be in sales, and I had a background in sales, so we came up with the idea and got it going. At the same time Juliet's girls went off to college and she had bookkeeping skills. She was looking for something to do, so we thought, why not. And we hired her.”

"Looks like you're successful."

"It's not easy to run your own business, but we've all worked in the industry, all except Juliet, of course. I was stupefied when she said she actually wanted to come on the boat when we took it to Annapolis to start the first sessions. I never figured she'd last. Mike and Guy and I go back a long time." She sipped her martini. "We knew what we were getting into. No illusions. But Juliet." She shook her head. "I didn't see that coming. She fell for Guy. He's an old divorcee. Married once, didn't really like being tied down and he's never been married since, but Juliet really got hooked on him. So, she decided to leave her husband and run away with him. I hope she doesn't really expect him to marry her. I'm afraid she's in for a rude awakening."

"He wouldn't?"

"I seriously doubt it. We've seen him go through women over the years. He's charming but no staying power. He manages to slither away when they're not looking. Besides, men get to that age and it's young blood they're really prone to fall for. It's a cliché but it's the truth." Lucy thought she sounded bitter. Rita stared back at her, then looked away to signal Delroy she wanted another drink. He finished the mixed drink for Norah and delivered it to Lucy with a flourish.

"I suppose that's pretty common," Lucy said. She hesitated, wanting to get as much as she could from Rita while she was in a talking mood.

"The one thing poor old Juliet has going for her is a pot at the end of the rainbow. I don't know how much she thinks she's getting from Tom, her husband, but she's pretty confident it will be enough. Or maybe she's got some other boat coming in, I don't know. She's not getting it from Last Resort, anyhow, we're all just about breaking even at this point."

Lucy considered this. "You mean if Juliet comes into some money, you think she'll be able to hold on to Guy Laurent?"

"Sounds pretty blunt but, truth is Guy has a style of living to which he is accustomed. It wouldn't be the first time he supplemented his income by accepting favors from a lady." She grinned. "I do like Guy, always have. I'm not sure if Juliet will pull it off, but if she doesn't, I can tell you as far as we're concerned, Guy is a necessity, Juliet is just a bookkeeper. We could do it with Quicken now that we're set up. I don't think she understands that. I'm a little concerned if Guy dumps her how she'll react."

"You think your husband would agree that Guy is more important to the business?"

"Mike will do what Guy and I tell him to do. He knows which side his bread is buttered on. Without us, he wouldn't have a business. And he wouldn't have a family and you can believe I make sure he understands that," she said.

Lucy was about to try to pump her for more information about Juliet Raymond when her cell phone rang. It was Mary. "Lucy, you have to come to the hospital. I need you," Mary told her.

FORTY-ONE

As Lucy headed for the lobby, she was waylaid by Anna Maria Vandergott. The girl looked upset.

"I'm sorry," Lucy said. "I have to get to the hospital."

"Is it Captain Neil? Is he worse?"

"I don't know, but I think so."

"Please, just give me a moment. They're waiting for me at the boat. I said I'd catch up with them. Livingston's going to take me. He can drive you to the hospital after he drops me off. Please."

Lucy accepted the suggestion and they hurried out to the waiting van. Anna Maria explained to Livingston where they were going.

As they started up, she turned to Lucy. "I'm worried. I know Juliet Raymond is up to something and I'm afraid of what she'll do. I've seen that kind of irrational jealousy before and it's just so unpredictable."

Lucy remembered the girl's affair with Neil and had the cynical thought that she might well have seen jealousy in action if that was how she conducted herself. She probably caused it. "Well, there's nothing I can do about it," Lucy said. "If you're that worried, why don't you speak to Rita Blaine yourself? I was just talking to her, and she didn't sound like she was particularly smitten with Guy Laurent. Sounded more like they were old friends."

Anna Maria shook her head in frustration. "You don't understand. Even if that's true, Juliet Raymond believes they are lovers and she's so jealous I think she will do something to harm Mrs. Blaine."

Rita Blain had also mentioned a concern about Juliet's reaction if Guy dropped her. Perhaps Anna Marie was right to worry. Lucy couldn't see that the dilemma had anything to do with Chin's murder, though. It was unlikely he had been the victim of Juliet Raymond's jealous rage, unless there was something they didn't know about. Lucy had to concentrate on Meilan's situation. She had no time for love triangles around the pool. Still, this was obviously bothering Anna Maria and if Lucy was wrong about it, she'd certainly live to regret it. She couldn't just ignore the girl's concerns.

"Listen, if you don't want to talk to Rita, why don't you talk to her husband, or Guy Laurent for that matter? I'm sure they're aware of the feelings and whether they'll boil over any time soon. And even if she is jealous of the Blaine woman, I think it's more likely she'd make a scene or something, rather than actually doing her harm."

"But don't you see? She's not the sort to make a scene. That's just what she's not doing. She's repressing it all and bottling it up until it's going to explode."

They had reached the dock where the Last Resort crew were waiting impatiently for Anna Maria.

"Go. It'll be all right," Lucy told her, reaching over to open the door. "Talk to Guy. Tell him to straighten it out. He's the cause of all the fuss. Just point out to him this isn't high school and they all need to start acting like grownups, and if they don't, stand back and let them take care of it."

Anna Maria was not satisfied, but she shrugged her shoulders and climbed from the van, shaking her head in frustration. Lucy waved as the car pulled away.

***

At the hospital, Lucy found Mary pacing outside the intensive care unit. It alarmed Lucy that she was nodding and talking to herself. Lucy steeled herself for bad news about Captain Neil. "Is he gone?" she asked quietly.

"What? Oh, no, no. He's in there. Jake is with him. There's something he needs to tell you. No, it's not just that he was having a fling with the Vandergott girl, I know about that. It's much worse. Go in." She took Lucy's arm and guided her to the door, exchanging a look with the nurse at the desk in the center of the area as she did so.

Lucy found Neil hooked up to beeping machines with Jake wide awake on a metal chair beside the bed. Jake rose and waved Lucy to the chair. "Tell her, Neil. Tell her all of it."

There was a bluish tint to Captain Neil's face, and he had a plastic tube in his nose. Lucy knew that would be for the oxygen that had saved him from the SUX injection earlier. She leaned her arm on the bed to get closer to hear him.

"I never thought she'd hurt anyone. She told me she was just afraid—of the step kids, you know?"

"What are you talking about?"

Jake lacked patience. "It's Anna Maria. She's not Anna Maria Vandergott, she's Ingrid Sobel."

Lucy was confused. Neil reached for her arm with a bony grasp. "It's true. She was married to Andy Sobel. I knew them—sort of. I knew she nursed his wife when she was dying and then she married the old guy. I knew his kids didn't like it, but I thought more power to him, and Andy was a man who could handle his own affairs."

"But if she's Ingrid Sobel, why would she pretend to be someone else? And if she's Mrs. Sobel, who died in that beach villa?"

"That's it, you know. She said it was just chance. She met Anna Maria Vandergott on the plane and, just like she told everybody, she invited her to spend some time at the villa she rented before the girl had to start her job." His eyes were wide, and he clutched Lucy's arm. She patted his hand trying to calm him. It seemed to help.

"She came to get away from Andy's kids, you see. They were persecuting her, suing her, calling her names to Andy's old friends. She said the girl, the real Anna Maria, was sympathetic and she thought she was the first friend she had been able to talk to for a long time. They got on. Then, it was just bad luck. When they called the cab to take Anna Maria that last day, Ingrid had to use it first to go to the pharmacy. When they got back, she went in and found her."

"You mean she found her beaten to death? And she didn't call the police? Why ever not?"

"Aye, she should have. She knew that. But she was a nurse. She knew there was nothing anyone could do for the poor girl, she was a gonner. Ingrid said she thought how it might have been her, it should have been her. It was all done for the emeralds Andy gave her, and they were gone. She knew Anna Maria had no relatives who would be looking for her. She made a wild choice and just stepped into one of the girl's dresses and into her life. She took the purse and the packed bags out to the taxi and went to Pelican Bay. She had nothing left, she said. No family, no husband, no house, and finally no emeralds. She was so tired of it all, she said. She would have to start all over, so, instead, she stepped into the girl's shoes."

"What about the cab driver?" Lucy found the story outlandish.

"He didn't know. He saw a woman in a different dress. He had his fare, he just took her."

"But he was accused of the murder. How could she not come forward?"

"And she was thinking she'd have to, but when she heard there was a bracelet with some of the emeralds found in the cab, she wasn't so sure. She thought he must have been involved, and then he was killed."

Neil started to cough, and Jake leaned over Lucy, putting a cup of water with a straw to the man's mouth. Neil closed his eyes and swallowed then Jake stepped back.

"All this time, you knew she was Ingrid Sobel, and you didn't tell anyone?" Lucy asked.

"She begged me not to tell. She said it was the only way she could start over."

Jake sputtered. "Come off it. She came on to him and seduced him into not telling anyone. And whenever it seemed like he might be slipping she'd show up at his place again. Right, Neil? Tell it like it is."

Neil kept his eyes shut. "I didn't see the harm in it."

"Did Eliot Chin recognize her?" Lucy asked. She could certainly picture how the beautiful young woman could get Neil to keep his peace. That body would be too enticing for a man of Neil's age to resist.

Neil's blue eyes opened at her question. "Oh, no. I don't think so, no."

"If he had, she'd probably have seduced him, too," Jake said.

Lucy wondered if that would have worked on the young Chin. If not that, perhaps something else would work to hold his tongue. If he even recognized her. "She's been impersonating Anna Maria Vandergott for months then." She suddenly thought of her nephew,

Steve, and wondered how big a blow it would be to him when he found out the truth. "She's got to tell the police about this."

"I agree," Jake said.

"She should," Neil said, then he sighed. "But I don't see how it matters. It was wrong, sure, but it didn't hurt anybody. It's not like the real Anna Maria had family and Ingrid's stepchildren were only too happy to be rid of her."

"She gave up the money? Don't the stepchildren get it with Mrs. Sobel dead?" Lucy was still having trouble believing this.

"She said there wasn't much left. The kids were just suing her for spite. It was the emeralds that she was meant to inherit, but with them gone, she had no reason to want to keep her name. If the emeralds had ever been recovered, she'd have admitted it all but they never were. She thought the renegade cops probably took them."

Lucy shook her head. "It's not clear how this figures into the investigation into Chin's death but the police need to know about it. At the very least it might be enough to keep them from letting the Chinese extradite Meilan. We've got to go tell the chief about this."

"I'll take you," Jake said. Lucy looked at him and decided it was time to trust him. She was sure that Neil had only come clean about Ingrid Sobel because Jake had badgered him. Besides, Jake was an old friend of the chief's so he might be able to get her through the door. They were both friends of Neil's and she found herself suspicious of his story. If he knew of Ingrid's impersonation all along, why hadn't he told anyone? But getting Meilan out of custody was the priority now.

FORTY-TWO

"We'll interview Ms. Vandergott and verify if she is really Mrs. Sobel," Chief Jackson told Lucy and Jake. "But that in no way proves the innocence of Mrs. Lin."

"You need to arrest that girl. She's pretending to be someone she isn't," Jake said.

"You can't let the Chinese extradite Meilan," Lucy said. "Even if you say it doesn't prove her innocence it raises all kinds of questions. If you aren't going to release Mrs. Lin, at least say you won't hand her over to the Chinese while you look into all of this."

Chief Jackson looked down and shuffled some papers on his desk. Lucy sat back, stunned by the reaction and she felt her stomach turn. This was not good.

"There's a lot of pressure to satisfy the complaints of the consul," the chief said.

"You've got to be kidding." Jake began to rise from one of the visitor's chairs in the chief's small office as he protested. Mary had stayed behind at the hospital while Livingston drove Jake and Lucy to the police station. They'd managed to bull their way into the office and now Livingston was leaning on the door frame, frowning at his brother while the other two sat in metal chairs across the desk from the chief.

"Look," the chief ignored Jake, but he raised his head to look Lucy in the eye. "It's out of my control. The governor is making a deal with them. The island is embarrassed by the death of a Chinese national. They want to cooperate and smooth ruffled feathers. You know how it is."

Livingston came to attention in the doorway and slapped his hands. "It's the stadium, right? They made a deal for the stadium, didn't they?"

Jake pounded a fist on the desk. "Wendell, what are you doing? Is that the truth? Did they make a deal?"

The chief closed his eyes and heaved a great sigh. "I'm tellin' ya, it's out of my hands." He glared at his brother. "And, yes, they made a deal. There'll be a stadium, but it'll be built with island labor, not a Chinese construction team."

"They got that for letting them have Meilan?" Lucy asked.

"That's no good, man," Jake said. "We'll go to the American embassy."

The chief put up his hands. "Do what you have to do, but don't you think they already ran it by the Americans? I don't know, but I'd bet on it."

"Jesus Christ," Jake said, then he flopped back into his chair.

Lucy knew the chief meant it when he said it was out of his hands. "So, are you going to stop the investigation? What if she didn't do it?"

Livingston put his hands on his hips, glaring at his brother.

The chief was frustrated. "No, of course we'll investigate. I'll find the truth no matter what they do, even if it costs me my job. What

I'm saying is, I can't do anything about Mrs. Lin. They're going to extradite her."

"She's got a green card but she's not a citizen," Lucy said. "No American bureaucrat is going to put their ass on the line for her. So, how much time do we have? When are they planning to take her?"

"Monday."

"Monday?" Lucy was shocked. She had promised Bin Yu his mother-in-law would still be on St. Hilaire when he arrived on Monday. But it would do no good to have him fly in earlier. It was already Saturday night. Lucy felt a surge of acid from her stomach to esophagus. How was she going to tell him?

"What do you have on Ingrid Sobel?" Lucy asked. She felt like sand was slipping away beneath her feet and she was about to plunge into an abyss. She needed to grab at anything to stop the disaster. She felt herself click into detective mode, listing in her mind all the facts and figures of the investigation. Chin's death was a murder investigation, like the scores of investigations she had done during her career.

The chief seemed grateful for the switch from recrimination to some kind of action. "I've got a report faxed from Australia about her." He dove into the pile of papers and pulled out a stack of faxes that he handed to her. "On the stepchildren, too. But Mrs. Lin admitted that she had the poison and was trying to implicate the old man by planting it on him. She as good as confessed."

"No, she said she didn't poison the son. She thinks the old man did it," Lucy said as she rifled through the faxes. She wondered briefly how Meilan had gotten more of the herb concoction to try to plant in Chin's room. Lucy still had the bottle she had confiscated in her purse. Meilan must have bought two.

While she perused the reports, Jake and Livingston tried to gang up on the chief by insulting him about giving in to pressure from above, but Lucy knew only too well that it was useless. She knew what he meant when he said it was out of his control. She'd been there.

She looked at the report on Ingrid Sobel. Her real name was plain Sally Jones. She was the only child of a prostitute, but she had grown up to train as a nurse. Lucy noted experience in an Intensive Care Unit. It clicked in Lucy's mind that she would have known how to use SUX. Apparently, the mother had been an invalid and finally died. After that, Sally turned up as Ingrid Van Ness and did private nursing under that name. Lucy wondered if she had married. It was as a private nurse that she went to the Sobel ranch and nursed the dying wife, then married the widower. All of that confirmed what Captain Neil had told her.

The Australian police had also checked on the stepchildren, verifying that both sons were in the country although the daughter was on a trip to the U.S. with her husband. They reported the suit against Ingrid Sobel had already been dismissed. The amount of money was a mere ten thousand dollars, most of which would have been eaten up by legal fees if the suit had gone ahead. The judge dismissed it as frivolous, and the police report commented that the suit was brought more to annoy the disliked stepmother than to achieve anything. Most of Sobel's money had been invested in emerald jewelry and the will clearly left all of that to the widow.

Watching her read, Chief Jackson typed on his keyboard, then turned his computer monitor so she and the others could see. "You see? The emeralds. This is the collection he bought for her. That's where the money went." He flicked the mouse to scroll down as Lucy, Jake and Livingston bent forward to look at the images of a dozen pieces of jewelry. Bracelets, earrings, several pendants and even a tiara where shown. Livingston whistled.

"All that was stolen?" Lucy asked. "Has any of it turned up?"

"Only the bracelet found in William Roberts' taxi and a single earring found in Louella Roberts' pocket."

"That's a lie," Livingston yelled. "She didn't steal."

"I know, I know," the chief said. "We don't want to believe it. But it was in her pocket. That's not to say she took it or even that her brother did. But it was there. That's a fact."

"Maybe she found it," Jake said. "And whoever had it killed her."

"Yeah, yeah," Livingston said.

"Or maybe whoever killed her planted it on her," Lucy said. The three men looked at her in confusion. "Chief, I see the name of a detective on this fax. Do you think I could call him to ask him a couple of follow up questions?"

His eyebrows rose but he nodded, pushing the phone around so she could use it.

It took some time to get through, but she was in luck as there was an older somewhat garrulous detective who had been given the assignment to do the research for them. His name was Macgregor and she thought she recognized the type. He was probably on the verge of retirement, no longer fit to chase down thugs so they put him on a desk and gave him the cold cases and background checks. He sounded like he had enjoyed tracking down information on Sally Jones who had become Ingrid Sobel.

Lucy reviewed the file with him while the others lost interest and chatted restlessly in the background. She covered her left ear to block out the noise. "One thing, did you happen to find out where the name Van Ness came from? Did she marry?" She listened intently. "I see. You actually talked to him then?" "And was there anything suspicious about the mother's death?"

"I see, that's interesting. How about Mrs. Sobel? Or the husband?" Lucy asked.

The chief had noticed the questions. Jake and Livingston also stopped talking, waiting for her to finish the call. Lucy thanked Detective Macgregor and hung up.

"Anything?" Jake asked.

"Sally Jones was an ICU nurse. Also, her mother used Chinese herbal remedies. She was already dying of liver failure when she overdosed on an aconite-type of remedy, but there was no suspicion of the daughter. She was out of town and had warned the mother repeatedly about the herbal remedies. We were lucky Detective Macgregor was so thorough. He had the time to look into it."

"She must have done it," Jake said. "She was a nurse, she knows about this stuff."

"It's suspicious, but so is Mrs. Lin's knowledge of Chinese herbs," the chief said.

"The Van Ness thing was interesting," Lucy said. "Apparently it wasn't really her name. At one point she was engaged to a doctor named Van Ness, but they never married. Macgregor managed to track him down and talk to him over the phone. He admitted that while he was engaged to the daughter, he had an affair with the mother. Sally found out and broke it off. For some reason she used his name after the mother died."

"And they don't think she killed her mother? She must have been ready to," Livingston said.

"No, Macgregor was quite sure she had nothing to do with her mother's death. It was a year later, and she had continued to support and nurse her mother during that time. There was no indication that she could have poisoned the Sobels either. The wife was already dying when she began nursing her and the husband was sick for a while, sold the ranch, and then passed away. Their death certificates say natural causes and the authorities aren't about to exhume them on the chance it might have been poison. No reason, from their point of view." She looked at Chief Jackson.

"I agree with them. It's not enough," he said. You can't prove anything with that. I can bring her in and question her, but nothing proves she had anything to do with Chin's death or Louella's. Why would she want to poison them?" No one had a ready answer. "Mrs. Lin did have a reason to poison Eliot Chin. Revenge. Old Chin caused her father's death during the Cultural Revolution, she got back at him by killing his son."

But why would she kill Louella?" Livingston asked.

"Louella must have seen something."

"How did Louella get the emerald earring?" Jake asked.

The chief threw up his hands. "I don't know." He looked at his brother warily. "I know we don't want to believe it, but maybe Louella knew something about her brother's involvement."

When Livingston began to protest Lucy raised a hand to stop them. "Chief, I need to see Meilan. Tonight. Please."

"All right, all right. But I'm warning you, there's nothing you can do to stop the extradition."

FORTY-THREE

Meilan was led into a small windowless interrogation room where Lucy was waiting. They sat down opposite each other at the grey steel table.

"Meilan, I'm really sorry about all of this," Lucy said. She knew the others were watching behind the obvious observation mirror. Just like in TV shows. How often had she witnessed interrogations from behind that screen? She knew how to conduct an interrogation and she knew how to evaluate responses. But it seemed wrong to turn that skill on a woman she'd invited on a vacation trip. She tried to block the idea of Bin Yu's reaction to the scene from her mind.

Meilan kept her mouth closed, folding her hands on the table in front of her as if she were preparing for a long session. Lucy wondered what kind of interrogations Meilan had experienced in her younger life. She knew Meilan had been sent to a reeducation camp at some point. Lucy hated to think what she had suffered during that experience.

"Listen, we're doing everything we can, but they're going to extradite you to China on Monday. Bin and Hong are coming, but they won't get here until then, and I'm afraid they might not let you see them. I promise you, if they do take you back, we'll do everything we can to help you."

Meilan's eyes narrowed but she kept quiet. Lucy found it disconcerting. She cleared her throat. "We've found out something that may help us. Anna Maria Vandergott is really Ingrid Sobel, the Australian woman who was supposedly killed. The real Anna Maria was killed, and this woman took her place, so she's an imposter. And she was a nurse, so we're thinking she may have poisoned Eliot Chin when he recognized her."

Meilan's frown turned into a pout, and she broke her silence. "Not true. Corrupt comrade Chin killed his son to hide bad practices. He is the criminal. I'm not afraid to go back to China. You just make sure there is a public trial. I'll tell Wang Qishao this dirty rat Chin is a tiger he needs to kill. A corrupt traitor, he killed his own son to cover up. I'll make sure everybody knows, you'll see." She sat back. "You tell Hong to stay in the States. No need to come back to China. I'm not afraid of Chin. The Party will purge him, you'll see."

Lucy had no idea whether Meilan had any justification for her confidence that by returning to China she would be able to expose Chin's supposedly corrupt dealings. As far as she could see it was beside the point. "I don't know why you think Chin killed his son. He may be a corrupt official, as you say, but there's no evidence he poisoned his son. None. That's what you're accused of, you know."

To Lucy's dismay, Meilan dismissed her statement with a flap of her hand. "All that'a just cover up," she said. "Cover up for a big corruption scandal. When China corruption czar finds out, Chin will face firing squad, you'll see."

"You are so stubborn. Chin didn't kill his son and we need to find out who did, or you'll never be released. Why can't you see that?"

When Meilan just relapsed into silence, Lucy tried to push her. She was aware that the chief was watching and might even be recording their conversation. By mentioning the herbal remedy she had taken from Meilan she might be hurting her case but she was desperate. "Meilan, where did you get the bottle of herbal remedy you were trying to plant on Chin when they arrested you? I took the bottle you showed me at lunch. Did you have another one? How did you get that anyhow? Come on, tell me. I need to know."

"From town, from town. I got herbs from a herbalist in town. Not Chinese guy but owned by Chinese."

"Did you know to go there from Lucky and the others at the warehouse?"

"No, no. Your nephew's girlfriend at the resort. She gets information on everything for everybody. Everybody knows that. Even that other woman going for stuff to fix yang wei, got direction from Vanderdander woman." When Lucy looked flabbergasted Meilan explained. "You know--man trouble with sex. Plenty of Chinese herbs help. That woman went in disguise. She thought I didn't know who she was, went to get stuff to boost her man up, you know. I saw her but didn't say so."

"You mean you saw one of the resort guests buying herbs from the Chinese herbalist?"

"He's not Chinese. Black guy, but Chinese herbs. Yes, Raymond woman, the one so hot on the tall guy with gray hair. He needs help I guess." She seemed amused. "Not all guys need help when they get older. She should look around."

"Meilan," Lucy tried to call back her attention. "Are you saying Anna Maria Vandergott was the one who told you where to buy the herbs? She knew about that?"

"Sure. Lots of other stuff, too. Very helpful." Meilan rolled her eyes as if she found Lucy somewhat stupid. Then she frowned again. "But she didn't poison young Chin, the father did it."

"Meilan, where did you get the herbal to try to plant on old Chin after I took away this bottle?" Lucy had pulled it out and put it on the table. She was glaring at Meilan. "Where did you get it? Tell me."

Meilan shrugged. "Vanderdander woman. I was going to get a ride to town to get more, but she had some. Very helpful."

FORTY-FOUR

"Captain Neil is dead? Oh, my goodness, that's terrible," Norah said. "Poor Mary, it must have been awful for you. Tell me what happened."

It was eleven o'clock when Lucy and Mary finally arrived back at the resort. They'd spent a considerable amount of time at the police station, after Lucy talked to Meilan. Lucy had not been able to get the extradition postponed, but there were a few things she and the chief could agree on. Mary and Lucy had promised not to tell Norah about Anna Maria until the police interviewed her.

When they finally got back, they found Norah on the balcony with Anna Maria. Lucy noticed that when she heard the news the girl looked shocked and grabbed the arms of the chair where she sat. She'd had a relationship with him after all. It was awkward. Lucy looked at Mary who excused herself, saying she was exhausted and wanted some sleep.

"Well at least they can't think Meilan did that," Norah said. "The police have her in custody."

"It's not that simple. He could have died from an earlier dose that was injected into the IV solution, and they think she got to him before she was arrested," Lucy said. "There's another possibility that the local police probably won't believe. Jake Flaherty was at the hospital visiting him again. I can't help wondering..." Lucy shifted uncomfortably in her chair.

"Oh, no," Anna Maria said. "Jake was his friend. He didn't like me, but he wouldn't hurt Captain Neil."

Lucy thought of what Jake and Neil had told her about the affair between Anna Maria and the dead man. Thinking of her nephew's interest in Anna Maria, which was one of the reasons they all were there at the resort made her tired. That and everything else she'd learned about the girl as well. Before she could say anything, Norah burst out just as she had anticipated.

"Jake Flaherty! You've got to be kidding. He's here? He's mental, you know that. I can believe he's behind all of this." Norah turned to Anna Maria, shaking her head. "We knew him years ago. He grew up with us. Lucy and he were a number, but he went to Vietnam and when he came back he lost it. He was a mad man. Lucy, you have to tell the police about his background. He's crazy. Of course, he must have done this."

Anna Maria stared at her with wide eyes.

"It's not that straight forward," Lucy said. "He's lived here for more than ten years and he's a friend of the chief of police. There's no proof he did anything, and without that, and with the Chinese pressing for extradition, accusing Jake Flaherty is not going to help Meilan."

"Since when did they need proof that a crazy man is acting crazy? They can't let the Chinese take Meilan. Honestly, Lucy, aren't you going to do anything?"

Norah and Anna Maria were looking at Lucy, waiting for a solution. She grimaced. "Jake wants me to help him sail Neil's catamaran in the race tomorrow. He says Neil would have wanted it and he got Delroy to agree when we were at the hospital. I said I'd help them."

"Are you out of your mind?" Norah yelled. Lucy hushed her, looking towards the bedroom door where Mary was trying to sleep. Norah took her tone down to a harsh whisper. "Lucy, what are you thinking of? You want to go out and sail a boat with a mad man? Whatever for?"

"Jake is a dangerous man," Anna Maria said. "You should tell the police, even if they won't do anything. He has always been strange. If he did as you said, he could hurt you, too."

"Listen," Lucy said. "When we were back at the hospital, I got a call from Chief Jackson. The Chinese are insisting that Meilan be released to them before Monday. That's before she even talks to her lawyer, or Bin Yu and Hong get here. I have to do something. They aren't going to believe Jake is a possibility unless I can provoke him into doing something."

"Like attacking you?" her sister said. "Good plan, Lucy."

"Delroy will be with me. Even if I don't get him to admit anything, I'm sure I can get under his skin enough to get a reaction."

"Yeah, like he could hit you over the head and throw you overboard. You're as nuts as he is. I'm going to call Jim," Norah said. She was keeping her voice down with a great effort. She shook her head. "That's our brother, another retired cop," she told Anna Maria. "He might be able to talk sense into her or talk to the local cops."

"He can't help," Lucy said. "If Jake tries anything, Delroy will be there and his brother will believe him, even if he doesn't believe me. I'm counting on that."

"But how will that help Mrs. Lin?" Anna Maria asked.

Lucy shrugged. "If I can provoke Jake into doing something that gets him arrested, I can accuse him of the poisonings. That should at least prevent them from turning Meilan over to the Chinese. It will buy us time to take legal action. If I don't do something, she'll be gone before Bin Yu and Hong even get here."

"Lucy, you are out of your mind. You're as crazy as Jake Flaherty. I'm going to bed." Norah was shaking her head all the way to the bedroom she had shared with Meilan.

"Are you sure you should do this?" Anna Maria asked Lucy. "Are you sure Jake is responsible? I was thinking it was Mrs. Raymond who might be related to Mrs. Sobel." She looked confused.

Lucy wondered what the girl was feeling after learning her lover was dead, but she didn't want Anna Maria to know that she knew about the affair with Neil or her real identity. She rubbed her hands on her face and realized she was extremely tired. "I don't know for sure," she said. "But Jake has always been very unstable. In any case, you're sailing on Blaine's boat, aren't you?"

"I'm supposed to, but perhaps I should go on the catamaran with you."

"No. Jake doesn't like you, remember? He wouldn't let you. Besides, you can keep an eye on Juliet Raymond."

"OK, but I think you really need to be careful."

"Oh, I will. Believe me," Lucy said.

FORTY-FIVE

Sunday afternoon, the Pelican Bay Resort was unusually quiet. Most of the guests had been invited to view the regatta on the other side of the island. School buses had been used for transportation and the resort van stood alone and empty in the driveway.

Livingston knocked and got no answer before he slid the master key card into the door slot. The door clicked open, and he stepped inside. It was a small neat room at the far end of the resort but there was a partial view of the ocean from the sliding doors to the balcony. White triangles on the horizon told him they had chosen the near shore course for the races. With a fresh breeze the race would not take long. He had to hurry.

Confident the owner would not return, he carefully opened drawers and checked behind cushions and furniture. He rifled through some papers in the desk drawer but found nothing of interest. Grinding his teeth, he stood in the bedroom and closed his eyes trying to blank out all his concerns, his grief about Louella, his anger about her death.

Breathing deeply, he opened his eyes and slowly moved his gaze around the room. It had the furnishings that were standard for the resort. The framed pictures were similar to those in the other rooms. Pastel watercolors of beaches and quaint island cottages, palm trees and boats. Except for one. He moved towards a medium sized watercolor of a local flea market. It stood out because it was more vivid and somehow portrayed movement, a gentle sway of people moving under the hot sun to the shade of a fruit stand. In the corner he saw the signature of Jake Flaherty.

Placing his hands on the edges he carefully lifted the picture from the wall and laid it down on the bed. Taped to the back were three plastic bags. Tiny stones gleamed green through the cloudy plastic. He took a cell phone from his pocket and snapped some pictures, turning towards a sliver of window for the last one. He saw the colorful chutes billowing out on the boats and calculated how long it would be before they returned to shore. He smiled grimly thinking of Louella and sending her a silent message. He was doing this for her.

It was four in the afternoon by the time Lucy had helped Jake and Delroy tidy the catamaran and get a ride to shore on the tender. They hadn't won the race, but they hadn't disgraced themselves either. Not that she cared about that. It had been a quiet boat, all things considered. They were all thinking of other things and their interest was only peaked when it was obvious that Mike Blaine's boat Last Resort was in the lead on the spinnaker run to the finish line. The boat Anna Maria had crewed on won the race and Lucy saw them celebrating at one of tables set up under tents on the lawn of the yacht club. She nodded to Anna Maria, but she changed direction to join Chief Wendell Jackson at a table in the corner.

Sitting, Lucy set down her beer bottle and leaned forward on her elbows. "How did you do?"

He raised an eyebrow. "Well enough. We don't like to show up the visitors too much."

"Right. That's a good excuse. How about the other thing?"

He took a sip from his beer. "Still waiting to hear." Looking around at the sweaty looking racers who were straggling in for a drink before cleaning up for the awards dinner, he said, "you know, in my father's time, most of us locals only ever got in here as waiters. We weren't allowed in the bar or dining room."

They looked around the tent where a third of the faces were black or brown. "Time was," he continued, "all the power on this island was centered right here. All the decisions that mattered were made at the big oak bar inside. But we weren't allowed in. Hmph." Two of his crew were at the table and they nodded in agreement.

Lucy looked out at the peaceful view of the harbor. Boats rocked gently at their moorings or docks and there was a tingle of metal halyards slapping masts like some huge wind chime making fleeting atonal music. Behind them the clapboards weathered gray with time defined the rambling structure that was the yacht club with a deep veranda wrapping all around it. Inside, waiters were setting linen draped tables. It was a picture of a certain kind of age-old privilege and an emblem of power. It reminded her of old Yankee institutions back in New England, but this power went back even further to the British roots of the island.

"Now they've had to let you in, they'll never be able to get rid of you—I hope." She raised her bottle in salute and the three of them joined in the toast. It was the sort of bittersweet victory Lucy had seen many times as the world had changed in the course of her life. Looking out at a crowd where there were more young people than old, she realized most of them didn't even remember those bad old times.

Her eyes swept across the scene of tired but happy sailors ribbing each other. The noise level rose, as more people entered and got drinks from the bars. The sides of the tent were rolled up to allow a gentle breeze to blow through, and people spilled out on to the lawn.

As she waited for news, she watched Mike Blaine's exhilarated crew raising their bottles in toasts while Mike exchanged jibes with the next table. When she noticed Rita Blaine walking unsteadily through the crowd, she took a sip of her beer and settled back to see what would happen. She was too far away to hear, but she could see the tipsy blond woman with a martini glass in her hand talking to a red faced and frowning Mike Blaine.

Lucy raised an eyebrow when she saw Guy Laurent remove his arm from Juliet Raymond's shoulders to stand and offer a steadying hand to Rita. Juliet glowered and Mike blustered as Guy obviously attempted to guide the drunken woman away. Anna Maria huddled in her seat as if trying to become invisible and Lucy wasn't surprised to notice the girl slip away into the crowd while the others were occupied with the dispute.

Lucy sat up impatiently and was about to rise when she saw Jake making his way through the crowd followed by Livingston who held up a plastic shopping bag as he approached. "Found it," he announced, dropping the bag on the table. Chief Jackson was paying attention. Lucy looked into the bag and recognized the emeralds that belonged to Ingrid Sobel.

FORTY-SIX

"Where did she go?" Lucy asked. She was frustrated. "She has to be here somewhere." After looking at the emeralds, they hurried over to Mike Blaine's table but only Mike and a couple of men from a rival boat remained. Mike denied knowledge of where his crew had gone and refused to be drawn away from his partying. They pushed their way out to the lawn.

"She can't have gone far," Jake said.

"Over there," Livingston pointed. There were two figures silhouetted against the setting sun. One stumbled.

"I think that's Rita Blaine," Lucy said. "She was pretty plastered. What the..."

As they watched the stumbling figure disappeared.

"That's the sea wall," Chief Jackson said. "She must have fallen."

"Or was pushed," Lucy murmured to herself.

The chief took off towards the spot with Lucy, Jake, Livingston, and the chief's two crew members running after him. When they caught up, he was peering down at the rocks below. "She's down there."

Lucy looked around. There was no sign of the other figure, but she thought she saw a shadow heading towards the parking lot. The gentle tingling of the metal halyards suddenly sounded more like a clang as a stiff wind hit them. When she looked back, the men were yelling, and she saw that Jake had grabbed the edge of the sea wall and was letting himself down. Livingston yelled and started to follow. The others leaned forward to watch in the gathering dusk. Chief Jackson sent one of his men back for help.

On the rocks below they could see the body of Rita Blaine draped between two boulders. She wasn't moving and waves were lapping up at her in a gentle rhythm. They couldn't see how badly she was hurt but Lucy saw Jake squat by her side and reach out to touch her throat.

"She's alive," he yelled back.

Lucy stood up frowning. What had just happened? They found the emeralds, Ingrid Sobel's emeralds. The jewels she'd convinced her wealthy husband to buy after he sold off his ranch, after he married her when his wife died. The wife that Ingrid Van Ness had nursed. Now, Rita Blaine, wife of a wealthy American had nearly died. Surely a woman who had benefited from a scenario once wouldn't be foolish enough to repeat it. Would she?

Lucy turned to Chief Jackson. "We have to find Juliet Raymond."

FORTY-SEVEN

She wasn't at Mike Blaine's table when they went to tell him his wife was badly injured and on the way to the hospital. When he tried to stand up, he staggered so they were helping him out to a police car that would take him to the hospital when Guy Laurent joined them.

"What happened? What is it?"

Lucy grabbed his arm to keep him from following Mike Blaine into the car. "It's his wife. She fell, or was pushed, from the sea wall. They pulled her out but she's unconscious and on the way to the hospital. Where's Juliet Raymond?"

"She was pushed? What are you saying?" He looked down at Lucy and she could see his square jaw setting like stone. "You want Juliet? But she would never harm Rita. Besides, she wasn't with Rita. I took Rita out. She was drunk. Anna Maria took her to the ladies room. Juliet wasn't with her."

They put Mike into the squad car. Lucy motioned for them to wait. "Mr. Laurent, where is Juliet Raymond?"

He looked around helplessly. "I don't know. I haven't seen her." He looked at the car. "She wasn't with Mike? She was there at the table with him the last time I saw her." He looked back at the crowded tent. "Juliet doesn't like crowds. If it got too noisy, she might have gone back to the boat. The Last Resort. At the marina." He looked around blankly. "She must have gone there I suppose."

Lucy put him into the squad car with Mike Blaine and sent them off. "We have to find Juliet Raymond," she told Chief Jackson. "There's a chance she went back to their boat."

The chief sent Livingston and Delroy off to check on whether Juliet had returned to Pelican Bay Resort. He organized his men to look for her at the yacht club and harbor, telling them to also look for Anna Maria and bring either or both to him. Lucy and Jake trotted after the chief looking down the string of docks for the Last Resort.

Lucy shook her head. "I didn't see this coming. I thought we could distract her with Jake. She must think if she can get rid of Rita she could marry the husband, just like she did in Australia."

"You think she killed Sobel's first wife in Australia?" Jake asked.

"She was the woman's nurse, I don't know. Maybe the woman just died of her illness. But she could marry Mike Blaine like she married Andrew Sobel."

"She's progressing, getting more active then? If she also killed the older husband that wouldn't bode well for Blaine," the chief said. He was straining to see the boat names on hulls tied off on the next dock.

"No kidding," Lucy said.

"But isn't it crazy to think she could keep doing that? Does she think no one would notice? I'll bet she wants him so she can enter the States. It's not that easy to get a visa these days, but if she got him to marry her, she'd get right in. It's insane though." The chief huffed a bit as he trotted along. So did Lucy.

Jake was moving quietly and surely beside them. He said, "If she's insane it may make perfect sense to her, though. She married an older man once and got his money once, she can do it again."

"But the guy's children were suing her," Lucy said. She felt uncomfortable about Jake's comment. It made her only too conscious of why he would know the ins and outs of insanity. She tried to shake off the thought.

"That would make her paranoid," Jake said. "All the more reason to run away again. She'd be driven to it. She thinks she's in danger, so she'll strike out."

"If she's that disturbed, we'd better be careful how we confront her," the chief said. "There, I think that's Blaine's boat over there."

They came to a stop at the end of a dock where a half dozen yachts were tied off. As they stood still, the only noise they heard was the music and chatter from the yacht club lawn off to the right. "Second to the last," Chief Jackson said softly as he stepped on to the dock.

Jake stepped in front of Lucy to creep along after the chief. She rolled her eyes in the darkness at this attempted gallantry. If they weren't in a hurry, she would have pointed out that her many years of police work trumped his short stint in the military as preparation for facing danger, but there was no time for a discussion.

A light was shining from the cabin of the Last Resort. Guy Laurent was right. Juliet must have retreated to the boat. As the men reached the boat slip, Lucy looked around. She had the feeling she was being watched. When Chief Jackson stood up straight, she shook herself and stood up too.

"Mrs. Raymond, it's Chief Wendell Jackson of St. Hilaire constabulary. I'd like to talk to you. Can you come out of the cabin, please."

There was no answer, so after another attempt, the chief stepped on to the boat followed by Jake. Lucy looked around again and suppressed a shiver. Halyards clanged in the breeze. She stepped on to the boat and down the short ladder into the bowels of the cabin where they found Juliet Raymond slumped over the built-in table. There was an empty glass in front of her, anchoring a piece of printer paper. Lucy turned and saw a laptop with a compact printer on a shelf. As the men felt for a pulse and Chief Jackson radioed for emergency help, she pressed a key on the laptop and the screen lit up.

A WORD document flashed on, and she knew she was looking at the text from the sheet of paper on the table.

Dear Guy,

I'm sorry I'm so sorry. We had so much. But I can see you want her. I'm sorry my love but I cannot stand it. Now you won't have either of us. I couldn't help myself. I pushed Rita. I was so angry but I see what I have done and I can't face it. I can't. Goodbye. Your Juliet

Jake had picked up the printed copy. "Suicide?" He and the chief both looked at Lucy with shock in their faces.

"No," she said. "It's Anna Maria. We have to find her."

After the EMT's arrived they returned to the regatta party where they finally found Anna Maria Vandergott at the bar.

"What happened?" she asked.

Jake grabbed her wrist before she could pick up her drink.

"Aouw," she said.

Chief Jackson stepped forward. "Ingrid Sobel, I am arresting you for the murders of Eliot Chin and Luella Roberts as well as the attempted murders of Rita Blaine and Juliet Raymond."

FORTY-EIGHT

Ingrid Sobel, or Anna Maria Vandergott as she insisted on being called, proclaimed her confusion and innocence all the way to the police station. When she was released from the hand cuffs and seated in a conference room for the interrogation, she pleaded with Lucy. "Please, Ms. O'Donnell, I don't understand any of this. Why are they calling me Ingrid Sobel? You know me. Your nephew Steve can tell you. I'm Anna Maria Vandergott. Please, call Steve. Talk to him. He'll tell you. This is a horrible mistake."

The girl had showered and changed at the yacht club. She wore an expensive looking silk sheath in a design of blurry blue waves like a watercolor. Her blond hair gleamed, and she wore white sandals of soft Italian leather. Lucy felt grubby in her sweat stained shorts and long-sleeved shirt. The chief had willingly ceded the interrogation to Lucy because she was an experienced homicide detective. Looking at the attractive young woman she saw the hundreds of murder suspects she had questioned over the years. No matter how different they were in religion, race, or upbringing, when they sat in that chair opposite her and had to face the facts, they all started huddling down in a congealed mess of mostly false but always fiercely asserted denial. This could not be happening to them.

"Yes, Steve knows you as Anna Maria Vandergott. It must have been a godsend for you to meet and befriend the real Anna Maria on the flight over. When you learned she had no family and was unknown to the staff of Pelican Bay, you saw an opportunity. She would be meeting the Pelican Bay staff for the first time after being hired by the company in Brussels. You realized how easy it would be to put the past behind you by stepping into her shoes."

"You're mistaken." She stared at Lucy with big blue eyes, appearing hurt by the accusation. "I am who I am. What makes you think I am not? You're wrong. Who's telling you these lies?"

Lucy stared back. Then she reached to the seat of the chair beside her and brought out the plastic bag, spilling the contents on to the table between them. Green emeralds glistened in the harsh fluorescent light.

The woman who insisted she was Anna Maria Vandergott gasped and sat back in her chair. Lucy fingered the stones. "These were found in your unit at Pelican Bay Resort. They were hidden behind a painting."

The girl leaned forward eagerly. "But I've never seen them before. I swear it. Someone put them there. Someone is trying to make it look like I stole them. I didn't."

"You didn't steal them, at least not from Ingrid Sobel because you are Ingrid Sobel. Or, that's your most recent name anyhow."

"No, you're wrong about me."

"Am I?" Lucy consulted the manila folder in front of her. "Actually, according to the Australian police you were born plain Sally Jones. You were a nurse. You nursed your mother until she died of, oh, guess what, she died of poison. How about that. The same poison that killed Eliot

Chin and Louella Roberts. You took the name Ingrid Van Ness, had it legally changed it says here. Then you married Andrew Sobel after his wife died and you inherited his money, much of which was invested in some very valuable emeralds. But when he died, his children started a suit against you, so you fled to St. Hilaire where you killed a young woman you befriended and took on her identity."

"No, no, you're so wrong. That's not true. I've never been to Australia, I'm from the Netherlands."

"So you wanted people to believe. That's why when Eliot Chin recognized you, you had to get rid of him. But what did Louella Roberts find out? Did she find the emeralds and guess the rest? Or was it something insignificant? What did she do for you to kill her too?"

"I don't know what you're talking about." The girl sat looking at Lucy with a completely blank look on her face.

Lucy found it spooky, so she withdrew her gaze and concentrated on her notes. "What were you afraid of? The terms of the will were clear. According to the Australian authorities you would have won the suit by Sobel's children. But you feared an investigation into your past.

"Just covering up your past and taking on Anna Maria Vandergott's identity still wasn't enough for you, though was it? You had the emeralds, but they weren't enough so you decided if it worked for you once, it would work again. You decided to kill Rita Blaine so you could marry Mike Blaine. And to be sure you got away with it, you staged a suicide of Juliet Raymond with a fake note that had her taking the blame for Rita's death."

The girl's face did not change expression, but Lucy thought she saw a gleam in her eyes. It must have taken a huge amount of self-restraint for her to repress her reaction like that.

"Oh, no, is Mrs. Blaine dead? But I told you. I was worried that Mrs. Raymond was so jealous of the way Mr. Laurent treated Mrs. Blaine she might do something. I warned you she might harm her, and she did, didn't she? Just like I said. And then she committed suicide. That is so awful." She raised her delicate hands to her face.

"That's what you wanted us to believe but it's not true."

"But it is. I don't know why you're doing this to me. I don't know why you think I'm someone else."

"Yes, you look enough like Anna Maria Vandergott to pass for her."

"I am Anna Maria Vandergott."

"And you took great care to remove anyone who recognized you as Ingrid Sobel. What bad luck to run into Chin and Captain Neil. They both recognized you, didn't they? Was Chin blackmailing you? Did you take care of more than his special drink for him? He was allergic to alcohol. His father was telling the truth about that. All his son drank was the special drink you made with no alcohol. He had bottles of colored water to replace the real alcohol in his suite. It was important to him to look like he fit in with westerners when they drank, so he pretended to gulp down drinks that were harmless. That's what Louella noticed and that's what made her suspicious of you. Why would he avoid alcohol in his room then drink some rum punch you mixed up? That convinced her there was something wrong and when she searched your room, she found the emeralds, didn't she? She knew her brother had a bracelet of emeralds planted in his taxi to implicate him in the murder. Did she confront you about that? Is that why you killed her?

"That special drink made it easy for you to poison Chin. You were careful to leave the pitcher out where someone else might get at it but you were the one who poisoned it, then you went back late at night, after he was dead, and replaced it. But did you work with old Chin to frame Mrs. Lin? What a pair of conspirators you made. Tell me, did you plan to get rid of the old man, too? Or was he too canny for you? You met your match in that old man, didn't you?"

"You're wrong. And you can't prove any of this. Why are you persecuting me? I'll tell Steve. He'll help me."

"You do have a way with men, getting them to come to your aid, don't you? Captain Neil knew you as Ingrid Sobel in Australia and he recognized you, but you knew his philosophy was to live and let live. You knew he thought everyone deserved a second chance, to start over. So, you went to him and asked him to conceal your identity. You seduced him by playing on his male vanity. How could he resist a beautiful young woman willing to go to bed with him? He was weak enough to want to believe you when you said you were starting over, so he kept your secret. And whenever it looked like he might tell someone, you had only to show up at his house and seduce him again."

"Poor Captain Neil. How can you tell lies about him when he's dead? You're horrible."

"Ingrid Sobel is a nurse. She knows how to inject SUX into a saline drip of a hospital patient. You did that. You did it more than once when you visited him."

"It's not true." She appealed to the chief and the other policemen at the table. "How can you let her lie about me like this?"

The chief rose and opened the door. Mary pushed in the wheelchair.

"Ingrid, it's over," Captain Neil said. "Tell them the truth."

FORTY-NINE

"You told me he was dead," Ingrid Sobel said to Lucy.

"I lied." Lucy turned to Captain Neil. "You knew she was Ingrid Sobel, but you kept her secret. Why?"

He sighed, looking at the young woman who had shrunk into a hunched over figure, like a little animal trying to make itself small enough to be overlooked by a predator. Lucy waited patiently. "Yes, I'm sorry. She told me it was the young woman she met on the plane who was killed at the villa. She said when it happened, she saw an opportunity to start a new life. She knew that I had done that when I came here. She knew I wasn't proud of some of the things in my past." He shrugged. "It was hard to resist her."

"In fact, you had an affair with her."

He reddened and looked away. "It wasn't serious, it was just an occasional thing. It was friendly."

Lucy doubted that, but it was beside the point. "You can identify her as Ingrid Sobel, wife of Andrew Sobel, now deceased?"

"Yes," he said. "But I never thought she'd harmed the real Anna Maria Vandergott."

The young woman now identified as Ingrid Sobel flinched.

"But she did harm Anna Maria Vandergott because she feared what Andrew Sobel's children would find out about her past. She came to the Sobels as Ingrid Van Ness but that was not her real name, was it, Sally Jones? That's your real name, isn't it? Plain old Jones."

The girl's mouth was working, whether to keep from crying or to try to speak, Lucy wasn't sure. She opened another folder of information from Australia. She needed to keep pounding away at the woman's story until she got a reaction. Once she started to speak, the flood gates would open, Lucy was sure of it.

"No, Van Ness. Mrs. Van Ness. It should have been that way," the girl glared at Lucy and all that damned up emotion was breached. "It should have been me, Mrs. Van Ness. We were engaged. He was a doctor. I was his nurse. He proposed. I picked out the dress. It was embroidered with tiny pearls, and it had a train. He was mine."

It began. Lucy remained receptively silent. The others in the room appeared to be holding their breath.

"Do you think I wanted to have to do all this?" She challenged Lucy, spreading her hands in supplication. "Do you think I wanted this? She always needed me. I took care of her. I paid the bills. I got the nursing degree because she wanted it. She knew she'd need me to take care of her."

"Your mother?" Lucy asked. She was gently pushing the flow of words to get what she needed. "What happened to her?"

Anna Maria's eyes were opened very wide, but she seemed to be seeing the past, not the room or Lucy sitting opposite her. "She said she was happy for me when Len proposed. We were engaged. She said it was good. She was supposed to come look for the dress, but she had one of her turns. Said she was dizzy." Anna Maria's face gathered into a sneer. "It was the gin, most likely. I didn't care. I went out and I found it. The perfect dress. I took pictures to show her. I rushed back but she was busy. In bed. I could tell by the noise. I knew to wait. She wouldn't put up with interruptions when she was seeing someone. I knew that. I always knew to be quiet as a mouse. Quiet as a mouse, that's what she told me from little. Until they came out and I saw it was Leonard. She slept with Leonard."

Lucy had a sudden perception. "Len was Leonard Van Ness?"

"Dr. Leonard Van Ness." She was wide eyed again. "She stole him. She ruined everything for me."

"Was that why you gave her aconite? To kill her? Because she slept with your fiancée?"

Anna Maria frowned. "Me? No, she did that to herself. She was careless. She was always so careless. Of course, I sent Len away. She ended that. I went back to the hospital. I paid the bills. Who else did I have? She took the aconite and drank the gin--not on purpose, she would never do that on purpose. She took aconite in a Chinese herb. She said it made her skin clearer. I made them do an autopsy. Aconite was what killed her."

"Did that give you the idea to use it on Mrs. Sobel and then on Andrew Sobel? Did you kill them with aconite?"

Her frown deepened, as if she was trying hard to remember. "They had plenty. They had more than they needed. Their kids were all grown up. Their kids knew their parents. They always had them. My father was a rock star, did you know that? My mother didn't want to tell me, but I got it out of her when she had too much gin. She was a groupie. She followed the band to Sydney. Then she got pregnant and had to stay. She wouldn't tell me which group or which guy it was. He was too big, too important, you know?"

"That must have been difficult for you. But what about Andrew Sobel and his wife?"

"Andrew was a nice man. And his wife, Mildred, was a luv. But she was suffering from colon cancer. That ranch was a horrible lonely old place out in the middle of nowhere. They were lucky to get me to come all the way out there to take care of her. They told me so. I took good care of her, but it was taking an awfully long time. She was going, but so slowly. I helped her. I got her something to clear up her skin. By then Andrew and I were friendly. We got used to each other. But I could see he'd never go further, not while she was alive and suffering in the next room. I stopped her suffering."

Lucy glanced down at the folder. "And you married Andrew, but you did it as Ingrid Van Ness which wasn't your real name."

"I should have been Mrs. Van Ness. I told you. If she hadn't spoiled it. I was a widow. He was dead to me, Dr. Leonard Van Ness. But we could have been married, we should have been, so I used his name."

"You knew Eliot Chin and Captain Neil when you were married to Andrew Sobel?"

"It was that awful ranch. Of course, he thought I could take it, because I lived there but I didn't want to stay there forever. Then Chin was one of the ones looking to buy and Neil was a salesman for a liquor company. Andy liked his single malt scotch. Andy used to have them stay out at the ranch. He wouldn't sell to the Chinese, though. He said it was unpatriotic. But I finally got him to sell to another rancher. He was getting sick by then."

"And you got him to invest in emeralds?"

She shrugged. "A lot of people were doing that. We heard about it and Andy decided it was a good place to put the money."

"Did you poison him?"

She batted her eyelashes. Lucy was slightly shocked by the action. Despite her experience with dozens of murderers it seemed a very strange reaction.

"Andy liked his scotch. He was seventy-five by then and his heart gave out. He had plenty of good times with me, but he kept saying he missed Mildred. It was time for him to go."

Lucy tried to repress a frown. "When he died, his children contested the will that left everything to you. But the Australian authorities say the will was quite proper and would have stood up to the challenge. Surely your own lawyer told you that. Why did you run?"

"They never liked me. Andrew Junior and Ralph and the daughter, Ivy. What right did they have to begrudge me the money? They grew up safe and taken care of, not like me with no father and a drunk for a mother. I needed it take care of myself. But their lawyer started routing around in my past. They just wanted to spoil it for me. I had to protect myself. They would find out about the name and try to get the marriage declared null because of that. They wanted to take it all away from me and then I'd have nothing."

Lucy knew that the name change had been legal. There was no reason for Ingrid to fear exposure. No one could have taken away the inheritance, but the woman was paranoid. "So you ran away to St. Hilaire and when you met Anna Maria Vandergott on the plane, you invited her to your villa. When you assured yourself you could step into her shoes, you killed her and framed the taxi driver."

"I had to use one of the bracelets. I stuffed it in the back seat. It was already done when he came to take me to the resort. But I had to leave something as evidence. It was the only way. I didn't want to leave it, but I had to."

Lucy looked at the seemingly sincere young woman before her. She had viciously beaten the Dutch girl to death with a brick from the patio. She must have showered and changed before calling the cab. But her only regret seemed to be that she had been forced to leave behind an emerald bracelet.

"What about Eliot Chin?" Lucy rested her chin on her hand, finding it hard to believe the false Anna Maria could be so callous.

"He recognized me, of course, from when he came to the ranch. I tried to tell him I just needed a new start. But he wasn't like Neil." Lucy saw Captain Neil flinch, but she concentrated on the girl. "He just wanted to get something so he could feel like he had power over me. He was ashamed that he couldn't drink alcohol. It embarrassed him when he was out with American businessmen. So, he had me make up that silly drink to look like it had rum and other stuff but really it didn't. It was a virgin punch. Like Chin, he was a virgin."

"That made it easy for you to poison him, didn't it, when the time came?"

"Didn't you hear him? That first day you were here, he called me Ingrid when I took you up to the roof. Didn't you notice? If he was going to be that stupid, I couldn't let him just go on like that. He was dangerous."

"Not nearly as dangerous as you," Lucy was thinking but she kept the comment to herself and looked down at her notes. She didn't remember Chin's slip of tongue that first day, but that was what had set off Anna Maria like a firecracker. "By then you had identified Mike Blaine as your next savior, right? You couldn't let Chin or Neil get in the way of that plan, could you?"

"I had to take care of myself. Mike liked me right away. That Guy Laurent tried to stop him but, you know, when men start to get older they're really very flattered by the interest of a younger woman He liked me and he wanted to help me."

"So you decided to get rid of his wife but you wanted to make it look like Juliet Raymond did it, just like you made it look like Billy Roberts, the taxi driver, killed Ms. Vandergott."

"That Mrs. Raymond, she came to me looking for a local aphrodisiac, can you imagine? She wanted to feed it to Mr. Laurent. She must have felt him slipping away from her."

"You sent her to the place where you had purchased the Chinese herb with the aconite?"

"I thought it was clever of me."

Lucy shook her head. "You pushed Rita Blaine off the cliff and then you poisoned Juliet Raymond and typed up a fake suicide note on her laptop."

"You are mistaken," Sally Jones said. "I don't know what you're talking about."

"Oh, really? Guess what, Rita Blaine is not dead and will recover. And, furthermore, Juliet Raymond's stomach was pumped out in time so she won't die either. We'll be interviewing both of them and there will be further charges. For now, we're charging you with the murder of Eliot Chin. You poisoned the drink you left for him and replaced the pitcher with another before morning. Chin's father has told us that his son recognized you as Ingrid Sobel from Australia. And he told us how you put the bottle of aconite in Meilan Lin's bag to make it appear that she had killed his son."

"What a double-crossing old liar! He paid me to do that."

"Yes, well, Mr. Chin has his own problems and is willing to swear to what you did."

The false Anna Maria scanned the room. Her eyes quickly passed over Lucy and Mary and Captain Neil to rest on Chief Jackson. She directed her appeal to him. "I don't know what to do, Chief Jackson. I was only trying to protect myself. I've never had anything. Do you think I wanted to do bad things? Do you think I don't regret it? I just need help. Don't you see?"

Lucy rolled her eyes and slammed the folder shut.

FIFTY

With the weekend on them it was difficult to get the paperwork done for Meilan's release. By the time it was completed, it was too late for Bin Yu and his wife to cancel their flight. Lucy had gotten permission for Norah and Mary to leave on the flight they originally scheduled on Saturday, but she stayed on to try to straighten out the mess with Meilan. Carlo Menotti arranged for a chauffeur driven limousine to bring them back to the resort where he moved them to a premium unit right under the Eye of Sauron. Lucy had no idea why the Italian timeshare salesman was so solicitous, but she was grateful.

Lucy and Meilan sat on the balcony watching the sky glow with the remains of a sunset. Lucy was sipping a local beer from the bottle while Meilan drank tea from a large mug decorated with palm trees.

"I'm sorry I couldn't convince Bin Yu and Hong to cancel their flight in time to save them from coming all the way down here," Lucy said.

Melan put down her mug. "Is OK. Good for them to see this." She gestured towards the sea. "Only, it would be better if old Chin was the villain not Vandergutter girl. Bad men don't get punished enough."

Lucy took a long pull from her beer. She couldn't decide if the mangling of the Dutch name was ironic or a true mistake. "Meilan, you and I are old enough to know that the guilty don't always pay for their crimes." Lucy thought of politicians and even clergymen she had come across who had managed to hide acts that would have destroyed ordinary people. "But they pay in other ways. Look at Chin. He didn't kill his son, but he didn't save him either. He'll have to live knowing his only child died before him. Isn't that a punishment?"

Lucy thought that having progeny was particularly important to the Chinese from what she had heard. And it seemed to her that scheming, amoral, corrupt officials she had seen either became estranged from their children or lived to see the next generation shock them with actions they found more despicable than anything they'd done themselves. Maybe she was deluding herself, but she had seen it happen. She and Meilan might not have easy relationships with their children, but at least they could look at them with pride.

"You've got Hong and Bin and the children. Chin has nothing now."

Meilan was sitting in a rigid posture staring out at the horizon. "Maybe I do not deserve such luck. Why should I? It's useless to have grandchildren to honor me when I have done such an awful thing to my father." She turned her head to look Lucy in the eye. Her round face with still chubby cheeks had always seemed ageless to Lucy but tonight the wrinkles showed. She was becoming an old woman. It occurred to Lucy that Meilan had reached an age that her father had never attained. He died in his forties; she was over sixty now.

"When I see Chin, I remember that day. I remember him beating my brother, disgracing my father. But more, I remember I cheered him on. Me. My father stood bent over with a sign hanging on his neck, hundreds, thousands of people yelling bad words, insults and I, his own daughter, I joined with them. The last time he sees me or hears me speak, I'm calling him traitor and running dog. That night he was beaten to death by Chin and others, but I think I already killed him. How would you feel if your daughter betrayed you like that? You don't want to live, right? Chin lost his son. He deserves it. I also deserve to lose Hong. I should suffer."

Lucy looked out at the horizon and tried to imagine what Meilan's father must have felt, caught up in the mass hysteria of a crowd. She'd seen crowds in action. She'd felt the rush that could flow through, lifting individual people's emotions like a wave rolling in to shore. She remembered the fierce emotions of the busing protests in Boston in the seventies. She had seen people driven to do things they regretted later. Being in uniform she'd resisted the sucking pull of that tide, but she witnessed people overcome and blinded by the scorching heat blast of emotion that spread like a mushroom cloud through a crowd of people.

What would it have felt like to have all that energy turned against you? In a way, she *had* felt it as one of the blue uniformed line of police trying to keep the crowd in check. She knew Meilan's father was an intellectual, a professor. He must have tried to stand against the wave of insanity that swept across a whole nation during those days of the Cultural Revolution. And as he was picked up by that wave and dashed to his destruction, he heard the voice of his own daughter condemning him. How had he felt?

"Meilan, how old were you when your father was killed?"

"Fourteen."

Lucy tried to conjure a picture of her daughter at that age. Oh, yes, she remembered it now. The accusations, the recriminations, the rebellions and acts of pettiness committed. "When my daughter was fourteen, she didn't like me very much. How about Hong. What was she like at that age?"

Meilan blinked, looked down at her hands and then back up at Lucy. "Different times. She didn't like that I told her she must study for university. Always excuses and complaints. She didn't understand why she has to do this instead of going to movies. She said because I don't have a university degree why should she. Only later did she understand. No degree, you only get manual work. She was too young then to know."

"Right. They really don't get it at that age. But what if the Cultural Revolution had happened then? What if you were in your father's place and Hong disavowed you? What would you think?"

Meilan began to speak but stopped. Lucy thought she was going to protest that the Cultural Revolution was a mistake that was rectified by the Party so it would never happen again. Lucy had heard her say so before, like she was repeating a slogan. But this time she lapsed into a moody silence.

Lucy let her mull it over for a while, then she said softly, "You were only fourteen."

Meilan clasped her mug and sipped the tea.

"Really, would you hate your fourteen-year-old daughter for doing such a stupid thing? I can imagine Janey doing it at that age and I can imagine myself just praying that whatever she was doing would save her from the crowd. Meilan, as a parent I would feel that I should be protecting my child. If rejecting me protected her and kept her alive, I would want her to do that, wouldn't you? If she jumped in and tried to defend me and was beaten to death for it, wouldn't that be worse?"

There were tears overflowing Meilan's eyes and falling down her cheeks. "Shang tried to defend our father."

"Your brother was older. Think of Hong at fourteen. What would you want for her?"

Meilan stared out at the horizon. Lucy noticed that she had slumped down in her chair as if some knot holding her together had been loosened. After a while she sniffed and said, "Hong's all grown up now. She thinks I'm old, she has to take care of me. I don't feel like an old woman. Still things to fix. I can't stop now, have to make better China for Mai and Xi." She named her grandchildren.

"I know what you mean. Every time I talk to my daughter, I feel like she's ready to commit me to an old folk's home. She wants to know am I seeing the doctor, do I need help with the grocery shopping, am I driving at night. For crying out loud, you'd think I was decrepit. I feel like telling her it's none of her god damn business how late I stay out, but I'm afraid I'll offend her, and she'll stop calling. We haven't always gotten along."

Meilan chuckled and Lucy was glad to hear the sound. Then Lucy's cell phone chirped with the tone she'd chosen for Chief Jackson. She answered and listened to him for a while, murmuring responses. When she hung up, she told Meilan, "Chief Jackson will be at the airport when we pick up Hong and Bin tomorrow. He has something he wants you to see."

FIFTY-ONE

When Carlo Menotti provided a limo for the ride to the airport the next day, Meilan mentioned in an offhand way that she and the Italian had been having a little affair all during the vacation week. Lucy nearly choked on a sip of beer when she heard that. It explained why Meilan had disappeared so often and how she had gotten information about banks and herbalists on the island. Lucy was also astounded to learn the relationship had developed during negotiations that led to purchase of a timeshare week by Meilan. "For Hong and Bin," she explained. "I can take care of kids. They need some 'alone time,'" she said. Lucy thought she was nowhere near as surprised by this as Bin would be.

"You and crazy painter have some 'alone time?'" Meilan asked on the way to the airport.

"Oh, no. It's not like that," Lucy said. She felt a bit affronted by this casual intrusion into her personal life but then she remembered the very personal conversation of the night before and relented. "Jake Flaherty and I were close many years ago. But we went our separate ways and haven't seen each other since."

Meilan grunted. "We're not getting younger. Silly to waste time. You want 'alone time' with this man, you need to take it when you have it. What does your nephew think of Vanderdander girl now?"

"Vandergott, and her real name is Sally Jones," Lucy said. She'd managed to have a private conversation with her nephew on Saturday, so she could tell him what had happened firsthand before Norah and Mary arrived home. News of the arrest had not reached the Boston papers or TV stations. She was relieved to find Stephen was not very upset. "Wow," he said, "You don't mean it." Lucy conjectured the relationship had, in fact, been much more informal than the mother and aunts had imagined. She told Meilan he was disappointed but not upset.

They met Bin and Hong at the baggage area and Hong gave her mother a big hug. The young couple were flabbergasted to learn they would remain in the luxury suite at Pelican Bay for the week while Meilan proposed returning to tend to the children. She had booked herself on the same flight as Lucy the next day.

There was one more thing to attend to and Chief Johnson arrived to lead them behind the scenes to a customs area where they could look out a plate glass window to where a small private jet was being boarded.

Lucy heard an exclamation in Chinese.

"Do you know who that is?" Bin Yu asked her. He was pointing at an official surrounded by bodyguards who was strolling out to the plane. "That's Wong Qishao, China's anti-corruption czar."

Meilan was clapping her hands with excitement. As they watched, they saw old Chin pushed out in his wheelchair then carried up the steps to the jet by one of the burly black suited bodyguards. Meilan said something in Chinese. Bin Yu replied at length then turned to Lucy to translate. "Hong's uncles in Beijing contacted the anti-corruption officials and told them what her mother found out about what Chin was doing here. He was offering to hide money for corrupt Chinese officials in secret bank accounts and island investments. They decided to make an example of him. Wong Qishao came over himself. Chin'll face charges back in China." Bin Yu made a slicing motion across his neck to suggest the likely result for Chin. Lucy raised her eyebrows and thought again of several corrupt officials back home who might have been discouraged by that kind of potential punishment. She shrugged. Not her problem.

The surprised young couple were ushered off to the limo with Meilan and Lucy. Lucy knew they had expected to spend anxious time with lawyers trying to get Meilan released, so it would be doubly relaxing for them to eat and drink and lie by the pool instead. Especially with Meilan out of their hair after tomorrow.

When they got back to Pelican Bay, Lucy watched her friend harry Carlo Menotti about the furnishings in the timeshare for her daughter and son-in-law. Suddenly Livingston appeared in the doorway with a six pack of local beer hanging from one hand. "Mrs. Lin thought you might want a ride out to Jake's," he said.

Meilan hurried over. "You go," she said, patting Lucy's arm. "Go see crazy painter. We leave tomorrow."

"But he didn't ask me, and I didn't tell him I was coming. Can I call him? Do you have his number Livingston?"

"Don't you worry," Livingston grinned. "S'long as you bring this," he held up the six pack, "he'll be plenty glad to see you. No problem."

"No problem," Meilan repeated.

Lucy shook her head. But the thought of the peaceful sunny little cottage was appealing, and she had promised to bring him up to date on news from Boston. What the heck. She took the six pack from

Livingston and led him out the door that Meilan slammed behind them.

Acknowledgments

Many thanks to Marie Donahue, retired deputy superintendent with the Boston Police Department who read and commented on a very early draft. She provided a number of useful recommendations for how to portray a police officer like Lucy O'Donnell. The characters are strictly fictional, and any errors or unbelievable situations are from my imagination, not drawn from my own life or anyone else's. As an author, I tend to spice things up to make a story more dramatic.

Thanks, too, to Diane Harvey an old friend of my sister-in-law who put me in touch with Marie Donahue

I studied Chinese language for a number of years and am very fond of the Chinese culture. I love Lu Hsun and lots of contemporary Chinese films. Xiaolong Qiu writes a series about a Shanghai detective who is also a poet, like P.D. James's detective. I recommend his stories for a great look at contemporary China for mystery lovers.

I want to thank Matthew Salesses author of *The Hundred-Year Flood* for doing a sensitivity reading and making a number of suggestions for corrections to the text. Any remaining issues are all my responsibility.

Finally, thanks to Emily Victorson, my longtime publisher and editor at Allium Press of Chicago for a critical reading that helped immensely. Once more, I have to say that any remaining flaws are owned by me, the author.

Also by Frances McNamara

E   *mily Cabot Mysteries*

Death at the Fair

The 1893 World's Columbian Exposition provides a vibrant back-drop for this exciting new mystery. Emily Cabot is one of the first women graduate students at the University of Chicago, eager to prove herself in the new field of sociology. While she is busy exploring the Exposition with her family and friends, her colleague, Dr. Stephen Chapman, is accused of murder. Emily sets out to search for the truth behind the crime, but is thwarted by the thieves, corrupt politicians, and gamblers who are ever-present in Chicago. A lynching that oc-curred in the dead man's past leads Emily to seek the assistance of the black activist Ida B. Wells. Rich with historical details that bring turn-of-the-century Chicago to life, this novel will appeal equally to history buffs and mystery fans.

Death at Hull House

It's Chicago in 1893 and Emily Cabot, an aspiring sociologist, finds work at Hull House, the famous settlement established by Jane Addams. There she quickly becomes involved in the political and social problems of the immigrant community. But when a man who works for a sweatshop owner is murdered in the Hull House parlor, Emily must determine whether one of her colleagues is responsible, or whether the real reason for the murder is revenge for a past tragedy in her own family. As a smallpox epidemic spreads through the impoverished West Side of Chicago, the very existence of the settlement is threatened and Emily finds herself in jeopardy from both the deadly disease and a killer. This is the exciting sequel to Death at the Fair.

Death at Pullman

A model town at war with itself . . . George Pullman created an ideal community for his railroad car workers, complete with every amenity they could want or need. But when hard economic times hit in 1894, lay-offs follow and the workers can no longer pay their rent or buy food at the company store. Starving and desperate, they turn against their once benevolent employer. Emily Cabot and her friend Dr. Stephen Chapman bring much needed food and medical supplies to the town, hoping they can meet the immediate needs of the workers and keep them from resorting to violence. But when one young worker-suspected of being a spy-is murdered, and a bomb plot comes to light, Emily must race to discover the truth behind a tangled web of family and company alliances.

Death at Woods Hole

Exhausted after the tumult of the Pullman Strike of 1894, Emily Cabot is looking forward to a restful summer visit to Cape Cod. She has plans to collect "beasties" for the Marine Biological Laboratory, alongside other visiting scientists from the University of Chicago. She also hopes to enjoy romantic clambakes with Dr. Stephen Chapman, although they must keep an important secret from their friends. But her summer takes a dramatic turn when she finds a dead man floating in a fish tank. In order to solve his murder she must first deal with dueling scientists, a testy local sheriff, the theft of a fortune, and uncooperative weather. This fourth book in the Emily Cabot Mysteries series will continue to delight history buffs and mystery lovers alike.

Death at Chinatown

In the summer of 1896, amateur sleuth Emily Cabot meets two young Chinese women who have recently received medical degrees. She is inspired to make an important decision about her own life when she learns about the difficult choices they have made in order to pursue their careers. When one of the women is accused of poisoning a Chinese herbalist, Emily once again finds herself in the midst of a murder investigation. But, before the case can be solved, she must first settle a serious quarrel with her husband, help quell a political uprising, and overcome threats against her family. Timeless issues, such as restrictions on immigration, the conflict between Western and Eastern medicine, and women's struggle to balance family and work, are woven seamlessly throughout this riveting historical mystery. Rich with fascinating details of life in Chicago's original Chinatown, this fifth book in the Emily Cabot Mysteries series will continue to delight history buffs and mystery lovers alike.

Death at the Paris Exposition

In the sixth Emily Cabot Mystery, the intrepid amateur sleuth's journey once again takes her to a world's fair—the Paris Exposition of 1900. Chicago socialite Bertha Palmer has been named the only female U. S. commissioner to the Exposition and she enlists Emily's services as her social secretary. Their visit to the House of Worth for the fitting of a couture gown is interrupted by the theft of Mrs. Palmer's famous pearl necklace. Before that crime can be solved, several young women meet untimely deaths and a member of the Palmer's inner circle is accused of the crimes. As Emily races to clear the family name she encounters jealous society ladies, American heiresses seeking titled European husbands, and more luscious gowns and priceless jewels. Along the way, she takes refuge from the tumult at the country estate of Impressionist painter Mary Cassatt. In between her work and sleuthing, she is able to share the Art Nouveau delights of the Exposition, and the enduring pleasures of the City of Light, with her husband and their young children.

Death at the Selig Studios

The early summer of 1909 finds Emily Cabot eagerly anticipating a relaxing vacation with her family. Before they can depart, however, she receives news that her brother, Alden, has been involved in a shooting death at the Selig Polyscope silent movie studios on Chicago's northwest side. She races to investigate, along with her friend Detective Henry Whitbread. There they discover a sprawling backlot, complete with ferocious jungle animals and the celluloid cowboys Tom Mix and Broncho Billy. As they dig deeper into the situation, they uncover furtive romantic liaisons between budding movie stars and an attempt by Thomas Edison to maintain his stranglehold over the emerging film industry. Before the intrepid amateur sleuth can clear her brother's name she faces a serious break with the detective; a struggle with her adolescent daughter, who is obsessed with the filming of the original Wizard of Oz movie; and threats upon her own life.

Death on the Homefront

With the United States on the verge of entering World War I, tensions run high in Chicago in the Spring of 1917, and the city simmers with anti-German sentiment mixed with virulent patriotism. Shockingly, amateur sleuth Emily Cabot is present when a young Chicago woman, who is about to make a brilliant society marriage, is murdered. Was her death retaliation for her pacifist activities, or was it linked to her romantic entanglements? Emily has a personal connection to the woman, but she's torn between her determination to solve the murder and her deep need to protect her newly adult children from the realities of a new world. As the country's entry into the war unfolds, Emily watches with trepidation as her sons and daughter make questionable choices about their own futures. Violent worker unrest and the tumultuous arena of automobile racing provide an emotionally charged backdrop for this compelling mystery.

Death in a Time of Spanish Flu

In fall of 1918, while the war is finally ending, the Spanish Flu is rampant in Chicago. Emily's husband is treating patients at Cook County Hospital but her son and daughter have been drawn into a scandalous murder trial of the wife of a local gambling king and ward boss. When Emily accompanies her children to the avantgarde Dil Pickle club a man is found shot do death. She works with Detective Henry Whitbread to save her children by finding the real murderer.

Death at the Chicago Trust

In February 1930, Emily Cabot is a widow who finds her funds have been lost in theWall Street Crash. After she witnesses the suicide of a banker, she's nearlykilled in a gangland style shootout. Her police mentor has retired, her friendat City Hall is demoted. She cant believe the way Chicago has dissolved intochaos. When her own family is threatened by the clash of the Secret Sixvigilantes and the Outfit gangsters, Emily meets Eliot Ness and Frank Nittiwhen she fights to protect the innocent and ensure some justice in a lawlesscity.

NUTSHELL MURDER MYSTERIES
"convict the guilty, clear the innocent, and find the truth in a nutshell."

This is a series of fictional stories roughly based on the *Nutshell Studies of Unexplained Death*. Over twenty miniature crime scenes were used from the 1940's to the present to train police detectives. Set in the 1920's these stories imagine Frances Glessner Lee working with Dr. George Magrath to learn about "legal medicine" as forensic science was known at the time. Working with Magrath provided the foundation for the miniatures for which Frances Glessner Lee has become known as the Mother of Forensic Science.

Molasses Murder in a Nutshell

In January 1919 a tank bursts in Boston's North End, flooding the neighborhood with molasses. When a woman is found murdered in the wreckage, Frances Glessner Lee asks her old friend, medical examiner Dr. George Magrath to help exonerate a young serviceman. Frustrated by her lack of education and skills, she wants the clear the young man's name and find the killer. Will creation of a miniature crime scene lead to the truth? It's the best she can do.

Three Decker Murder in a Nutshell

n November 1919 a woman is found dead. Police assume she fell from the back porch of a three-decker in East Boston. At the funeral home, they discover she was shot. Medical examiner Magrath is furious at newly hired police detective Peter Attwood for the mistake. Since the police strike in September, experienced Irish detectives like McNally have been blackballed and inexperienced men like the Harvard student have been hired. Frances Glessner Lee is determined to help both Magrath and young Peter who is grandson to her widowed friend. Lives of Boston Brahmins and Irish clash as they hunt for the truth.

Joy Street Jail Murder in a Nutshell

A man found drunk on a sidewalk in Boston's West End is taken to Joy Street Jail, he's found dead in the morning. Young Peter Attwood is the policeman who brought him in. When local politician Martin Lomasney gets complaints from his Jewish voters that the man was a well-known jeweler, medical examiner Dr. Jake Magrath is called on the carpet. Morphine poisoning caused the death. Frustrated by the shoddy police work that threatens to convict Peter of negligence, Magrath is near resigning his job. But Frances Glessner Lee and Magrath's staff are determined to clear Peter. Blacklisted policeman Mack plunges into the multi-ethnic culture of the West End to find the truth. There are secrets buried in the depths of the settlement houses and tenements of the vibrant section of the city and they have to be exposed to exonerate the young policeman.

www.ingramcontent.com/pod-product-compliance
Lightning Source LLC
Chambersburg PA
CBHW032055050726
47590CB00001B/277